LITTLE WOMAN IN BLUE

Published 2015
Printed in the United States of America
ISBN: 978-1-63152-987-0
Library of Congress Control Number: 2015935726

Book design by Stacey Aaronson

For information, address:
She Writes Press
1563 Solano Ave #546
Berkeley, CA 94707

She Writes Press is a division of SparkPoint Studio, LLC.

LITTLE WOMAN

 in

BLUE

A Novel of
MAY ALCOTT

BY
JEANNINE ATKINS

SHE WRITES PRESS

For my husband and our daughter,
Peter and Emily Laird, with love.

CONTENTS

1

VOWS

May's nightgown brushed her feet as she and her sister climbed the hill behind their house. They clipped enough pine branches to overflow their baskets. When Louisa started to turn back, May grabbed her arm and said, "We need more boughs to hide the cracks in the paint."

"No one will be looking at the walls." Louisa stepped away.

"Everyone will see the chipped paint and peeling wall-paper and pretend not to."

"Anna said she wanted to keep her wedding simple."

"And you believed her?" May broke another branch. But the sun was rising, and there was a lot to do before guests arrived, so she hurried behind Louisa back to the house. They twisted evergreen branches over windows they'd scrubbed with crumpled newspapers and vinegar. Then May brought lilies of the valley upstairs. She twined the cream-colored flowers through Anna's hair. She fastened buttons on the back of her gray poplin gown, wishing her sister had chosen to wear white, like Princess Victoria, instead of stitching a dress she thought was more suitable for a bride who was turning thirty. May tossed her a soft, apple-sized bundle and said, "For you."

Anna unrolled the silk stockings, which wavered like smoke. "Thank you! But what an extravagance for something no one will see."

"You'll see them. So will your husband."

Anna's face turned pink.

May put on her best blue gown and arranged her light hair so it fell in waves between her shoulder blades. She hurried downstairs to help Father carry a table outside. She covered it with a cloth and set out the good green-and-white china, strategically placing plates over stains. She picked more lilies of the valley and slipped some through a buttonhole of Father's wrinkled linen frock coat.

"Mother will like that." May added, in case he forgot: "Her favorite flower."

She went into the kitchen to squeeze lemons, while Mother sliced bread on the board May had decorated years ago, using a hot poker to burn an impression of an Italian artist. She cringed at the amateurish attempt. Hearing hooves *clip-clop* and the rattle of wheels, she stepped outside to greet Mr. and Mrs. Emerson, who were lending their horses and carriage so the newlyweds could leave in style for their new home just north of Boston. May fetched a pail of water for the horses, made sure John didn't see his bride until the last moment, and welcomed his family, other relatives, and a few neighbors. After collecting wedding presents, grape wine, and pies brought by guests, May glanced at the clock. Anna was superstitious and wanted to say her vows while the clock's hands swept up to eleven.

May showed people inside, hoping the crowded room might distract them from noticing the slanting floorboards and shabby furniture. And of course they'd be looking at Anna, who'd chosen to stand by John without a maid of honor. She'd said she didn't want to fuss, but May expected she wanted to avoid any rites that could stir sisterly rivalry. She stepped between Mother and Louisa, whose eyes were fixed on the picture of Beth, with violets twined around the frame. Louisa hunched the way she did over her paper and pen, her curved back a dare to interrupt. Still, May offered her hand. At least Louisa had been with Beth when she passed over, while she . . . No, she wouldn't think about why she'd been away, not as Anna and John took their places before Father and Uncle Samuel, who'd once been a minister, and who'd arrived from Syracuse yesterday and made May a kind but unappealing offer that she'd promised to reply to soon.

Father pushed his hair behind his shoulders. He said, "Let us pray," though the words that followed seemed more like an editorial on the wrongs between North and South. After the murmurs of *Amen,* Uncle Samuel spoke the vows. Anna looked into John Pratt's eyes. His sun-weathered face was framed by a brown beard and wavy hair. Anna leaned forward over her wide skirt for a kiss. When she turned and raised her hand with a slim gold ring, people rushed forward with blessings and congratulations.

May cheered the loudest. She'd once imagined a more brilliant match for her oldest sister, but John was good, handsome, and dependable, which wasn't a romantic word, but one dear to daughters whose father scorned making money, which he believed could corrupt, tied as it was to evils such as slavery. Who could argue, but May had hated going hungry and wearing cast-off clothing, and she was certain Anna had, too. Father had a deep, persuasive voice, but he'd never convince May that a pumpkin was as good as a throne or a wreath of daisies as splendid as a tiara.

She held open the door, then followed everyone into the yard, which was scented by lilacs. Already conversations were turning from the short ceremony to the war some predicted would break out between the states soon or whether the lemonade was sweet enough. Louisa had her eyes on Mr. Thoreau's shaggy beard, which looked as if it had been trimmed with a penknife. Wearing a straw hat, threadbare coat, and trousers tucked into scuffed boots, he kept his eyes on the ground, as if scouting for mushrooms. May was fond of the man who years before had taught her and other children the names of wildflowers. Mr. Thoreau stopped by in early spring to announce when the bluebirds had returned. But he was awfully short, and one of the few people in Concord who might be poorer than the Alcotts. Louisa, who was canny about so much, couldn't seem to see that a middle-aged man who lived with his mother and couldn't look a woman in the eye or anywhere else wasn't one to pin her hopes on.

May took her aside. "It was a lovely wedding, though I'm not going to get married in a parlor. Or a backyard."

"The sky is church enough," Louisa said.

"But not as reliable as a ceiling. Thank goodness it didn't rain." May thought stained glass flattered a bride. And she'd make sure her mother wouldn't be clearing tables at her wedding. She said, "Father must have been more pliable when Mother convinced him to marry in King's Chapel."

"Mother's pleased that Anna chose to marry on their anniversary."

"I just wish they were taking a real honeymoon."

"They're wise to save their money."

May wasn't opposed to them being practical. Marrying in a breathless rush was no proof of ardor. "But I wanted more for her."

"She has tenderness and loyalty."

"You want more than that. Why shouldn't she?" May wondered if Louisa buttoned conversations with morals only with her younger sister. She wished she didn't speak as if she hadn't seen the bleak apartment Anna and John were renting, where they'd scrubbed windows bound to blacken with the next passing train. Of course May was glad that John cherished Anna, but was she the only Alcott who understood that love needn't be the opposite of good fortune? At twenty-one, May felt ready to end her flirtations and get serious about finding a man who might not be the prince she'd once dreamed of, but who would take her to tour art museums in Paris and ruins in Rome. She wasn't in a hurry, for it was nicest for older sisters to marry first. But she wished Louisa would get to work.

"What are you doing talking to me when you could be with Mr. Thoreau? Look, he's taking out his flute." May grabbed Louisa's hand and pulled her toward the guests who danced in the old German style around the elm tree, skipping, twisting, swinging their arms. Louisa laughed and kicked higher than anyone else, until May swung her legs still higher.

The dancers dropped each other's hands. The circle unwound. Mr. Thoreau put down his flute, then coughed while bending into a handkerchief, which he unfolded and inspected. May turned to the table where the linen napkins were now crumpled. Crumbs littered the tablecloth. The signs of polishing, ironing, and bleaching she'd done to show this day mattered had disappeared. She stacked the scattered teacups that came from Mother's family and were printed with *M*'s, which made her hopeful that one day she, rather than her sisters, might inherit them, though that wasn't why she'd recently asked to be called by Mother's maiden name as well as her and Louisa's middle name. "May" was prettier than "Abigail." She carried the cups and plates through the parlor, where the pine garlands smelled more fragrant as they wilted.

She returned outside and stood by Louisa, watching John gently touch Anna's waist as they headed to the carriage. Anna lifted her skirt to climb up, showing a glimpse of stocking.

"Gracious, where did she get those?" Louisa said.

"Do you think she'll tell us what it's like?" May asked.

"The truth about marriage? No one tells that."

"I was hoping for just the wedding night. You'll confide in me, won't you?"

"You might tell me."

"Mother says you just need to find the right man. But we shouldn't wait too long. We could help watch each other's babies. Imagine cousins playing croquet or skating together.

But first there's the marriage. How good it must be to live with someone who knows everything about you."

"That sounds like a sister more than a husband."

May caught her breath. Did Louisa really think she knew her? "I never felt I knew much about Beth. She seemed patient, then had such spells."

"Let's not talk about her today. First I lose her, now Anna."

"Aren't you going back to Boston? You'll be closer to Anna there than you are here." May had sometimes felt jealous of the bond between her two oldest sisters, who were just about a year apart in age, and nine and eight years older than she. Maybe she and Louisa would become closer now that they were the sisters yet to marry.

People cheered as the horses began pulling the carriage, where Anna and John sat close. Louisa kicked off her shoes, grabbed May's hand, and raced behind them, shouting, "Farewell!"

They ran until the carriage was nearly out of sight and they were out of breath. They turned and headed home, stopping by the house next to their own, where they'd lived some fifteen years ago. They had moved about once a year when they were growing up, as Father looked for work, loans, or distance from people to whom he owed money.

"Of all the places we lived, I loved this house most." Louisa kept her eyes on the house that was now shuttered. Ladders leaned against the walls. "The Hawthornes were wise to have the roof repaired before they return from Europe. Mr. Hawthorne won't want to write while hearing hammering over his head."

"Mr. Wetherbee isn't just replacing slates," May said. "See how they took out the garret and are adding some sort of turret? What's wrong?"

"They can't take down the garret! That's where we played! Don't you remember? I suppose everything's gone now. That chest filled with old clothes and boots we used for dress-up."

"For those theatricals you wrote? I always got roles like the castle cat."

"You wouldn't learn your lines."

"I must have been five. You couldn't expect a professional actress." May linked her arm through Louisa's as they headed home. "Now you can see real productions."

"Our cousins are generous with tickets they can't always use. Don't tell Mother, but I think of Boston as my home now. I find ideas there. I can hardly write about women who bring soup to sick neighbors or the trials girls have with lemonade-stained gloves."

"I want to live in Boston, too. I could take art classes again. Lu, we could share a room!"

"I thought Uncle Samuel found you a job in Syracuse."

"He meant well, offering me a place with his family so I can send home the money I earn. But I don't want to teach at a sanitarium, no matter how refined he says it is. That spa in Maine where Mother worked was probably called 'elegant,' too." May had been seven when she accompanied her mother, who'd been hired to help with water cures. She remembered hollow-eyed women sinking into warm baths in narrow tubs, then bracing themselves against hoses that sprayed cold water.

Louisa stopped at the gate Father had built from branches.

"Anyway, I'm not looking for a roommate. Annie Fields, our second, or is it third, cousin, offered me a place with them."

"I know who Mrs. Fields is. She's famously pretty and married to that editor who must be twenty years older. Isn't he the one who sent back your story with advice to stick to your teaching?"

"To emphasize his point, he offered to loan me forty dollars to start a kindergarten. The worst part is that I can't refuse. I hate being the poor relation, but I'll save on rent. I mean to pay back that loan as soon as I can."

"You'd rather live with them than me? I want the freedom of a city, too."

"But Mother's relatives are everywhere. I went to the Parker House for coffee after a meeting, and the next morning, half the family knew I'd been seen dining with two men."

"You never told me."

"We were discussing abolition."

May was glad that perhaps Louisa didn't pin all her hopes on Mr. Thoreau. "I could help you cook and mend and . . ."

"No. It's not like when you were a girl and you widened your eyes, shook your curls, and got your way."

"That's what I want to show you. You don't know me now that I've grown up."

"Maybe. I'm impressed that you'd even consider working with deranged or delicate girls. But Mother needs you here."

May looked at the brown clapboard house, where she'd now be the only daughter. She said, "Though I might do some good helping those poor girls in Syracuse."

2

N E İ G H B O R S

*D*r. Wilbur's Idiot Asylum stood amid gardens on a hill overlooking a lake and the city. The tall brick building with turrets was the nearest thing May had seen to a palace, though with locks on the gates and iron grilles on the arched windows. But after just one day inside, she wondered how much any of these girls, some with eyes as shiny and vacant as ponds, could be soothed by her introduction to art and music. One girl had bandaged wrists. Another had jumped from a window of her family's home. Each morning, May set out paint and paper and reminded everyone which end of the brush to dip. While she wiped spit from one girl's chin, another hurled a pot of paint across the room. She spent part of the afternoon mopping the floors and walls. Music lessons didn't go much better. While she played "Home, Sweet Home" on the piano, some girls laughed shrilly, while others gazed straight ahead. No one sang along.

May convinced few of the peace to be found by trying to hold beauty within the borders of paper, and she had hardly made any art herself since moving to upstate New York. She didn't paint in Uncle Samuel's elegant home, for fear of accidents on the antiques or Brussels carpets, but stuck to an embroidery hoop, which she thought looked pretty on her lap as she spoke with the young men invited to dine with her and her cousins. Talk often turned to the presidential election. Conversations grew heated after the lanky young man from the West was inaugurated and didn't immediately outlaw slavery. Apparently the new president wasn't any more popular in the South, for states kept seceding from the Union. One evening in April, news arrived that Fort Sumter had been attacked and war was declared between the states.

During the following weeks, guests still gathered in the parlor, but now there were usually more young women than men, with less laughter and fewer games of charades. Early in the summer, after some sad good-byes to men who looked younger instead of older in their new blue frock coats and caps, and more failures at teaching about color and chords, May returned to Concord.

Mother listened to her tales, then spoke of how Anna fretted that she'd been married a year and still showed no signs of a baby. Louisa had published a patriotic poem. Mr. Thoreau never got over a cough that started after being out in the snow counting rings on tree stumps. "Some think it's consumption, though your father believes it's the broken Union that ruined his health. And we have neighbors again."

"Mr. and Mrs. Hawthorne are back, with their children?"

"Not really children any more, except for Rose. Una and Julian are grown." Mother picked up the blue socks with red and white trim she was knitting.

"I suppose I should call on them," May said.

A few days later, May picked huckleberries from the hill behind their houses, and she brought over a pie. The parlor looked finer than it had when the Alcotts had lived there, with velvet drapes and shiny wallpaper. A marble mantelpiece had been put over the hearth. Busts of Roman gods stood on the piano.

As Mrs. Hawthorne poured tea from a silver pot, she said, "Una will be sorry to have missed you, but she's resting, poor dear. She never quite recovered from a fever she got in Rome. We want to add a room where she'll get more sun, but Mr. Wetherbee left without a day's notice when war was declared, leaving Mr. Hawthorne's tower room unfinished. I know it's necessary to save the Union, but my husband needs a peaceful place to work."

May looked up as Julian entered. His jacket and slim pants were as dark as his thick hair. He was tall with wide shoulders, though the way his jacket fell suggested they were soft, not necessarily from laziness, but because he was young enough for his muscles not to have yet hardened. She put out her hand, which he took in his. Its pulse cast a heat.

After some conversation, while Julian finished a quarter of the pie, they stepped outside. May looked back at the house. Ivy grew toward the gables and a room, without shingles or shutters by the windows, that rose above the roof.

"My father hopes that being a floor above everyone else will inspire him," Julian said.

"I wish I had a tower."

"And be cut off from your admirers?"

"I wouldn't miss people asking why I was painting when I might be helping my dear mother." She shook her head, hoping he wouldn't see her flush from his tossed-off compliment. "Concord must seem dull after Europe."

"My father believes that since no one can understand him, he might as well live in exile. But he was afraid his children would forget we're Americans."

"Did you get to Paris? How I envy you seeing all that art!"

"Masterpieces get tiring after one or two. Except for those my mother tried to rush us by. That Venus statue. Quite right she shouldn't bother with clothes."

"All that art was wasted on you."

"I suppose it was." He rested his blue-brown eyes on hers. "Europe had nothing like what I find right here."

"I want to see the Louvre for myself." She tried to make her voice prim.

"Why don't you?"

She was relieved that he didn't guess that she was not someone who'd be sent on the Grand Tour to become cultured and meet eligible expatriates. She said, "How can I paint when I've seen prints borrowed from the Emersons but not a real brushstroke from Michelangelo's hand? No one expects Louisa to write without having read great books."

"Surely you're not serious about art."

"I hope you don't say that because I'm a woman."

"I don't believe a single painting in the Louvre was made by one."

Turning her face to mask her irritation, she started across the meadow between their houses. He seemed to see this as an invitation, and he walked beside her. When she stumbled over a stone, he threw an arm around her waist, then didn't let go. She tried to step away, but he squeezed tighter, so she had to separate herself with some force.

"Did you learn to take such liberties on the continent?" she asked.

"No, I thought of them all myself."

She stepped away and headed home, telling herself that she didn't want a frivolous suitor.

That fall she began teaching penmanship, composition, and elementary French at Mr. Sanborn's school. She drew gods, goddesses, cherubs, and horses on her bedroom walls and up the sides of windows, and she gave private drawing lessons to two girls. On Wednesday evenings, she joined ladies to roll bandages torn from old muslin or scrape linen tablecloths with a pine shingle, collecting lint to send south to dress wounds. Sometimes she borrowed a horse from the Emersons, who were grateful that she kept Dolly and Grace exercised. She paid calls on veterans, who mostly wanted to talk about almost anything except what they'd seen.

Life was meant to be more than work. While May still had misgivings about Julian, she couldn't refuse his invitation to gather chestnuts at a neighbor's farm one Saturday. Afterward, they sat close in the hay wagon and by the bonfire under starlight. On Thursday evenings that winter, May set out bowls of popcorn and homemade root beer and invited neighbors for games of whist, euchre, or Generals, which was currently more popular than Authors. She teamed up with Julian and slipped off her pumps, tapping his toes or feeling his boot on her ankles, not just to win at cards, but because cheating held its own pleasures. They played charades and danced the polka, while Ellen Emerson played the piano. One night, when the moon was full, everyone left to skate on the river. May and Julian ducked behind trees, where his warm lips softened against hers. Something shifted like ocean waves above and below her belly. May thought her sisters would be horrified, for Anna had confided that she'd kissed John only after they were betrothed. But the old rules were changing. News from battlefields made May loath to spurn any chance to feel the strength of her own body.

That spring, May watched Julian drill on Lexington Road. There was nothing like a musket on a shoulder to make a lad look older, though she hoped he wouldn't go off to war. There was grief enough at home. One day, when it was warm enough to go out without a shawl, Mother asked her to bring a basket of Father's apples and some of her tincture of spearmint to Mr. Thoreau, with instructions to take it cold with cream and sugar.

In his parlor, May looked at a stack of books, a vase of hyacinths, a music box, a cane bed, and blood-stained cloths. His aunt tucked a Bible under her elbow, leaned toward the man whose eyes looked big in his gaunt face, and said, "Have you made your peace with God?"

"I didn't know we ever quarreled," Mr. Thoreau replied.

May told him about the return of bluebirds, robins, spiders, violets, and fiddleheads, for he could only see bluebottle flies at the window. He talked about the water lilies that opened on Concord River in July, and she told him the ice had broken there. She'd heard phoebes, meadowlarks, and peepers, and she had seen boys crouch to catch tadpoles near the skunk cabbage and pussy willows.

Later in April, the beaks of starlings turned yellow. In May, church bells rang forty-four times, one for every year of Mr. Thoreau's life. Louisa hiked in from Boston, clutching andromeda, which hadn't yet bloomed into bell-shaped flowers, but whose deep green leaves were fragrant, like the pine boughs piled before the altar. Schools had been closed for the day, and children had picked violets now spread on his casket. Louisa and May sat by their parents in front of crowded pews.

"He hated churches," Louisa whispered.

"Mr. Emerson said he didn't want to mourn alone. When people die, little goes the way they hoped." May watched Louisa press her lips together, supposing she was angry about more than the church. May was sorry she'd ever thought Mr. Thoreau was too old and short for her sister, or that he wore his trousers too low.

After the service, May walked between Julian and Louisa in a procession to the cemetery, which included philosophers, writers, editors, and hundreds of children whose necks smelled of soap.

"Mr. Thoreau showed me how to catch pickerel and chub with blades of grass when I was a boy. We twisted the grass into loops," Julian said.

"He must have liked you," May said.

"He put up with anyone who was willing to follow him around the woods and not bother him with talking."

"He told me how the water lilies near Egg Rock open all at once, with the first touch of sunlight." May squeezed Louisa's hand. "Sometime we should go there at dawn."

"When did he say that?" Louisa asked.

"The last time I saw him. Not long ago."

Louisa didn't reply. When they reached the gravesite in Sleepy Hollow, she stood still and silent. Louisa didn't cry until they were home and May told her about bringing him apples and spearmint. Then Louisa yelled, too. "You take what you don't even want!"

May explained that she'd been doing Mother a favor, reminding Louisa that she hadn't been around. This didn't seem to matter. Louisa hardly spoke to her before she returned to Boston, though when she came back in July, she acted as if she'd never raised her voice. Her forehead smoothed as she told May she was writing about a woman in doomed love with a woodsman philosopher. May thought such writing was a peculiar way to mourn, and she couldn't imagine such a book selling, even if Louisa came up with a better title than *Moods*. She didn't say this, but, grateful that she seemed happier, invited her to swim with her and Julian.

"Is it proper for you to traipse about with him?" Louisa asked.

"Weren't we taught to go where we please? Besides, we usually go with Ellen and Edith, or Julian's sisters, after convincing their mother that the farmer boys keep to the side of the pond by the railroad."

"So I'm to be chaperone."

"That's not why I ask. Some cool water will do you a world of good."

On the next hot afternoon, May, Louisa, and Julian walked through shadows cast by high branches that arched from one side of the dirt road to the other. Orange day lilies grew by cornfields.

"Julian gets up early every morning to practice marching with the Concord Auxiliary." May hoped to impress Louisa.

"Lexington Road could be the closest I'll get to the front," Julian said. "My mother says I'm too young to go to war, though plenty of fellows my age are signing up."

"Our father is writing letters begging for a place in the army. He admits sixty-one is rather elderly to be a soldier, but he reminds them he's a vegetarian and teetotaler and couldn't be in finer health," May said.

"He wants to show the South whose side God is on," Louisa said. "I wish I could fight, too. All women can do is roll bandages and make jam for hospital raffles. Julian, I hope you do enlist."

"You look good in blue. But you mustn't break your mother's heart," May said.

"People say your father is on the southern side." Louisa looked at Julian.

"He's not, but he thinks southerners have good manners, which he finds lacking around here."

"He should hardly comment on etiquette when he walks the long way through the woods into town, rather than pass our yard and risk conversation with our father," Louisa said.

"My father never quite recovered from a long poem yours brought over to recite."

"Louisa admires your father's novels." May changed the subject. "What is he writing now?"

"No one knows. When he worked as a consul in Europe, he kept saying how he needed solitude and silence to write. Now that he has it, he mostly paces."

"What I'd give to travel and find dastardly dukes and corrupt ladies-in-waiting for my tales," Louisa said.

"I'm not much of a reader, but I'm looking forward to your novel if it's as immoral as May says it is," Julian said.

"May, what did you tell him?"

"Only that it's hard to please editors in a city where some ladies put books by men and women on different shelves to avoid a hint of scandal."

They reached Walden Pond, which reflected the pointed tops of spruce trees and rounded silhouettes of maples. Red-winged black birds and yellow warblers sipped water by blueberry bushes. May and Louisa took sheets from their baskets and wound them around a few birches to make a space where they could change into flannel tunics and pantaloons. Louisa unpinned her chestnut-colored hair and let it fall to her waist, reminding May how she'd grown up thinking Louisa was the most beautiful sister. This role seemed bequeathed to May as her sisters brushed her light hair, casting such a spell of confidence that by the time she began to depend more upon mirrors than her sisters' touches, and saw that her looks were ordinary, her belief in her own allure didn't dim with the recognition that her nose was too long to be classical, her eyes, neither gray nor green, were too small, and she was starting to tower over her friends.

When she and Louisa stepped away from the cloth-wound trees, Julian was already swimming. Louisa dragged in a yellow rowboat that belonged to the Emersons, who welcomed borrowers. She slung her legs over the side and took the oars. May waded until the water reached her waist, then plunged in and swam toward Julian. Her soaked tunic was heavy, but her swift strokes and kicks kept her buoyant. Flannel pressed against her legs, a pleasurable sensation, as was noticing Julian's eyes on her arms as they arced over the pond's surface.

He swam toward her. His wet hair and eyelashes were black. He pressed his wide hands on her shoulders and pushed her down. Water filled her eyes and mouth. She felt the ache of a shriek caught in her throat, then burst back into the air. She shook her hair off her face, laughed, caught Julian's waist in her hands, and pulled him under. Her mouth trailed over his neck, which was slick, though prickly under his chin.

He grabbed her foot and slid his hand up her calf. As his palm reached her thigh, her legs opened. She twisted around, raised her arms over the surface, and swam toward the rowboat. Julian grabbed her foot again. She kicked it away, so that her bathing costume billowed. She reached the boat before him. Louisa gave her a hand as she tried to scramble in.

Julian clutched the rim of the rowboat and pulled it down. May let go of Louisa's hand, slid back into the water, and helped Julian rock the boat. It tipped over. Louisa tumbled in. She flung up her arms to propel herself out of the water, sputtering and laughing. All three splashed and dunked each other until they were breathless. Then May and Louisa swam to shore, dragged the boat up the pebbly beach, and changed from their clinging clothes into dry dresses. They sat where moss and dried pine needles made the ground pale green and burnt orange. May spread her fingers to comb Louisa's hair, watching Julian wade from the water. As he headed behind some pines to change into dry trousers and a shirt, she glimpsed his broad pale back.

"He's not a bad fellow," Louisa said.

"I prefer his company to that of the scholars who tell Father how our New England granite is more precious than emeralds from afar or farmers who can't carry on a conversation." May stopped talking as Julian emerged from the woods, pushing back his damp dark hair.

"Do you want to row across the pond? I want to try out for the crew team, and I should practice," he said.

"He's going to Harvard soon," May reminded Louisa.

"If I pass the examinations," he said.

"You should be grateful for the chance at college," Louisa said.

"You aren't going to give me one of your suffragist talks, are you?" Julian started shoving out the boat. "Aren't some colleges open to women?"

"Not many. And all require money," Louisa said.

"Our cousin Lucy is going to medical school." May shook her head as Julian beckoned. "I'll stay and keep my sister company."

She saw Louisa's mouth soften, as if touched that she'd choose to be with her. They looked at the pond, which was partly shadowed this late in the day, but some water still shimmered a jewel-like blue. A muskrat paddled to shore. A heron spread its wide wings.

"I can't see the use of art, when beauty is right here." Louisa took a notebook from her basket and propped it on her knees.

"But not everyone sees it. Artists try to point out the ordinary splendors." May borrowed paper and a pencil to sketch the pond and hill where Mr. Thoreau had lived for two years, two months, and two days. She even drew the cabin. The world seemed to turn quiet while she moved her hand.

Louisa glanced at her paper. "His little house is gone."

"Can't you see it?" May squinted at the pines and hemlocks.

"Across town, where it was hauled to store grain."

"Look harder."

"I liked him."

"I know." May touched her hand, then added a rowboat to the picture, showing the back of a man holding oars. The more she moved her pencil, the more shapes and hues she saw in the shadows. "A view like this seems like a message from the world. Drawing is my way to keep up my end of the conversation. I've missed it."

"Too busy with card games, I hear."

"Making tea and conversation, hanging the wash, and sorting the mail for bills. The lot of the unmarried daughter."

Louisa watched Julian rowing back and asked, "Are you smitten?"

"He'll be off to Harvard soon." May thought of how Cambridge was a good afternoon's hike from Concord and how Julian would surely meet more young ladies there. She said, "I want a beau who will take me to Europe, not tell me about it."

"You don't still have that dream?"

"My art would improve with Michelangelo and Raphael to teach me."

"Perhaps you should look for a living tutor. There must be some in Boston. Maybe we should find a place to room together."

"What?"

"Do you still want to live with me?"

"I don't want to be the girl who's left behind."

"And I wouldn't want anyone to speak of my sister that way. You could take my place at the kindergarten, so I'd have more time for writing. But you should remember that Chapel Street is where immigrants come for help. These aren't the little girls in fresh frocks or the boys with ringlets you see with governesses in the park."

"Did you forget I taught girls in an asylum? If I can calm girls who consider jumping off bridges, I can manage children's tantrums. Lu, you won't regret it. I can help fix up your wardrobe and cook us lovely suppers."

"I can't have you fussing with clothes or clever dishes, banning drinking from jam jars. I like to put a few apples in the stove, then pick up my pen. If my writing is going well, I don't want someone telling me to put out the lamp."

"You can write until morning. Something dazzling enough to make a fortune."

"I don't know. But I dream of hiring a cook and servant for Mother."

"We could become famous together!"

"I'd just like to earn enough to pay back Mr. Fields."

"And it's not wrong to remember ourselves. Should we tour France first, then Italy? Do you think that's greedy?"

"Men call it ambition. I've been writing every day since I was fifteen. I suppose I'm ready for some acclaim."

May squeezed her pencil. Perhaps as much as meeting gentlemen, she wanted more time like this, drawing while her sister wrote beside her. Did Louisa want that, too? Or did she hear May's breath deepen as Julian pulled up the boat, then walked closer? Was she afraid May might marry first? She asked, "What made you change your mind about my joining you?"

Louisa responded, "And there can't be a lot of questions. Sisters should have some secrets."

3

CHANDELİERS

*B*oston's brick sidewalks were crowded with ladies wearing skirts puffed out by crinolines. Many wore hats with wider brims than those worn in Concord, and ribbons seemed chosen to swish, not just hold on in the wind. Shorter steps and slower gaits suggested some ladies were aware they'd be seen, which was reason enough to step outside. May kept her small-town habit of scanning faces she expected to recognize, but she had little time for strolling. At the kindergarten, she led songs about ducks and helped children conduct experiments with prisms, mold clay nests, weave strips of colored paper, and count on an abacus. Many of the children were Irish, with green eyes, pale foreheads, rosy cheeks, red or black hair, and lilting voices. They made May laugh and could be coaxed out of mischief with the promise of sitting on her lap.

After putting away wooden blocks and wiping low tables,

she often set off to handsome townhouses where she'd arranged to teach piano to girls of about sixteen. Most had finished their formal educations but were either deemed too young to be courting or thwarted because so many men had joined the Union Army. The girls dutifully practiced scales, but were more charmed by the way May admired paintings they'd passed thousands of times but had never really seen. Charlotte, one of her most devoted students, urged her to teach art as well as music. May knew most parents would frown on paints in their parlors, so she looked for lodgings where students might come to her.

"I found a place not far from the Old Corner Bookshop and the Music Hall," May told Louisa one evening as she painted flowers on lampshades to sell at charity fairs. "The room has a sofa that changes to a bed. A lovely doorman stands by potted palms in the entryway."

"May, pay attention to your purse. You just spent a week's salary on silk."

"My muslins are fine to wear among the sticky children at Chapel Street, but I can't arrive in Beacon Hill and be sent to back doors. Charlotte tells me all her friends will want to take art lessons. We won't have to fret about money."

Louisa bent over her paper. "I can't think about potted palms or other luxuries until I pay back Mr. Fields."

"I can't believe he's in a hurry. Julian says he's quite jolly. He not only edits his father's novels, but also brings him cigars and whiskey and keeps track of his accounts so he doesn't have to bother."

"I will repay that loan, and I don't want to move."

May had enough experience hearing her older sisters tell her *no* to recognize the varieties of breath within the word. She thought there was hope, but not now, so she changed the subject. "Are you writing more patriotic poems?"

"No. Remember that story about a girl going out to service that Mr. Fields turned down? Instead of putting it away, I'm adding episodes to turn it into a novel I'm calling *Work.*"

"Will it chronicle all the dreadful jobs you took?"

"And show how a girl learns from making sacrifices."

"Good for you, writing more instead of less. But you might want this book to have a happy ending."

"I intend my heroine to join a union of women workers, after surviving horrors some will say I shouldn't mention. I didn't invent human nature. I merely record it, but people blame me."

May thought that living with Louisa made her more of a mystery instead of less of one. She wondered if she told Anna things she never told her. She looked for signs when they visited Anna in her small home. Lace doilies covered chairs and tables. The handles of the teacups in the cupboard faced the same direction. Spoons and forks nested in their proper slots within drawers. May felt alarmed when Anna burst into tears after finding ants in the sugar bin. Could a woman spend too much time in one home, especially one where windows rattled when trains sped by on the nearby tracks? She urged Anna to join them for a night of theater or opera.

"Don't think I'm not busy," Anna said. "I knit and bake with some ladies from church. We bring baskets to the sick and those in need, as Mother always did."

"Except she used to invite the sick and needy right into our house. Baskets sound better," May said. Still, she thought that making things for strangers must be lonely. "Come look at pictures in the Athenæum with me. Aunt Bond lent me her pass."

Anna shook her head and turned the conversation back to her worry about time passing with no signs of a baby on the way.

A few weeks later, May convinced her to join her and Louisa at a fair to raise funds for Union hospitals. The sandal-wood fans and letter openers that May had decorated were for sale along with wax flowers under glass globes, jars of jam covered with calico swatches, and woven potholders. Three panels May had painted of morning glories had already sold.

Making their way through the crowded hall, May studied busts of John Brown and other eminent abolitionists, which were displayed under bunting. She admired the colors and patterns of Log Cabin, Joseph's Coat, Sixteen Blossoms, Broken Star, and Oak Leaf quilts, while Anna peered at stitches, as if to measure signs of diligence or haste.

When they returned to the table where May's painted fans and lampshades had been displayed, Anna grabbed her wrist. "All your work has sold! I'm so proud of you!"

"No, here's a paperweight." Louisa pushed forward a smooth stone May had painted, which had been half-hidden. "I'd recognize your lilies anywhere. But it's too bad you can't put your name on them."

"Painters sign their names in the corners of canvas. Decorative paperweights aren't the same kind of art," May said.

"The charity the sales benefit is what's important," Anna said.

"The money goes to hospitals for our brave boys, but you don't see men giving away their work, at least without acknowledgement. When I publish a book, you can be sure I'll put my name on it. No pseudonym, no initials. I won't masquerade." Louisa glanced at a table holding a collection of stories inscribed by Nathaniel Hawthorne and *Uncle Tom's Cabin* signed by Harriet Beecher Stowe. The books were offered as prizes for a raffle, along with a white ox and piano lessons.

May turned as she was greeted by Charlotte. She introduced her to a friend named Alice Bartlett, who said, "We were looking for your work."

"All her panels and fans have sold," Louisa said.

"I told you we should have come earlier," Charlotte said. "Alice, we beg her to give art lessons and reveal her secrets."

"I taught in Concord, but there are so many fine artists here," May said.

"And all are curmudgeonly. I was promised the Grand Tour to cap my education, but the war means we're stuck at home for now. A class would be some consolation." Alice smiled as two gentlemen approached. "May, you must meet my brother and his chum."

May slightly dropped her knees while greeting a tall young man with curly blond hair. She batted words as lightly and deliberately as she'd swing a croquet mallet, paying attention to the rhythm as she would doing the Virginia reel, leaning just close enough to suggest both hesitation and promise. But she didn't mind when Ellen Emerson interrupted to say hello. Ellen told them that her sister Edith's beau had enlisted, and their brother Edward had left Harvard, to their father's distress.

"Will he join the army?" May wondered if there was a discreet way to ask about news of Julian.

"He wants to. Our mother says she'll allow it only if emancipation is proclaimed."

"If all mothers were like yours, the war would end sooner. Bells ring here at two o'clock to close shops for recruitment, but freeing the slaves would do more for the Union than the draft. Men would sign up in droves." Louisa grabbed May's hand as she fixed her eyes on a thin, stern-faced woman who stepped behind a table. "That's Dorothea Dix."

"Who?" May asked.

"She's behind these fundraisers to set up hospitals. I heard she's looking for more ladies to sign on as nurses."

"Women do such work?" May asked.

"Now that so many men are soldiers, there aren't enough left to care for the wounded."

"Surely you're not considering doing that!"

"They're looking for women who are either married or at least plain and thirty-five."

"You're beautiful and thirty."

"If the war doesn't end soon, they might take younger women." Louisa's mouth tightened as she walked toward the woman with her hair simply pulled back, standing behind a table with a stack of papers.

May thought Louisa was getting rather too old to waste time on impossible people and causes, but she supposed there was no harm in talking. She looked at portraits of military heroes while calculating how much she might charge for lessons and if she could make enough to afford a sky parlor for rent near the Public Garden. The last time she'd mentioned moving, Louisa's protests had seemed to weaken. Teaching art would give her more chances to paint, something she would emphasize to the young ladies, implying that her fees were almost inconsequential.

❧

AS SOON AS MAY ANNOUNCED SHE'D BE GIVING ART lessons, Charlotte, Alice, and two of their friends signed up. May asked Father to help her build some easels, which she squeezed into the sky parlor after pushing back the bed and then hiding it with a screen she painted with a landscape of Roman ruins. She showed the girls how to shape their hands into small frames to look through and compose. They each closed one eye and squinted to flatten a vase of wildflowers that May had arranged. The goldenrod, Queen Anne's Lace, and asters had looked lovelier by the road, even tangled on the table, but one couldn't paint such a jumble.

Late one afternoon, May bid her students good-bye, put two potatoes in the stove, and pushed the easels behind the screen. Louisa returned from a meeting with bright cheeks. She tossed her cloak over the back of a chair, put up her feet, took a letter from her carpetbag, scanned it, then slipped it back into a worn envelope. May wondered if she was stirred by more than political passion.

"Two more girls enrolled in my classes. We haven't enough chairs, but I told them that standing while working keeps the mind clear." She pulled the potatoes from the coals, dropped them on a plate she handed Louisa, then glanced at a bowl of russet apples. "Please don't eat the still life. I should keep it here for a month, but the girls are in a hurry to bring home something pretty. They don't understand that art isn't a race." She took her Eugénie blue dress from the wardrobe and finished stitching lace over the fraying cuffs.

"Aren't you eating?" Louisa asked.

"Alice invited me to dinner. She wants me to get to know her brother and tells me they have some masterpieces from Italy. Her grandfather made a fortune importing marble and silk."

"And probably immigrants, who traveled in worse conditions than his wares. But I suppose you're lucky to be asked. I'm glad you're not pining over Julian."

"You should be thinking about meeting bachelors, too. Or have you found someone?"

"I'm staying home to work."

"Attending dinner parties is work, too. Writers can slip manuscripts into envelopes and duck away, but artists must go into society. We depend on wealthy people with walls to adorn."

"I suppose Alice's brother is handsome as well as rich. How old is he?"

"Since when are you so preoccupied with numbers?"

"You're right. Why should I care? Mr. Fields marries a girl seventeen years younger, and few raise an eyebrow. Why shouldn't women also marry who they please?"

May hooked on a corset, dropped a crinoline over her head, and wiggled her hips until the hoops fell into place. She put on her dress, shook her curls so they spread down her back, pulled back her shoulders to stand to her full height, and breathed deeply. She turned to Louisa. "How do I look?"

"If I told you, you'd get vain."

"My favorite sin." May kissed the top of her head and put on her woolen shawl, hoping the traces left by nibbling moths couldn't be seen in the dark. "I'll bring you back descriptions of jewels and jam tarts. Even if your hero is more taken with squirrels and acorns than finery, there's no reason the heroine can't be well dressed. No one wants to read about girls wearing hand-me-downs who eat crackers and potatoes."

She hurried down the stairs to the lobby, where she asked for a carriage. Alice's home wasn't far, but May's morocco kid boots had delicate heels that weren't designed for walking, and a wide skirt in a narrow street made being spattered with mud too likely. Besides, there was no telling who might arrive at the Bartletts' as she did and admire the way she angled her toes as she stepped from the carriage. She supposed such thoughts *were* vain, but she'd never understood why a bit of conceit should be placed with stealing, murder, or even coveting. Had she missed something by seldom going to church, something that seemed to have gotten lost in all their moving? She knew she was ignorant of much doctrine but was certain the Creator reveled in beauty. Why shouldn't people?

The sky was turning dark as she settled into the coach and looked out the window. A boy lifted a rod to light a streetlamp. Vendors cried, "Oysters! Hot on the shell!"

"Chestnuts, don't burn your fingers!"

"Fresh flowers for your sweetheart!"

They drove past Faneuil Hall, which had been turned into an enlistment center. Soldiers who mustered in the Boston Common during the day now sang and drank around pitched tents. Past elm and chestnut trees, May saw the frog pond, where Louisa had taught her to skate. She wished that pretty memory of skidding over ice were her first one. She scarcely remembered living in a dilapidated farmhouse filled with philosophers, only faintly recalled being terribly hungry and cold when leaving Fruitlands. The Alcott family had been offered temporary lodgings here and there, before May left with Mother when she took a job helping with water cures. After that, relatives arranged a job for Mother in Boston, finding homes for beaten wives or sick children and households where their Irish immigrant neighbors could work as washerwomen and cooks. Louisa and Anna found positions as servants, while Beth looked after the basement apartment that smelled of wet wool stockings hung by the stove. Even at eight years old, May helped out by walking down the pebbled sidewalks in the Common, waving papers advertising Father's lectures on transcendence.

The bells on the horses' bridles jingled as the carriage pulled up to the Bartletts' town house. May walked with the footman to the grand entryway, where another man escorted her upstairs. She left her shawl among fur stoles and cashmere cloaks. One maid brushed the hem of her dress, while another smoothed her hair. Then a man offered his arm to guide her back downstairs. May met each servant as she would a partner in a dance. If she let herself be guided, she hoped no one would guess that she hadn't been raised with these rituals of wealth.

In the drawing room, the rustle of silk and the tap of fashionably heeled shoes sounded lovelier than cheap fabric or worn soles. Solid silver laid on mahogany rang more musically than tin on pine. Alice, who wore a striped taffeta gown, greeted her. "I'm sorry my brother won't join us tonight. I'm afraid he isn't feeling well."

"That's a shame." May's disappointment was diverted as she overhead a gentleman in a fashionable frock coat referred to as being in the publishing business. She was used to more ragtag literary sorts. She thought that if this evening didn't turn out to be entertaining, she might make it useful for Louisa. She asked Alice to introduce her.

A few minutes later, Mr. Niles offered his elbow on their way to the dining room, where he pulled out a chair upholstered in claret-colored velvet. A servant unfolded a linen napkin and placed it on her lap. Guests nodded at a butler holding a silver soup tureen, then waited to be served. May surveyed the goblets and crystal glasses and a bowl holding a pyramid of sugared pears and grapes. Like the other ladies, she shook her head when offered wine, though she wouldn't have minded a glass.

Mr. Niles, whose eyes were as dark as his waxed mustache, asked her a few questions that called for short answers, then told her about a séance he'd attended. "The piano moved. A mahogany table spun around while the chandelier rattled. I am a rational man, but can you give me a rational explanation for that?"

As he went on to describe an experience with a mesmerist, May leaned to the left while a servant took her majolica plate and gave her another one with a slice of beef pie. Her knife felt pleasantly hefty. She'd been raised to think that all people were equal and money didn't matter much, but wouldn't it be easier to give bread to the poor if her mother hadn't kept an anxious eye on the levels of flour barrels? It would be easier to be kind if she could afford all colors of oil paint and not have to scrimp on cobalt blue and crimson.

Around her, guests discussed whether ice water was unhealthy, the accident on Tremont Street, and the reckless way young men drove their horses. Mention of cranberries or lumber, hints of the shipping business that must have made the fortunes of several men there, were hushed. References to Shenandoah Valley and Stonewall Jackson prompted Mrs. Bartlett to steer conversations from battlefields and generals back to more appropriate subjects. Ladies here disapproved of politics and religion as topics for the table, while in Concord people talked about little else.

Mr. Niles took a bite of haddock. "It reminds me of the delicious turbot I recently enjoyed in Rome."

May supposed that everyone here had tasted seafood from the Mediterranean. She glanced at a gentleman who was discussing *The Scarlet Letter*.

"Did you read it, Miss Alcott? What do you think?" Mr. Niles asked.

"I found the ending disappointing." May thought that was a safe comment for any Hawthorne novel.

"I used to work with his editor, but I left Ticknor and Fields to help start a company specializing in memory albums. The war means there's a call for books with blank pages for pictures and inscriptions," Mr. Niles said.

"But novels will always be needed. Even in these hard times, people want to read about love and tragedy."

"And what does a young lady like you know of such goings on?"

"Not a thing, but my sister does. She's a writer."

Mr. Niles's eyelids fell. As a maid set down bowls of water with rose petals floating on top, he dipped his fingers, then stood and pulled out her chair. He didn't look back as he joined the gentlemen filing out. May followed the ladies down a hall, then heard the clacking of billiard balls and smelled cigar smoke wafting from the next room as ladies stirred sugar into cups of Darjeeling tea and chatted about an uppity cook, bouts with influenza, the quest for an honest butcher, and a curiously short engagement. Alice spoke near her ear. "I'm afraid we bored you at dinner."

May hooked her arm into hers. "Didn't you tell me that your father has a drawing by Michelangelo?"

"It's in his study. I'm not supposed to go there."

"Please. I want to see art as it was intended, not copies. The sketches tourists bring home are like being given a taste of something fine, then having the feast pulled away."

Alice glanced around, then showed May into a room lined with cases of leather-bound books. May turned slowly, stopping when she saw strong chalk lines depicting a man shown naked from the hips up. The sketch of the head and torso seemed unfinished, though the lines depicting muscles looked both confident and swift, so the portrait seemed to rise from the paper. The places where the red chalk thickened then turned paler suggested a face aching to change expression, a body about to move.

"My mother doesn't think it belongs even on a private wall, but she allows it as it's supposed to be someone from the Bible. Whoever it is, I'm sure he'd look nicer dressed," Alice said.

"Artists have worked from the nude for thousands of years."

"Not in Boston."

"You must get used to nudity if you hope to take the Grand Tour with your mother."

"She says the most eligible men can be met in Europe, where the best families spend some time. May, wouldn't it be bonny if we went together? I'm sure our mothers would adore each other."

May turned to a plaster cast of a gladiator struggling to stand. His head was thrown back in agony, with taut and rippling muscles in his neck and gored chest. The clenched toes and fingers looked rigid, as if he were desperate to hold onto life. "Who sculpted this?"

"Dr. Rimmer, a talented but rather odd friend of my father's," Alice said. "I think art should be uplifting, don't you? What's the point of depicting something gruesome? There's talk of raising money to have it cast in bronze and sent to Paris, where it might be shown in the Salon des Beaux-Arts. Its chances of getting past the jury don't seem good."

"Surely this would find a place! The artist won't send it himself?"

"I presume shipping is expensive. Dr. Rimmer teaches an anatomy class for artists and also works as a doctor for poor people out in Quincy, but he can scarcely put food on the table for his passel of children."

"He teaches? Are women allowed?"

"I believe he has one class of young ladies."

"Imagine how much better we could paint portraits if we knew what's under the surface. Does he use nude models?"

"Gracious, not in his classes! He has daughters of his own and knows what's good for them. All his subjects are gloomy or violent. Cain and Abel. Saint Stephen being stoned to death. I suppose such things used to happen, but must we dwell on them? My mother says it's no wonder his art doesn't sell."

May looked back at the statue, feeling the heat of life and death twisting together. No matter how Alice might praise her, whether anyone here knew her name or not, May knew her paintings did not belong on these walls. But she vowed to someday make one that would. She wondered how much the sculptor's lessons cost as she heard doors open and gentlemen's voices get louder.

She and Alice left for a drawing room, where butlers passed out fruit and ices. May asked Alice to find out the details of Dr. Rimmer's classes, then asked if she could call a carriage for her.

"It won't be easy finding one at this hour." Alice glanced at men collecting hats and helping ladies into ermine stoles or mink wraps. "Maybe someone could give you a ride. I don't suppose there will be talk if you leave with Mr. Niles."

May wondered if she recalled that the fares doubled after eleven o'clock and was being considerate, trying to conceal, just as May did, that she taught not just for pleasure, but to earn a living. A few minutes later, May walked with Mr. Niles to his carriage. After they settled on seats across from each other, May asked a few careful questions about his work. He spoke of locating books that had proved popular in England to sell in the United States. "I work about half the year in London."

"What do you do there for entertainment?"

"I go to an opera now and then."

"My sisters would give anything to see the London theaters. When we were little, we used to make pasteboard crowns and perform plays my sister wrote."

As the carriage passed the Common, May glanced out the window. Once again, she remembered standing under the bare gray branches of elms, passing out handbills. One morning, a gentleman had pressed a nickel into her hand and asked, "Does your father know where you are?"

"Yes, he sent me," she'd replied brightly. Her smile fell as he'd said, "Tell him to get a job instead of sending his children out begging."

May's face grew warm, as if those words had been spoken moments instead of years ago. The coin had felt heavy in her palm. The blue sky had seemed to rise, clearly too high to touch. For the first time in her life, she'd felt all alone, knowing that the parents she loved weren't loved by all the rest of the world.

Now she pointed out the frog pond, sparkling in the moonlight. "That's where my sisters taught me how to skate."

"It sounds like you had jolly times," Mr. Niles said.

"It was the happiest of childhoods."

The horses clattered over cobblestones, then stopped in front of the rooming house. May stepped out of the carriage carefully, so that only the tips of her boots showed.

◈

RATHER THAN LEAVING HER DISCOURAGED, THE ART SHE'D seen at the Bartlett's home made May determined to work harder. She remained proud of her past paintings but also aware of how much she still must do. The following evening, she sketched Louisa in the room that smelled of lemon drops and pickled limes. It was impossible to convey the light on Louisa's long, thick hair, the amber flecks in her eyes. May rubbed out lines.

"You didn't tell me about Alice's brother." Louisa clasped her hands over her head.

"Sit still, please. There's nothing to tell, though that family is wealthier than Julian's."

"I suppose that's all you need to know."

May didn't just compare Julian's house with its claret-colored carpets and brocatelle-covered cushions on the window seats to one that was even more elegant. She also wanted distance from a town where most people not only didn't notice what was hung on a wall, but also called that a virtue. She missed kisses that felt like opening a door between a stuffy room and the outdoors, but she said, "There's nothing wrong with looking out for not only my future, but our whole family's. Who will take care of Mother and Father one day? Anna married a poor fellow, and you claim to be uninterested, though you're coy about that letter you carry around."

"I have more on my mind than fortunes or romance."

"Yes, you're noble, with your old story about how Father returned from his lecture tour and I was the only one who asked what was in his pocket. When he took out a single dollar, Mother said, 'All that matters is that you're safely home.'"

"I tell that to show her goodness."

"With me as the villain. But what's wrong with having

more to eat than stale bread or wrinkled apples? Or saying what everyone else is thinking? Anyway, your luck may change soon. I met an editor who works for a new company that specializes in diaries and albums."

"He thinks people want books without words?"

"Maybe he hasn't found the right ones yet. You should send him one of your plays or stories. You might even find you have more than literature in common. It seems he often goes to Europe on business."

"I didn't ask you to look for a beau for me! Or an editor."

"Everyone can use some help." May rubbed out most of the portrait.

❧

A FEW DAYS LATER, MAY WALKED UP TREMONT STREET and entered the Art Studio Building, where Alice had told her Dr. Rimmer taught. She heard a harp, scuffing slippers, numbers called in French from a ballet studio, shouts from rehearsing actors, and a pounding mallet from behind a door with a handle streaked with clay. She climbed the stairs and peeked into a room where charts of bones and organs were tacked to the walls. A human skeleton hung in a corner. A chalkboard was covered with sketches labeled *frontal, parietal,* and *occipital bones.* May touched a drawing showing what was under a turned neck. The strands of muscles looked as hidden and complicated as the currents of a river. She vowed to never again draw a few lines and a smudge of shadow for a neck.

May left the studio to call on Aunt Bond. She didn't ask for a loan but for references for women who might need mending done. By the following week, May was letting out waistbands for young women expecting babies or hemming linens for beds she wouldn't sleep in. She kept accounts of what she spent on thread and trim and how much she'd need to pay for classes. As her needle circled, her thoughts of the future turned less to the sort of gown she might wear to a show that included her paintings and more to her hand painting eyes that properly flickered, mouths on the verge of moving.

One evening, Louisa frowned at the black silk dress on May's lap. "Where did that come from?"

"I'm taking in sewing."

"Why? You have more students each week."

May felt proud that Louisa noticed. "A new series of anatomy classes starts in January. If I improve at drawing faces and figures, I might earn a living painting portraits of sons and husbands before they leave for war."

"When will you find time for classes between sewing and teaching? May, you did what you said when we moved to this neighborhood. You got more students. I'm not surprised they adore you, and they take you seriously, too. You've accomplished something. It's a shame you should sew so much when you might be improving your craft. I'm putting money aside to send home, but the next time I sell a story, I'll help pay for lessons."

"You're too generous! I'll get commissions, I'm sure, and it won't be long before I can pay you back."

"It's a gift. There are enough debts in this family."

"Just your wanting to do this means a lot."

"You didn't think I'd help out a sister?"

"I didn't think you'd help out an artist."

May's anticipation of classes over the following weeks lightened all her chores. Louisa also often seemed in a bright mood, crumpling fewer sheets of paper. One night, when she took out a worn letter, May said, "You might tell your sister if you were courting."

"I'm not." Louisa's voice was firm, but color rose on her face. "I have a plan. It may come to nothing. I must talk to Mother first."

"Then it's time for a trip home. Let's ask Anna and John to join us for your and Father's birthday."

❦

ON A CHILLY MORNING LATE IN NOVEMBER, MAY AND Louisa headed to the train station. Louisa whistled as they walked, though her birthday often made her gloomy. Father had been born on the same day and had long preached that it should be an occasion to give rather than get. Louisa had often spoken of being a little girl who was asked to smile while passing around plum cakes to the students who Father then taught, though she didn't get to taste one. May didn't bring this up, but she'd packed dried plums, hoping to bake a cake.

They got off at the depot and walked by arbors covered with vines shorn of grapes and leaves. Cornstalks had turned brown and brittle. On their way through town, they passed the general store, the apothecary, the redbrick town hall, the blacksmith shop, and a church. They turned at the rustic fence

Father had made from twisted branches and gnarled roots he'd dragged from the woods.

As May opened their kitchen door, she heard Mother, Anna, and Father talking all at once. The sputter of flames from the hearth suggested a generous fire. Before May had put down her bonnet, she learned the festive air had nothing to do with birthdays.

"I wanted to wait until everyone was here to tell," Anna said. "But I couldn't keep quiet. John and I expect a baby in spring!"

May hugged her, then let go to throw her arms around Mother, John, then Father. Everyone repeated the usual questions about whether Anna was sure and well and if she suspected exactly when the baby might come.

"This is the best gift a daughter could give us. Motherhood is woman's highest calling," Father said. His long hair was the color of butter and tarnished silver.

"Of course, but I worked hard in the kindergarten, as May does now," Louisa said.

"Teaching is noble, but it's not the same as being a parent. You girls will understand when you have your own," Mother said.

"Mother, I'm thirty years old. I'm not going to get married," Louisa said.

"You just haven't met the right man yet," Anna said.

"We don't know if she has." May made her voice light, hoping Louisa would smile again. "I don't know how she keeps so mum, but she won't even hint about who wrote the letter she's been carting around."

"I told you, there's no one." Louisa pulled the letter from her satchel, shook it dramatically, and read: "'We seek mature ladies who are diligent, clean, healthy, sober, and industrious. No jewelry, bows, or hoop skirts are allowed.'" She straightened her back. "The nation won't let me fight, but I can help the men who do."

"I'm not sure I understand," Mother said.

"Dorothea Dix is looking for nurses and said I might join," Louisa said.

"You can't be serious," May exclaimed.

"I want to do more than sew blue shirts."

"It's an honorable idea. Who would have thought I'd have a child who might help turn this war around?" Father said.

"Bronson, please!" Mother turned from him to Louisa. "You'd be so near the fighting! And we've heard these hospitals are breeding grounds for sickness."

"That's why I'm going. They need help. I'm strong and healthy, just the sort they're looking for. I thought you'd be proud."

Louisa looked so stricken that May said, "Mother, you shouldn't worry. Louisa has never been sick a day in her life."

"You're the one who taught us to help others," Louisa said.

"It's dangerous," Mother replied. "Pneumonia, typhoid, and measles spread from one person to another."

"It's nothing compared to what our good men risk," Louisa said. "People say that President Lincoln will soon free the slaves, and Governor Andrew is already looking for colored men to make up a regiment. They'll fight like no one else, and the war will be over soon."

May wrapped an arm around her oldest sister, who seemed forgotten as Father read aloud the letter in his rich voice. May knew Louisa deserved praise for meaning to bathe and bandage men whose arms and legs were cut off, men who bled and coughed and needed bedpans, but did she have to announce this plan minutes after Anna's news? John seemed agitated, too, as if about to defend his wife. Or was he hoping to become invisible, sorry that the hero in the family wasn't him? No one found fault with him for staying out of God's war, not when they knew he endured constant pain in his legs. But May supposed he must dread silent criticism.

"I suppose we all must make sacrifices in these times," Mother said.

"Then it's settled," Louisa said. "May and I will move our things back here, and as soon as I get notice, I'll be off to the front."

"Move back here? I was going to start art lessons in January," May said.

"Lessons?" Mother asked. "You're the finest artist in town. Louisa never took classes in writing."

"Art is different. I'll look for cheaper lodgings," May said.

"Mercy, you can't live in Boston by yourself," Mother said.

"The kindergarten has been losing students and has been advised to close for the duration," Louisa said. "And your young ladies will make do without your fruit bowls for a while."

"Won't you be glad to be near Julian again? When he's home from college," Anna said.

"His mother tells me he sometimes dines at Judge Hoar's house. Carrie is quite pretty," Mother said.

"Judge Hoar graduated from Harvard and likes to make sure the college boys get a good meal now and then. A lot of them go." May thought Carrie seemed a churchy sort who wouldn't even play croquet lest someone catch sight of her ankles. "Julian can do as he pleases, as will I. Maybe Louisa and I will go to Europe together, when she gets back from the front."

"Why not?" Louisa said.

Everyone returned to talking again about her, as if Louisa were the sort of swashbuckling hero she'd acted in the plays she wrote. Didn't she remember that somebody always died? That in this case, there might be no curtsy before an improvised curtain? No, everything would be all right. May knew she couldn't complain about putting off drawing classes when others gave up so much more for the war. She stood up. "I'll make tea."

Mother squeezed her hand. "It's good to have you back here. You know just the way I like it. Strong, but not bitter."

As May rummaged for cups, she moved the breadboard with the burnt impression of Raphael she'd made with a hot poker on wood. As if she could know what one of her favorite painters would look like, when she'd never even been to Italy. She set the teapot over a low flame and thought how foolish she'd been to think she might save the day with a plum cake. She looked through the window to bent, blackened sunflowers and larches between their house and Julian's, then carefully measured spoonfuls of tea. How many cups would she brew while Louisa was gone?

She snatched up the breadboard and tried to cram it into the woodstove, but the iron door was too small. She threw it hard, so it slammed against the wall.

"Is everything all right?" Mother called.

"Yes." May took a breath, so her voice would carry to the next room. "Of course."

4

NORTH AND SOUTH

he Emerson family and Mrs. Hawthorne joined the Alcotts at the train station. Louisa held a basket of apples, gingerbread, a copper teakettle, paper, and a brass inkstand. Mr. Emerson kissed the top of her head and gave her two Dickens novels to pass the time on the train. Father clapped his hands on her shoulders and said, "I'm sending my only son to war."

May stamped her feet to keep warm. She reminded herself that Louisa was leaving for Washington, D.C., not Paris or Rome. She knew she should be grateful that Mr. Sanborn had told her he could use another teacher. But she couldn't help feeling forgotten.

"Are you sure you know what to do?" Mother asked.

"Miss Dix wrote down directions. I change trains in New London, take a ferry to Jersey City, then catch another train to an inn, where I'll spend the night." Louisa whispered to May. "I should have written a will, but I have so little. If something happens, will you see that everyone chooses a memento, as we did with Beth?"

"Don't be theatrical. You're coming back." May regretted her words even as they left her mouth. She softened her voice. "I'm sorry you'll have to leave your writing."

"I might find something really worth writing about there." Louisa turned to Mother. "Am I doing the right thing? Should I stay here?"

May pulled her cloak tighter. She felt the fear she'd tamped inside her tighten then lift. She could smell Mother's woolen scarf, sprinkled with pepper, which she used to keep off moths, and willed her to say: *No. It's ridiculous. It's risky. Stay home.*

"Of course it's the right thing." Mother hugged Louisa. They didn't drop their arms even when the locomotive's whistle shrieked and the smell of burning coal deepened, so May threw her arms around them both. Amid lots of wishes for good luck, Louisa pulled away and climbed aboard.

The next day, May walked to the schoolhouse run by Mr. Sanborn. She spent the morning between the blackboard and the girls who sat on one side of the room, teaching composition and introductory French. These lessons weren't much different from those given to the boys, but the school was already considered advanced enough without them sharing recess. While the boys went outside to wrestle, aim imaginary rifles at imaginary Confederate soldiers, and throw snowballs at horses, May listened to the girls recite poetry and supervised their knitting.

Ten days after Louisa left, May trekked over the packed snow into town. The general store smelled of pickles, coffee, and molasses. Men huddled around the woodstove, arguing about Generals Sherman and McClellan. A woman asked May about Louisa while keeping an eye on Mr. Stacy, who broke up lumps of sugar and put them on his scale. "How your mother must worry!"

"She's proud." May winked at some children pressing against the glass case displaying lemon drops and cinnamon candies. She picked up the mail and hurried home.

Kicking snow from her boots, she called, "A letter from Louisa!" and she read it aloud to Mother:

December 16, 1862

My dearest family,

I meant to write the minute I arrived to tell you of my journey, but I fell asleep with pen in hand, only to be awakened by shouts and the rumble of wheels outside my window. Wagons, pulled by tired horses, were full of soldiers from Fredericksburg. I hurried downstairs where towels and a block of brown soap such as we use for laundry were thrust into my arms. I was told to take off boots, socks, and shirts. Attendants are supposed to wash the rest, but they are convalescents themselves, some barely able to stand. The good men had waited for days in the rain for wagons. Until we cleaned off the layers of mud, we couldn't know their injuries.

Some nurses ask to be spared witnessing amputations, but I came here to help every way I can. One poor fellow had to have

his leg cut off when we were out of ether. His lips turned white,
but he did not make a sound. I couldn't comfort, but recited
Dickens from memory in an effort to take his thoughts off the
saw.

I am blessed to be here. I know your prayers are with me.

Your loving Louisa

May was touched by the letter, but was it necessary for
Mother to carry it on all of her errands and read it aloud to
neighbors? Mrs. Hawthorne, who stopped by every day for
news, must have heard it a dozen times.

"Poor Louisa. They say the wounded drink and use foul
language," she said. "I know they undergo dreadful amputations, but there's never a reason to take the Lord's name in
vain."

Mother fretted about the long hours Louisa worked and
about Anna, whose back ached, which was common among
women carrying babies, but which could also be a sign of
something wrong. May knew it was natural for a mother to be
concerned about a daughter living where she could hear
cannons fire and another expecting her first child. She wished
she could be more like Beth, who'd seemed to take satisfaction
in perfectly plumped pillows and the view from twelve well-
scrubbed panes of glass. But she missed kindergartners' round
faces, their eyes and noses the size of buttons, and the occasional
dinner parties at her students' houses. Instead, she joined a
group of ladies who made dominoes, chessboards, and
conundrum books to send to hospitalized soldiers.

The Saturday-night dances had been called off for the war.

Molasses candy scrapes were thought unpatriotic, too. May was happy when Julian came home for the Christmas break, having grown a mustache and looking handsome in his blue Prince Albert coat. Skates were slung over his shoulders, which looked wider, probably from having joined the crew team.

"What brought you into town, besides to brighten your mother's day?" she asked.

"Only that, of course. And perhaps to ask my father for some money."

His slow smile forming with soft, beautifully shaped lips made her belly lurch. She said, "I suppose a college boy has lots of expenses. How are your classes?"

"All my professors see me as Nathaniel Hawthorne's son. They compare my work to *The Scarlet Letter*, and my prose style comes out as wanting."

"We've always been Bronson Alcott's daughters. I know comparisons hurt."

"The one good thing about my father being unwell is that he doesn't know how badly I'm doing at college."

"I hope your father's troubles aren't serious." May thought of how he'd always seemed absentminded but had recently walked through their kitchen door and stood at the bottom of the stairs before realizing he was in the wrong house.

"My mother says it's Concord that threatens his health. Maybe they'll travel."

May got her skates, and they walked to the frozen river, which glinted in the sunlight. Julian hurled a few rocks, which slammed and skidded, to be sure the ice was safe in the middle. They sat on a stone between the old North Bridge and the house where his parents had lived when they were first married to strap on their skates. Wrapping their arms around each other's waists, they wobbled down the slope to the lace-like edge of ice. They headed down the river and made a few circles before skating side by side.

"Have you settled on a course of studies?" she asked.

"What I really want is a chance to do my part to save the Union. But after the war, I'd be glad to just row and wander, like Mr. Thoreau. Or sail, like my ancestors did."

"And go into trade?"

"I know little of that. But I'd like living on a ship."

"Become a pirate?"

"Why not? And you a pirate queen!" He grabbed her hands, and they spun over the ice. As he let her go, he said, "A chap came to the college and spoke about searching for the origin of the Nile. There are fortunes to be found in Africa. Wouldn't it be exciting? I want to see the world."

"You've lived in Rome and London. You've seen Paris!"

"I'm not talking about seeing things from trains. Traveling to and from Italy, we passed by the Alps, but I wanted to climb them."

"And what could you do with that?" May felt a flash of impatience, though she told herself it must be hard for some people to learn what they are best at. She supposed she was lucky to have known for so long what she could do, though her love of art might have fallen to her simply because it was what was left after Louisa claimed theater and writing, Beth music, and Anna a devotion to making sure clean linen was distributed fairly through the household and plum preserves through the neighborhood. She said, "You're a dreamer."

"And aren't you? There have never been lady painters."

"There's a lot we don't know." Her father's library contained no books by women, but that didn't mean that they hadn't been written. She wondered if women's work wasn't displayed in the galleries she'd seen because of something besides lack of worth. "Julian, it's jolly to think of adventures, but you must make other plans, too. What will your friends do after college?"

"I suppose those with proper connections can study whatever they please and end up as lawyers or bankers of some sort."

"Your father knows people in high places."

"Most are men of letters, who are as penniless as we are."

"Don't exaggerate." Such talk annoyed her. While his father's books might not have been widely beloved, educated people liked having them on their shelves.

"I could hunt whales. All the retiring captains means a shortage of lamp oil. There are still fortunes to be made," he said. "Or maybe I'll become an artist. At the library, I found some missals from the Middle Ages with intriguing borders. I copied some illustrations, and the fellow at the college bookstore said he might put them up for sale."

Pushing away jealousy, May skated farther down the river, past dried grasses bent by glistening ice. Soon Julian glided behind, then around her. He hummed a tune she didn't know, but she recognized its waltz pace. They took each other's hands and spun. She let go, slipped her hands back in her muff, and continued up the river, slowing down by a big rock. She heard the snap of splitting ice, the swallowing sounds of warmer currents clashing with cold. She said, "We should turn back."

"The river often sounds like that." He spread his long legs, sailed over a crack, then sped toward her. She threw out her hands so they wouldn't collide, but he dragged the tip of his skate and stopped close enough so she could smell the tobacco on his woolen jacket. He said, "I think this is where the water lilies grow."

"The ones Mr. Thoreau said open at dawn?"

"Yes. And where my father found a dead body, a long time ago."

"Someone drowned here? The river isn't that deep. And slow."

"Apparently this girl worked at it. She was lonely and saw no chances for marriage or leaving town."

"There must be other ways to get out of Concord." May headed back toward the bridge. Seeing Julian skate around another split in the ice, she called, "Be careful!"

He leapt over a narrow channel, landing on ice that broke under the impact. She slapped her hand over her mouth but kept her eyes wide open as his foot, then ankle, and half his leg plunged into the water. He threw himself flat on the surrounding ice, which split. Black water rose and rippled, but Julian pulled up his leg and wiggled to ice that was thick enough to hold him as he squirmed to safety. May sped to the riverbank as he crawled toward it. He stood, hunching over, then lunged to the frozen ground.

"I'm all right." He tried to wring out his trousers.

"How could you be so reckless?"

"I'm just a bit wet."

"We should get back before your boots freeze."

They walked silently and briskly, though he hobbled slightly. She wondered whether it was the stories of exploring Africa or the drowned girl or his soaked boots that kept him from kissing her before they reached the door.

⌘

THE FACT OF MAIL OR NO MAIL COLORED THE FOLLOWING afternoons. When Louisa wrote about a persistent cough and fever, May reassured Mother. "She's surrounded by doctors. She'll get help if it gets worse."

May noticed that Louisa's recent letters contained no more pathetic passages about dying boys asking nurses to send locks of their hair to their sweethearts or descriptions of the unfinished Capitol dome. The shortness of the letters unsettled her, with little more than references to typhoid and pneumonia. The more Louisa wrote, "Don't worry," the more May did.

Late one afternoon, she heard a man trudging through snow toward the house. She swung open the door, took a telegram from him, and stared at the return address: "Washington, D.C." She read: "January 16, 1863. Miss Alcott very ill. Come immediately. Dorothea Dix."

May raced into Father's study, with Mother right behind her. She read the telegram aloud, then said, "I'll go. I wonder if any trains will head south tonight."

Mother twined her wrinkled fingers between May's soft ones. "I'd never forgive myself if you caught the fever from her."

"We can't afford two train tickets." Father's voice was firm, but his blue eyes looked frightened. "I'll go."

"Then let's not wait for the train in town," May said. "I'll borrow the Emersons' horses and sleigh and take you to Boston, where you can catch the earliest train to Washington."

May helped him pack, hitched up the horses, brought Father to the depot, and waited for the train with him. On the platform, a man with one leg leaned on a cane. Another veteran with a bent back muttered to himself. After Father boarded, May watched while the train rumbled out of sight. She knew the journey would last through the night and most of the next day. Even if Louisa were well enough to travel, Father would be bound to stay a day or two. Longer if she'd become more ill since the telegram had been sent. And if . . . No, May wouldn't let herself think of the worst. She remembered standing with Louisa at the depot. Why hadn't she told her that she loved her? Instead, she'd only said, "Don't be theatrical."

She returned home, offering fresh handkerchiefs to Mother as she blamed herself for having let Louisa go.

"No one can tell her what to do. Did you get supper? Some chamomile tea and toast will settle your stomach." May crouched by the hearth and slipped a slice of bread into a wire holder. A mouse scurried across the floor, startling her so she dropped the holder in the flames. She scorched her hand as she tried to snatch it, and she burst into tears. She cried, "Everything's wrong. I hate the war!"

"But it's necessary. In the end, our nation may become as just as our ancestors meant it to be. Your children will go to schools and sit side by side with the children of former slaves."

"Oh, Mother, I just want Lu to come home safe. You were right. We shouldn't have let her go."

The next days seemed long with the work of waiting. May agreed to stop teaching to keep Mother company, but she needed to leave the house sometimes, and she told Mother she was going to the general store for cornmeal, even though there was some left in the bin. While Mr. Stacy scooped tea into white paper he tied with a striped string, May listened to the men talking by the woodstove and made silent wagers: If they decided the last battle had been a Union victory, Louisa would be all right. May wanted to stay among the barrels of pickles and apples, shelves and drawers of marbles, preserved quince, spools of thread, packets of needles, hammers, axes, red flannel petticoats, and brass doorknobs, but she left before the men came to a conclusion. Louisa had to be all right.

Father had been gone almost two weeks when a letter from him arrived. May read aloud his accounts of hearing President Lincoln speak in the Senate and how doctors brought Louisa logs and kindling, making sure the fire in her room didn't go out. May hurried through his explanation that he'd been waiting to see whether Louisa's health would take a turn before putting her on a train, scanned the date, and said, "That means they should arrive tomorrow!"

Father didn't mention whether Louisa had become worse or better, but at least now they knew she was alive. Or she had been when he wrote.

THE NEXT DAY, MAY WAS RELIEVED WHEN JULIAN visited his parents' house, and learning about Louisa, offered to come with her to the depot. He said his mother would wait with hers and might distract her with her own worries about Una, who was late returning from visiting her aunt in Boston. May and Julian trudged into the cold wind on their way to the Emersons' house, where they hitched the horses to the sleigh. May pulled the bearskin left on the seat over her thin boots, woolen dress, and cloak. Julian snapped the reins, but when Grace and Dolly balked, he passed them to May, who was familiar with the old horses.

She steered onto the packed snow, which reflected moonlight, rode for about ten minutes, and turned at the depot. Sharing the bearskin, she and Julian held hands, but they didn't talk. An owl called. Then a long whistle pierced the black sky. May didn't move until Julian leapt down, and he reached for her as she jumped onto the tramped-down snow. The gaslights caught smoke rising from the locomotive. Doors clattered open. May saw Father, with his with light hair billowing, walking among other old, tired men. He was alone.

May's knees buckled. She might have fallen if Julian hadn't grabbed her waist. She saw a feeble woman clinging to the elbow of a slender, redheaded young lady. It took a moment to recognize Louisa being helped by Julian's sister, Una. May opened her mouth to cry out their names, but her voice caught. Even in the dim light, she could see that Louisa's face was pale, with purple sores around her mouth. Her eyes rolled as she looked up. They cast over May but didn't rest on her.

Julian wrapped an arm around Louisa, but she wrenched

herself away, spread her fingers, and scratched at the air. When her head wobbled, her bonnet slipped so that May could see that her hair was matted and thin.

"I was coming back from visiting my aunt when I saw your father trying to help her through the Boston station." Una choked back tears. "I told him I'd sit with her in the ladies' compartment. I didn't recognize her."

May squeezed her hand. Father and Julian helped Louisa onto the sleigh's backseat. She screamed when they pulled up the bearskin and shoved it to the floor. As Father sat beside her and tugged it back up, May stepped into the front, turned around, and said, "Lu, you must stay warm."

"Who are you?"

"I'm May. Abbie. Your sister. We're going home." May picked up the reins, then dropped them. She couldn't see the road, which seemed hidden by more than darkness. She couldn't remember which way anything was. She just sat, her chest heaving with sobs. She whispered, "Help."

Julian placed the reins back in her hands.

"Grace, Dolly, run." May lifted the reins with heavy arms, and they headed home.

⌘

DURING THE FOLLOWING NIGHTS AND DAYS, MAY PUT compresses on Louisa's forehead. She changed her nightgown often and rubbed her arms with cool cloths. Mother consulted a homeopath, who suggested herbs to bring down her dangerously high fever. Father was loyal to Dr. Bartlett, whose son was an army lieutenant and who burned his patients' old bills every January so that they could start the New Year fresh. He used herbs, too, but also prescribed laudanum, which contained opium to dull the pain.

May sat by Louisa for hours. Her eyes rolled up, opened wide, and then the lids slipped back down. She babbled about men with rifles, then screamed, "There's a witch on the rafters." As May tried to still Louisa's flailing arms, she cried, "The roof is spinning off! Get out!"

"I'm staying with you." May pushed down her arms.

At last Louisa grew calmer and slept. May twined ivy around her head, for she'd heard its leaves kept hair from falling out. She dozed in a chair, waking when she heard Louisa slide off the bed. Louisa tried to push herself to her knees, collapsed, and cried, "Someone's calling me."

May's hands turned cold. She bent over, gently shook her shoulders, and whispered, "Lu! Lu," which blended with a *whoo whoo* from the darkness outside.

"It's an owl." May helped her up.

Louisa sobbed. "Why did you leave me alone with all those naked men?"

"You're safe in your room. Mother is downstairs." May got her back into bed. "Anna would be here, but we can't risk her catching your fever, endangering the baby."

"There's a baby?"

"There will be soon, the good Lord willing." May stirred medicine and honey into lukewarm mint tea. She rocked Louisa until she slept. Instead of a lullaby, she murmured a litany of places they'd never seen, but must: Buckingham

Palace, Notre Dame, the Louvre, Versailles, St. Peter's, and the Parthenon.

"Think of London, where you can see boys like the ones we read about in Dickens." May knelt beside her, rubbed her back, and felt sharp bones protruding, like the wooden slats of a loom. Louisa's legs were still muscular, hardly seeming to belong to the thin face that looked alternately flushed, gray, and tinted pale yellow. May brushed her hair, then pulling out loose strands that twisted through the bristles, she took out her sewing shears. She cut what was left of Louisa's hair to just past her ears. When she slept, May prayed, "Please let her get well," saying the words over and over like the hollow, stuttering cries of an owl. She wouldn't ask for more.

Another night, both May and Mother sat beside Louisa while she slept.

"Her skin's cooler. That's a good sign," Mother said.

"She doesn't know us half the time!" May couldn't tell the disease from the medicines.

"Of course she knows us. The doctor is coming to-morrow."

"What if she doesn't live that long?"

"She'll be all right."

"How do you know? That's what you said about Beth."

"I never said it about Beth. At least not when . . ."

"I wasn't there." May broke in. "I should have brushed *her* hair. Instead you sent me to live with Aunt Bond."

"I didn't want you to see Beth like that."

"I wasn't a little girl to be sheltered. I was eighteen!"

"We couldn't take a chance with your health."

"You and Louisa took a chance. I should have insisted on staying. I was too old to let myself be convinced by letters saying that Beth seemed to be getting better."

"I don't suppose it would have made a difference."

"It would have made a difference to me. I lost my last chance to know her more. Louisa said a mist rose from her body when she died. I wish I'd seen that."

"It was her soul." Mother kept her eyes on the wall. "It was more than the fever with Beth. She wouldn't eat. I tried tea cakes and puddings, all the things she used to like."

"Could someone fall sick from not wanting enough?" When Mother didn't reply, May asked, "Was it a sort of melancholia?"

"Dear me, Beth was never sad. She was the most peaceful soul I've ever known."

"She gave up too much. She should have fought instead of smiling and sewing pen wipers and needle cases for us."

May wept for the sister whose brow she'd never tried to cool. She'd been away, embroidering daisies onto the corners of handkerchiefs, conjugating French verbs, and making watercolors instead of singing her to sleep, tightening the ropes beneath her mattress, emptying chamber pots, doing all the things she now did for Louisa.

One evening, May arranged pine boughs on the mantel to distract from the smells of sickness. She read aloud from one of Mr. Emerson's essays. The simple words about moods like a string of beads slipped over her tongue like smooth pebbles, and seemed to calm Louisa. May went to the window and peered into the branches of the old elm, but she couldn't spot the owl.

If she were quiet enough, would the bird tell her something? Such a soft *whoo whoo* must matter. This was the sort of faith she sometimes felt when drawing. That a sound or sight was important just because it was there. And if she kept looking, listening, and drawing, she would know something she hadn't when she began. She picked up a pencil and sketched one side of Louisa's gaunt face. Looking was a form of love, a way to hold on.

Then May must have slept. She heard chickadees before she felt light's warmth on her eyelids, and she looked out to see the first traces of sun. She wound a shawl over her head, shoulders, and chest. Seeing her breath in the cold air, she added sticks to the fire. She went to the kitchen and brought up a tray she'd arranged with porridge, rose geranium leaves tucked under the warm teapot, toast, and jam.

She forced open a window, its panes crackled with frost, and sprinkled sunflower seeds on the snow-covered sills. She loved the round bodies of chickadees, the swift hammering motion of their striped heads. She sat in the rocking chair, straightened Louisa's lace cap, and slipped broken pieces of toast between her chapped lips. Voices rose from downstairs, from Mrs. Hawthorne, who brought her sewing over every morning to stitch while listening to Mother's worries. May heard a log fall, the hiss of ashes. A shadow fell from the windowsill across the pine plank floor. It might be as beautiful as anything in Paris.

No, she didn't think so. She wrapped her arm around Louisa's head and said, "You must get well, my owl. Please. We haven't been to Europe yet. We haven't seen the water lilies open at dawn."

5

SISTERS

*M*ay didn't know if it was prayers, Dr. Bartlett's homeopathic remedies and opium, or the chants of Mrs. Bliss, a mesmerist recommended by Mrs. Emerson, but late in February, Louisa's hallucinations became less frequent. She recognized everyone through entire afternoons. Her shoulders didn't buckle when she coughed. She stumbled and had difficulty with balance, but she sat up for longer spells. Her eyes grew strong enough for her to stitch "L. C. P." on a bib for the baby Anna felt certain would be a girl and planned to name Louisa Caroline Pratt.

May still kept her company, but she no longer had to watch her as carefully as she had. She spent a few afternoons drawing an owl over Louisa's hearth. After Father sawed planks of wood with curved edges, May held them in place between two windows in Louisa's room. The half-moon shaped desk was set at the level of the windowsills to give Louisa the fullest view of the yard and road. May coated the left side of the beam above the desk with black, then painted over it with red and white blossoms.

"Won't you paint the other side of the beam, so anyone who comes in can see your work?" Mother asked.

"These are just for Louisa," May said. She added a moth in flight, a pale creature that was almost entirely wings.

Louisa wasn't well enough for May to return to teaching, but almost every day at noon now, she went next door for lunches of potatoes, carrots, and whortleberry pudding. May was glad for a respite from penning thank-you notes for broth and jellies neighbors brought, or listening to Mother, who, waiting for news from Anna, brooded about her past miscarriages and her only son, who'd died at less than a day old. Mrs. Hawthorne welcomed May's company, as her husband, whose hair had turned almost entirely white, was often distracted. Their youngest daughter, Rose, seemed sullen, too, and Una often stayed in her room with headaches, which her mother said were worsened by the clatter of forks and spoons.

When May returned home one afternoon, she curled up in an armchair by Louisa's bed and hummed "Oh, Shenandoah" while taking in the waistband of one of Louisa's dresses, so it wouldn't sag and call attention to the weight she'd lost. The shadows around Louisa's eyes had grown fainter. She said her mouth remained sore, but her tongue no longer looked swollen. As she tilted her head, May admired the line between her chin and throat. She said, "I want to draw your portrait, but wish I knew more about bones and muscles."

"You talked about anatomy classes before I went away. Didn't I say I'd help you pay for them?" Louisa said.

"You have other responsibilities now. After the Union triumphs, we can go back to Boston, and I'll earn money teaching." May put down her needle. "Lu, what was it like in Washington? You haven't said much. I know Mother says you should put it all behind you, but talking might bring you some relief."

Louisa shut her eyes, then said, "I saw mules drawing Army wagons filled with flag-covered coffins over muddy streets. Pigs ate from the gutters."

"No dashing officers?"

"There were some, wearing capes with scarlet lining and swords at their sides. But I was mostly in the wards, which smelled terrible, with the windows nailed shut to keep out the cold. We nurses had to shout to be heard over the sounds of coughing. When I offered to help one man sit up for some soup, he said, 'Thank you, ma'am. But I don't think I'll ever eat again, for I was shot in the stomach.' He asked for only a sip of water before he died."

"I don't know whether to call you a hero or a saint."

"Neither. I wanted to help, but I made a muddle of everything. Now I'm sick and a burden to everyone. Did I really talk to people no one else could see?"

"It doesn't matter."

"I want to know."

"Nothing was worse than anything I saw when Mother took me to that sanitarium in Maine."

"Was it awful there? You didn't complain."

"I was seven, old enough to know Mother was counting on what she could earn there."

"Everything comes down to money, doesn't it? I earned just ten dollars for my weeks as a nurse. Before I went to Washington, I was getting a start on paying off some of what Father owes."

"You mustn't fret about debts that have been around forever. All that matters is that you're getting well."

Louisa looked down, the way Mother sometimes frowned at her knitting, trying to figure out where a stitch had been dropped. "Beth got me through the hardest moments. I thought about how she was so cheerful, when she had less than any of us. It was a consolation to pray that I'd been good enough to see her in Heaven."

"You'll see her again. But not soon."

"She once told me that she was grateful she was sick. She said that of us four sisters, she was the one who would be least missed."

"I hope she didn't really believe that."

"She wanted to comfort us. Mother sent you to Aunt Bond's so you could be spared."

"But I wasn't! None of us were spared. I wish I'd known her more. Was she always so shy? What was she afraid of?"

"What makes you think she was scared? She just liked home."

"We all like home, but we leave it, too."

"Everyone isn't like you, needing to gallivant. I admired her more than anyone. It's not easy to be good." Louisa sighed. "I'll never be like her. Her soul was as pure as could be, but when she was dying, she told me she had one regret. That only our family would remember her. May, it's selfish, but I can't help it. I'd still like to make a mark. And pay for my own keep."

"And you will." May, too, missed earning a small salary for teaching. She'd inquired about work sewing, but prices were rising and banks closing because of the war, so many ladies had not only stopped buying new gowns, but did alterations themselves. "Will you return to your tale about the girl who stood up to dishonest and worse employers?"

"I sent *Work* to editors before I went to Washington. Every one turned it down."

"You should send it to Mr. Niles."

"The gentleman you told me about who publishes books without words?"

"Diaries and souvenir albums, but other books besides."

"Anyway, now I'm going to write something new, set in a hospital. Maybe I can do a bit of good by telling some of what I saw our brave soldiers endure. Nobody will like it."

"Mother will. And you'll feel more like your old self if you write."

The next morning, May helped Louisa to the desk, where she'd set out a steel pen, a bottle of ink, and paper. As the days passed, the room smelled less of medicine and more of a cidery scent from apple cores that had rolled under her desk. She got a letter asking for some stories for children. May exclaimed, but Louisa said, "I'd rather write about schemers, swindlers, and damsels in distress. I'm hoping to hear back from Frank Leslie: You've seen his name on all the tabloids. Don't tell anyone, but before the war, I wrote *Pauline's Passion and Punishment*."

"That story about a lady who's abandoned by a count, so she shoves him off a cliff?" May laughed.

"Such sensational tales let people forget their troubles for a few minutes. I used a pen name and risked it because no one in Concord buys such nonsense."

"Or they hide their tabloids under Spenser poems and translations of Greek plays."

After Louisa settled back at her desk, May brought the mail to the steps. She opened a letter from Alice, telling her that her brother had died, not on the battlefield, but of a fever that might strike anyone. May's shoulders sank as she cried not only for the boy she'd met just once, but for Louisa, who'd been too close to dying, and for herself, too. May hadn't helped nurse her sister for thanks or praise. She'd done what was necessary, as she never had a chance to do for Beth. But she wished Louisa would acknowledge that she'd thought beyond herself and see that she was no longer a girl tagging after her older sister, wanting to be that confident, free, and wise.

⁂

ONE SPRING AFTERNOON, MAY WAS STARTLED BY A shout from Mother. "Anna had a boy! We just got word!"

Louisa rolled up the bib she'd embroidered with initials for Louisa Caroline Pratt, and said, "Lucky Anna. Boys are easier to understand than girls."

May packed some things so Mother could take the next morning's train, leaving her to make sure Louisa and Father got proper rest and meals. For the following few days, they spoke of little besides the baby. Was he healthy, they wondered, and was Anna? They repeated, "A boy, imagine. What do you suppose he looks like?"

Finally a letter came from Mother. May helped Louisa into the parlor, where Father was reading, and she scanned and summarized the letter. "They named the baby Frederick. Anna's bleeding and has a temperature, but cousin Lucy says it's not the baby fever that's so dangerous in the lying-in wards, but seen less in the new hospital for women and children. They've found simply asking doctors to wash their hands makes a difference, but some gentlemen are insulted by such requests. Leave it to Mother to fit in a lecture, but she sounds worried. I should go."

"I'll go," Father said.

May nodded. She was eager to see Anna and the baby, but Father wouldn't be much help to Louisa.

The morning after he left, May walked into town, where people asked after Anna and Louisa, glad to hear that one's baby was thriving and the other was feeling well enough to write. May bought some beef and meant to swiftly leave the store, but on a whim, she selected some wallpaper to hang in the parlor as a surprise for Mother when she returned. She looked forward to the task. Since painting the owl, flowers, and moth in Louisa's room, May hadn't opened her paint box. Maybe she was being faithful, casting aside her old ambitions in trade for Louisa's good health. Or maybe she'd simply lost the kind of concentration she'd taken for granted at fifteen. Tasks such as baking or keeping a vigilant eye on medicine were easier than facing doubts about her worthiness, the way she had to when she put colors on paper. The line between good art and bad never seemed as clear as the one between a pie and an empty oven.

"I thought I'd make stew to build back your strength, without Father around to warn that meat brings out our animal nature," she told Louisa.

"And makes us bloodthirsty. Angry."

"Where would you be without your temper and stubbornness? You might have listened to those like Mr. Fields who advised you to stop writing."

"He might have been right. I should be grateful for my magazine and tabloid stories, but I'm afraid I'll never sell something with hard covers."

"That doesn't mean you shouldn't write."

"I won't waste my time on something no one will see."

"You'll see it. That matters. And you should think of the world beyond your desk. Mr. Emerson is lecturing at the town hall next week. If we borrowed a horse and carriage, you could go."

"People only attend those talks to criticize them."

"Mrs. Mann wants you to come to a tea party."

"Ladies only hold such parties for the pleasure of not inviting people. It's you who needs to get out more. Why don't you visit Anna? I'll be fine alone for a while."

"Are you sure? If I took the early train, I could get back in the late afternoon."

"Spend the night. I'll sleep in the parlor, so no one has to worry about me falling down stairs."

May wrote to her friend, Alice, to see if she could stay with her, and she asked Mrs. Hawthorne to stop by and check on

Louisa. On the next half-bright morning, she walked past snowbanks to the depot. After changing trains in Boston, then getting off in Chelsea, she saw crocuses and snowdrops blooming near puddles. May knocked on Anna's door, stepped in, and called, "Hello!"

Mother hurried in to hug her and said, "Shhh. The baby's sleeping."

They tiptoed into the parlor, where Anna and John were huddled around a cradle. Anna's brown hair fell limply from her pins. The skin beneath her eyes was dark, but pleasure hovered around the corners of her mouth as she lifted the baby and leaned back so that his downy head could rest in the hollow of her shoulder. When her shawl slipped to the floor, John picked it up and smoothed it back over her shoulders. He looked exhausted, too, but seemed unable to stop grinning.

"Look at those long fingers. Maybe he'll be an artist. Or play the piano, like Beth," May said.

"I can already see that our little Frederick is strong and will make an excellent soldier. But pray we will be a peaceful, united nation long before he comes of age. If only infants could teach the rest of us their wisdom," Father said.

May touched the baby's round head, which was as soft as the blanket he was loosely wrapped in. "He's darling, Anna. And I'm glad to see you sitting up and looking well."

"I was weak for a while, but the baby was all right. That was my one prayer."

May's face grew hot. She already adored the baby's bundled fingers, scrunched-up knees, and tucked elbows, but he wasn't her sister. "You're important, too!"

"You're sweet, but a baby starts out with all the chances in the world," Anna said. "You'll understand when you have your own."

"Did it hurt terribly?"

"Having a baby?" Anna glanced at John. "It's strange, but it already seems so long ago. Cousin Lucy knew what to do."

"May I hold him?" May asked.

"Of course," Anna said, but she didn't open her arms.

"No one could paint a finer picture than that. There's nothing like a mother with child," Father said.

With his tiny arms and legs crunched and crisscrossed, the baby reminded May of a plump rosebud, with petals folded over another. She gently pried him from Anna, whose forehead wrinkled as if he were going miles away instead of inches. He felt warm and startlingly light against May's chest. When he bobbed his head and opened his nut-sized mouth, she passed him back to Anna. "He's magnificent."

"I'll be happy if he's good, like his father." Anna looked at Mother. "You don't think he can be hungry again?"

After the clock chimed, May told everyone she had a train to catch. She didn't mention that she'd be going only as far as Boston, as she didn't want Mother to fret about Louisa being alone for the night. Though maybe she wouldn't worry. Mother didn't look up from the baby after May said her good-byes and headed to the door.

May was glad to see Alice, though concerned that her mother didn't join them for dinner or breakfast at the long table. Alice confided that her mother took her brother's death hard, though a hesitation in her voice hinted that Mrs. Bartlett kept to her room for troubles even beyond grief. May and Alice went to the Athenæum to look at prints of frescoes from the Sistine Chapel, Rembrandt paintings of Biblical scenes, and a Madonna done by Rubens. May loved the colors but wished for landscapes as well as people. She liked the Chinese scrolls showing pines and mountains. She and Alice entered the chalky-smelling sculpture gallery with its plaster copies of works from Greece and Rome. May admired the arc of a raised arm forever about to throw a disc, and a Venus with arms crossing her chest. She understood why one shouldn't touch the silk scrolls that were thousands of years old, but these sculptures were meant to last. She whispered to Alice, "Tell me if anyone is looking," and she ran her fingertips along a smooth stone shoulder.

When May returned home, she painted. She was glad that Louisa now felt hearty enough to walk down the road and write, though she wasn't yet strong enough for them to consider moving to Boston. That fall, Louisa read a poem called *Thoreau's Flute* to Mrs. Hawthorne. She encouraged Louisa to send it to Mr. Fields, and after she demurred, she sent it herself. He wrote back asking for permission to publish it in the *Atlantic Monthly*, an offer which helped Louisa forgive him for his slight on her writing a few years before. It bolstered her courage enough to send a story about life in a military hospital to another magazine, where it was published.

A few weeks later, Louisa's face turned pink as she opened her mail, while the family sat around the table eating pears. She stood and waved the letter. "It's from Mr. Redpath. He wants to gather my hospital stories into a book!"

May leapt up to hug her. Louisa swiftly kissed her and said,

"He'll print five hundred copies. I'll get ten percent of sales. The advance is about what Mr. Niles suggested. Maybe a little less."

"You had an offer from Mr. Niles?" May asked. "No one tells me anything. Why, I met him in Boston some time ago. He was quite dashing."

"I don't choose my publishers by how well they dress. Mr. Redpath promises that some of the profits will go to the Union hospitals. He does a lot for the war effort."

"And so have you. Now you deserve some pleasures," May said.

"Mrs. Stowe's *Uncle Tom's Cabin* helped start the war. Perhaps your book will end it," Mother said.

"It hasn't even been published," Louisa said. "And I don't expect . . ."

"Why not expect wonders for once?" May interrupted. "People will line up for blocks to hear you read, just like Charles Dickens. You'll be rich and famous. We need champagne!"

"Don't be silly," Louisa said, but she laughed. "It's wrong to want such things. I should be glad for what I have. To be alive."

"You are grateful, and so are we. It doesn't mean we can't want more. We'll celebrate in style when the book is in covers. And tonight, I'll bake you a plum cake and break open the currant wine." May carried some dishes into the kitchen.

Louisa followed and said, "After it's published, I might earn enough to pay for those lessons you've wanted."

"I'd hate to take from you, though classes would be a good investment. I might be able to make a living doing portraits for those who want more than a tintype or daguerreotype of those they lost in the war."

"I used to think you'd be married by now, not thinking of earning a living."

"I'm not who you thought I was. Though I can't entirely shake the notion that men should provide, even though Mother brought in most of our family's income."

"That's because she was secretive about it. Pretending boarders were guests and that she sewed only out of kindness, not for pay. One day, she won't have to accept gifts of cast-off clothing. I'll see to that." Louisa's voice softened. "Of course, you take care of so much now, May. Mother says it's the people who aren't seen who do most of the world's good work."

"She may be right. You know I admire her more than anyone. But I don't want to be as angry as she is."

"Angry? Our dear Marmee never raises her voice!"

"She counts under her breath. And tells us good lessons. But I don't think those are what have ground down her teeth."

"She's a good woman!"

"Can't good women get angry? I love Mother with all my heart, but do you think she was ever truly happy?"

"She was happy with her children."

"And now we're grown. She gave us everything, and I'm grateful. But she gave up too much," May said.

"She had her diaries. I'd rather have written one of the good, true sentences than all of my foolish tales."

"Who will ever read those diaries?"

"We will, one day. Mother is leaving them to us."

"I expect she'd rather have written epics and romances. Don't you want to write more than diaries?"

"Yes."

"Good." May was glad that Louisa was finally well. Now both of them could move into a wider world. She said, "You'll make us proud. But I plan to be famous first."

6

VİOLETS

After a long winter, robins flew over yards where snow lingered only in shadows. May held Freddy's hand as her nephew, now just over a year old, practiced a wobbly walk. Leaning to the side, she tried to steer him around puddles as he crouched to pick up stones. He laughed at a toad. As they made their slow way up the road, he waved at the flags hung in windows to honor that spring's victorious battles.

After they came into the kitchen, she tried to dry his hair, but he scooted under the table. Anna, who'd caught a bad cold and had moved into what the family called Orchard House until she recovered, called from the parlor for him to quiet down. Instead, he shrieked until May spread jam on bread for his lunch. She let him help her mix up some lip balm she scooped into a small pot for Rose Hawthorne's thirteenth birthday. Then they joined the rest of the family in the parlor.

"I hope the downpour doesn't keep Mr. Hawthorne from getting back from his trip." May hoped Julian would come for his sister's birthday, too.

"The excursion was meant to lift his spirits, but did it have to be with Mr. Pierce?" Mother said. "If he'd done a better job as president, we might not be suffering through a war now. He did nothing to help free the slaves."

"They were college friends. Naturally, they're loyal to each other." May heard a knock and headed to the door, stopping to tousle Freddy's hair. She greeted Mr. Emerson and reached for his black umbrella, but he walked past as if he didn't see her. He stopped before the hearth, his eyes on a picture May had hung of a Madonna with her feet just over the moon. He put his large, wrinkled hand on top of May's head, as if she were still a girl. "Abbie, Mr. Hawthorne has passed over. I got a telegram from Mr. Pierce, who asked me to break the news to his wife."

Two days later, May and Louisa picked violets from the ridge behind their houses, then joined Anna in the kitchen. They baked custard pies for the company who'd arrived next door. May was rolling more dough when Julian came in with a box of cups to hold the wildflowers they'd told his mother they'd bring to the church. May embraced him while her sisters murmured condolences.

"Two more loaves of gingerbread are coming out of the oven, if you can wait," Anna told him. "Would you hold the baby while I find a basket so you can bring home the pies?"

Julian bounced Freddy on his knees. His face looked

strained even as he picked up a newspaper and folded a section into a sailboat. Julian made the little boy laugh by waving it over his head, but his eyes remained wide, like someone coming in from the dark.

The next day, chapters from Nathaniel Hawthorne's unfinished novel were set on top of his casket at the front of the church. Julian wore a black jacket that looked a bit too small: May guessed it had been his father's. He held one arm around his mother and the other around Una and Rose.

After the service and procession to the cemetery, May carried platters between the Hawthorne's kitchen and sitting room. She heard their dog whimper behind a closed door, where he must have been put to keep from tripping the mourners. She slipped in to give him a broken cookie, then passed around cake and kept Father away from Mr. Pierce. She noticed the grateful way peoples' eyes fell on Anna, who smiled when asked about her baby and said, "He's growing up so fast. Walking and talking. John's watching him now." But when someone said, "I suppose the little chap will want a brother or sister soon," Anna's mouth stiffened.

May spoke with Una and Rose, their aunts, and Mr. Fields and his wife, who took her hand and said, "You must come visit us."

"Louisa told me you have paintings I should see in your lovely home."

"And I heard you are talented with a paintbrush."

"Louisa said that?"

"I know your friend, Alice, who told me."

May turned to watch Julian pace as if the crowded parlor

were a cage. When Mr. Pierce steered him to a corner, his shoulders rose enough to pull the fabric of his jacket. A few minutes later, she took his hand and led him outside. After days of rain, the grasses were bright green. They climbed past the blossoming apple trees toward the ferns, blackberry bushes, and pine grove.

The following weekend, when Julian came back again from college, they returned to the woods. He seemed more distraught than he'd been the week before, walking briskly after they reached the hilltop. He said, "I knew he was sick, but he was my father. You never think of them dying. I suppose that sounds childish. When I was little, he used to let me sit with him and pretend to write." Julian strode through some violets, whose leaves waved in a breeze. "His desk had slices in the sides where he scratched it with his penknife while lost in thought. Mother gave me his knife. I don't want it! He used to carve whistles, or cut off bits of licorice for us."

She took his hand and rubbed his knuckles. "Shortly before Mr. Thoreau died, his aunt asked if he'd made his peace with God. He said that he didn't know they'd ever quarreled."

"I expect my father did nothing but quarrel. It wasn't always that way. I remember clamboring onto his lap when I was small, lifting the cover of his inkstand, carved with the baby Hercules strangling a goose. He climbed hickory trees and shook nuts from the branches for us to pick."

She glanced at the treetops and imagined Mr. Hawthorne in one of his immaculate jackets balancing on a limb. She said, "He was a good father. He cared for his family. He took jobs he didn't like to make sure you had what you needed."

"Mr. Pierce says I'm the man of the family now. Without the faintest idea of what I'll do after college."

"Your father just died. Of course you don't know what you'll do next."

"May, the last time I saw him, I asked for money. Now all I can think about is how thin he looked. Ashen-faced and worried, probably about me. I whistled as I walked out the door, stashing dollars in my pocket. When I should have done something for him."

"What could you do?"

"Anything. He didn't eat. He barely slept. We should have made him see a doctor."

"He listened to no one."

"He kept asking what I planned to do, and I had no answer."

"You'll do something to make him proud."

"He's dead! He can't be proud. Please don't talk to me about Heaven."

"I meant . . . if he could see you."

"And what is there to be proud of? Not everyone is like you, finding your best talent at ten years old. All I know is that I don't want to write. Now I can't even join the army, and leave my mother to worry herself sick."

She knew how it felt to disappoint your parents, to be uncertain of the future, but she didn't have words. All she could think to do was brush her fingertips beside his blue-brown eyes and down the side of his face, feeling the slight stubble over the muscle of his jaw. She covered most of his mouth with hers. His lips opened. Their tongues slid together. She pressed his upper lip between hers, then gently bit a corner of his mouth. She could smell moss. His hands slid from her arms to her hips as they lay under the pines on the patch of small purple flowers.

∞

WHEN JULIAN CAME HOME FROM COLLEGE, THEY OFTEN walked on the hillside where Father had cut down junipers and pines. Sunlight fell over saplings and stumps to his garden and small orchard. May admired a view of meadows, woods, and Walden Pond, which looked like a patch of blue caught in treetops. Julian's lips softened under hers, opening slightly in kisses she didn't want to end. That fall and winter, May began wondering what his back looked like under his coat and what it might be like to be addressed as Mrs. Hawthorne. Sometimes she imagined holding an infant of her own, brushing the red hair of a little girl or chasing a little boy with Mr. Hawthorne's expressive eyebrows and Julian's fine eyes and nose. And with a daydream's shunning of chronology and logic, she lit on a proposal by a château in France, though of course they couldn't travel together until they were married.

But it was hard to have weeks go by in which she didn't see him. Her loneliness deepened when she read a black-bordered note from Alice, though she'd hardly known her mother. There was too much news of death. In April, less than two weeks after she set candles in the windows to mark the end of the war, she cut armbands from the hem of a black dress to mourn President Lincoln. She was glad that no more young men would be heading south, no more church bells would too often toll about twenty, or twenty-one, or twenty-two times. Soon the yard would be fragrant with lilacs, but the most welcome news for the Alcotts was that Anna was carrying another baby.

One afternoon, May sat on a stone sketching the ivy growing under her bedroom window, trying to suggest the flutter of leaves, the way light tugged and shadows slid, and thinking about how Julian would be back from college soon. On the hillside, Father was planting cabbages, squash, and beans. Louisa rolled a ball back and forth to Freddy, who Anna had sent to stay with them, since she'd experienced some bleeding and had been ordered to stay in bed. Catbirds and song sparrows flew among the apple trees. The Hawthorne's dog bounded out from the larches. May saw Julian heading over. She put down her sketchbook, stood up, and smoothed her dress.

"You don't have to stop. You look fetching with a sketchpad." Julian lifted Freddy high, which made his eyes widen and Louisa laugh. He chatted with her about Freddy's ball-catching skills, then looked at May's drawing and said, "That's nice."

"I spent the morning erasing more lines than I kept. I began a portrait of your house, too, seen from the side."

"I bought some Windsor and Newton paints and gold ink to copy some medieval manuscripts. Sketching is relaxing after a morning of lectures."

"Art should be more than relaxing. Perhaps I can teach you a few things this summer."

"There's nothing I'd like more, but I'm afraid I won't be

around much. I failed several classes, so I will go to the Berkshires for tutoring in chemistry and Latin."

"You'll be gone all summer?" May saw Louisa look over from where she'd joined Freddy, who was trying to get the dog interested in the ball.

"I got a job doing yard work at an inn, too. I told my mother I'd be doing bookkeeping, as she believes the son of Nathaniel Hawthorne should make more gentlemanly use of his hands than digging holes. What's wrong? You're not like her, thinking such labor is beneath me?"

"I'm certain I'd like what shovels and shears would do for your arms and shoulders. But aren't there bushes to trim around here?"

"I have to make up those courses. My mother says it's to be expected, that I'm grieving for my father, but the truth is, I was never meant for classrooms. I'm more like Mr. Thoreau. I'd rather hoe beans or tramp through the woods."

"Which he did after graduating from Harvard. And he didn't have a wife or children to think about."

"Neither do I. Don't look so forlorn. I'll come home for your birthday. Let's go see the water lilies Mr. Thoreau talked about."

"I thought you and I were going to see those, May," Louisa said as she strolled back to join them. "Though I never believed you could get up before dawn."

"I'm used to waking up for crew," Julian said. "Una and I had a trick we used with the governess we had in Rome, when we wanted to explore the city in the morning. She tied a long piece of string around her toe and let the other end trail out the window for us to give it a tug."

❧

LATER, AS MAY AND LOUISA FIXED SUPPER, MAY
reminded herself that July wasn't terribly far.

"Have you and Julian talked of a wedding?" Louisa asked.

"Certainly not."

"I suppose he isn't wealthy enough for you."

"Don't say that with such disdain. You hate poverty as
much as I do. I was eight when we lived in that basement in
Boston and went with handbills for Father's lectures. People
thought I was begging. I don't want my children to be hungry
and ashamed."

"You're right. I hated that. But if Julian's off to work with
scythe and hoe, is it because the Hawthornes need his salary?
Mother told me they let go of the housemaid and cook."

"Mrs. Hawthorne always complained about how they put
the ivory handles of knives in the dishwater and washed silver
last instead of first. And she's got two girls who can make the
whortleberry pudding and iron their own dresses."

"Of course. Though they must have doctor bills left from
poor Mr. Hawthorne's illness. Anyway, if you're not serious
about Julian, you shouldn't wander about with him. People will
talk."

"I'm not the sort who can court in a parlor, and neither are
you."

"I'm not the sort to court at all. I don't care to tie myself to
anyone who might try to tell me what to do."

"John and Anna are happy."

"Anna is different from us. She's contented with her

husband, son, and a baby on the way. She doesn't want more."

"Is that a curse?"

"I'm not the one who wants both marriage and art. For me, writing is enough."

"Don't you get lonely?"

"I have my family."

"I meant . . ."

"Ever since I was sick, my hair is thin, which was my only good feature. Though I wouldn't want a man who cared only about my hair."

"People see your hair. They can't see what's inside you."

"They can when I write." Louisa's face turned faintly red as she said, "I can write about a long, fatal love chase, but I never really understood such an impulse."

"It might be different if you let yourself stop criticizing. If you'd stand a little closer."

"That's just it. I see you step toward men as if you can't help yourself, but I've never felt that. And around babies, too, your arms open."

"Don't you yearn for children?"

Louisa shook her head. "It's like with you and painting. I can never truly see what the fuss is all about."

May struggled to make her voice even. "I know you can't walk far, the way you used to, but you could come along with Julian and me to see the lilies."

"Don't pity me. Anyway, I expect I'll be gone by mid-summer. I might take a job as companion to a wealthy young lady touring Europe."

"You're going to Europe! No one tells me anything!"

"It's not quite been decided. Miss Weld suffers from melancholia or neurasthenia. Her father heard I'd been a nurse during the war."

"We were going to see England and France together!"

"It's not a pleasure jaunt. I'd watch over her medicines and moods."

"I could help."

"You, a nurse?"

May blinked, stunned, though she supposed she shouldn't be, that her sister remembered so little about the weeks when she'd been so sick. May knew such care wasn't like working in a hospital, but it would certainly make her capable of escorting a frail woman to museums and historical sites. "You won't even go to tea parties with me, and you're crossing the ocean!"

"I told you, it's work."

"As an educated but poor companion. I expect this young lady just needs someone to make sure she gets on the proper trains, sees the necessary sights, and keeps out of drafts and away from the wrong sort of men. Carrying shawls, plumping pillows. You'll be bored to death."

"Perhaps I will. And Europe isn't likely to be all we hoped, back when we set plays in castles and dungeons. You'll have to wait for your chance to show everyone you're a lady of culture."

"I don't want to go just to tell people I've been overseas! I need differently shaped trees, differently colored flowers, homes made of stone or stucco, not just shingles. Sights talk to me, Lu. You wouldn't want to see the same people over and over. You thrive on varied conversations."

"Mother needs you."

"Father can watch over her for a while."

"I think she's a little glad when he goes away. I'm sorry, May. But Mother says that making sacrifices makes you stronger."

"So does doing what you love."

⊗

NOT LONG AFTER ANNA GAVE BIRTH TO ANOTHER boy, who they named after his father, she brought her sons to Concord. Instead of pouring over newspapers, Mother left them folded to hold the blanket-swaddled baby, watching his soft lips wobble as he breathed. His large eyelids had the same curves as his round head. Mother marveled at both cousin Lucy's skill as a doctor and her modest claim that all a safe delivery needed was sharp, sympathetic eyes and clean hands. Father carried Johnny around the yard, whispering the names of flowers, telling anyone who would listen, "Infants are natural philosophers, physicians, and priests."

May helped Louisa sew two new traveling dresses. She went with her to get a passport and ordered one of her own. Maybe she couldn't use it soon, but she'd be ready. In July, she escorted Louisa to the harbor.

Thunderstorms kept the ship from leaving on schedule, so they stayed overnight at Mr. and Mrs. Fields's townhouse. Mr. Fields was stout, with small eyes and a wiry white-and-brown beard. May knew he was distinguished, and some women, even those as pretty as his wife, chose older men for practical reasons, but May couldn't help thinking Mrs. Fields might have found happiness beyond signaling the maid for more cake and sherry among shelves of leather-bound books, a grand piano, and marble busts of Dante, Socrates, and Mr. Longfellow.

As she and Louisa talked, May picked up a book and examined hand-colored engravings of birds, then another with pictures of historic homes in Boston. She said, "I wonder that there isn't such a book like this about Concord. Showing the homes of luminaries, not just their faces."

"Yes, dear Mr. Hawthorne should be memorialized in such a way. And Mr. Thoreau, your father, and Mr. Emerson," Mrs. Fields said.

"I've done some sketches of the Hawthorne's house and Walden Pond. Maybe I could compile a book like that." May spoke before she had a chance to lose her courage. "Is there any chance Mr. Fields would consider publishing such a collection?"

"It sounds charming. Next time you visit, you must bring your portfolio."

May grinned. Books were what was needed to be taken seriously in her family. A book could fall into anyone's hands, perhaps those of someone who'd buy original art. Not that there was a guarantee one such as this would be published. Mr. Fields might tell her to stick to teaching. But the hope helped May feel strong the next day as she stood on a wharf with Louisa.

"I'll be gone almost a year," she said. "Anna's baby may be walking and talking when I get back. Freddy may know the alphabet. I'll miss so much. And what if, oh, I couldn't bear it if . . ."

"Mother and Father are healthy as horses," May interrupted.

"I already lost a sister. I can't risk losing my mother. You should have seen the care she lavished over Beth. And I don't remember much of when I was ill, but I know she barely ever left my side."

"She'll be fine. And maybe I'll be engaged."

"Weren't you waiting for someone with more prospects than Julian?"

"I'm only saying that anything can happen."

"Of course. And if something should happen to me . . ."

"Ships sail all the time without calamity. They're waiting." May hugged her good-bye, then stepped back among women waving handkerchiefs and men lifting caps. She watched the ship glide past frigates and schooners. Sails slivered the sky. Men in blue-and-white-checked shirts hauled up anchors or crawled over spars. May felt like the sister left behind, the way she'd been when she was young and Anna and Louisa had curled their hair and ironed gowns, getting ready for parties.

But she was not that girl. Her hands opened with an ache to draw as she watched gulls swoop for fish. Fog bells rang. Waves splashed on wharves. May felt full of possibilities, as if she were about to sail herself. She vowed she would one day.

7

WATER LİLİES

As May sat with Mrs. Hawthorne, she wondered why she'd been asked to her parlor. She thought of how Julian hadn't written since he'd left to work in the Berkshires. Her gaze moved from the music box to what looked like worn diaries as Mrs. Hawthorne asked, "What have you heard from Louisa?"

"We got a letter a few days ago. She and her companion were taking a river tour into Germany," May said.

"Germany! My one regret was that we never got there. The literature can be ponderous, but there's Bach."

"You saw so much else. You must be proud that your husband took all of you to Europe."

"It was his friend Franklin Pierce who saw that he got work as a consul. Everyone in town found fault with the poor man as president, as if they didn't criticize Mr. Lincoln, too. Until he passed over, and now no one breathes a word of reproach." Mrs. Hawthorne wore a maroon velvet dress, faded to mauve at the elbows, which must have been in fashion when she got married. She tucked back a strand of hair that had fallen from a slim band of pearls. "But I didn't invite you here to speak of politics. My husband's editor told me his books won't sell as they once did, now that readers know no more will come out. He says people crave the new, and an author's name must be kept before the public's eye. He wants to publish a biography and suggested Oliver Wendell Holmes as author. Mercy! I won't say the man isn't a good doctor, but I still shudder over the piece he wrote for the *Atlantic Monthly* baring details of my husband's final illness. As if the world needs to know about his stomach distention."

"Perhaps *you* should write about him."

"There's nothing he would have liked less. You know what he thought of women writers. Why, when Rose was ten and penned a story, he put a quick stop to that. But Mr. Fields proposed publishing selections from his letters and diaries. I removed some pages and crossed out lines and paragraphs where the veil should not be lifted. I hoped you might help by copying them. Una's hand is lovely, but her headaches have come back, and she mustn't strain her eyes."

"How could I refuse, after all you did keeping my mother serene when Louisa was so ill."

"I don't ask just as a favor. Mr. Fields offers a small salary."

May hoped this work would leave her time for drawing houses and might pay enough so she could afford art anatomy lessons. "I can start whenever you like."

"I think some of his diaries are in the room where we stored things after taking down the old garret to make way for the tower room. Would you come look with me?"

As they passed the cupboard under the stairs where Mrs. Hawthorne stored pies, May remembered calling that the Slough of Despond when she and her sisters had played Pilgrim's Progress here long ago, strapping on bundles of paper and cloth they called burdens. At the top of the stairs, she and Mrs. Hawthorne turned and entered a room crowded with chests, an old butter churn, a spinning wheel, and a green rocking horse. May opened a trunk that held a torn petticoat Anna had swirled in as if it were a ball gown, a flag made from a red flannel petticoat, and a pair of cracked leather boots Louisa had worn as a prince or pirate, back when they'd been girls who thought they could be anyone.

"Here are Una's baby socks! And my sketchbooks from Italy." Mrs. Hawthorne opened an old tin of paints with dried-up colors and faded labels. *Cremisi* was an orange-red and *azzurro* the color May imagined Italian skies.

They brought diaries, letters, and sketchbooks down to the parlor. After a few days of copying there, with Una playing passages from Bach, Rose complaining about the verses her mother had asked her to memorize, and Mrs. Hawthorne critiquing the novel she was reading, May suggested she might work more efficiently in the tower room. On her way up, she peeked past the open door to Julian's bedroom. She caught her breath at the sight of his blue jacket hanging from a hook, remembering its scent of wool, tobacco, pine, and boy. She continued to the room where Mr. Hawthorne had once paced. She copied the thin, slanting script he'd written on pale blue paper when he and Sophia had been engaged or separated during the early years of their marriage. May skipped over words and passages that Mrs. Hawthorne had drawn a line through, reading how her husband not only longed to see her, but to see her quite specifically in bed. "Desire," "yearning," "kisses," and the names of parts of the body were at the center of many stricken phrases.

May spent many early summer afternoons growing more familiar with the Hawthorne's first year of marriage, when Sophia had painted in the Old Manse and Nathaniel wrote stories. Mr. Hawthorne bathed in the river and picked his wife bouquets of cardinal flowers that grew along the banks. In winter, they skated on the frozen river, then warmed up by the fire, dancing to strains from the Swiss music box. Closing her eyes to rest them, May allowed herself to daydream. Why shouldn't she and Julian live simply but happily by the river, as his parents had? She'd like to have a ring to show Louisa when she returned from Europe and boasted about all the palaces she'd seen. May went on to wish for four children, though she wouldn't want them to be spread as far apart in age as she and her sisters had been. The youngest should never be lonely.

When she came downstairs one afternoon, she said, "I finished copying the diary you and your husband shared in the Old Manse."

"Where he wrote some of his best tales. Poor Elizabeth Ripley lives there now. When I feel sorry for myself, I think of her, a widow in her early twenties. That dreadful war."

"How is Julian?" May wondered if it had been a mistake to try to keep their romance from their parents.

"I expect him back from Lenox for a visit soon. It's good for him there, where he remembers happy times with his father when he was a boy."

"Sophia . . . oh, pardon me. It's reading those diaries . . ."

"Please, call me that. My husband is in a better place, but it's the small things I miss, like hearing my name."

"Reading the letters he wrote when you were engaged made me curious about the ones you must have written back."

"He burned them."

"Your letters!"

"We couldn't bring everything on the ship to Europe, and as no one can tell God's purpose, it seemed wiser not to store them and worry they'd be seen by strangers' eyes in the event the voyage turned tragic." She picked up a sketchbook she'd brought down. "Did I show you the drawings I did when we lived in Rome?"

May looked through pen-and-ink renderings of broken marble pillars, ruins, and ancient fountains and watercolor copies of paintings by Raphael and Correggio. "These are exquisite!"

"When we were first married, I helped make ends meet by decorating fireplace screens and lampshades. I illustrated some of Mr. Hawthorne's stories."

"He didn't mind that you made art?"

"He had no patience with suffragists but knew I wouldn't be happy if I didn't do some kind of artwork. Of course, that was before we had children."

"And now they're mostly grown. Will you paint again?"

"That's all in the past. It was my husband who was a genius.

He thought painting was a gracious refinement for a lady, but indelicate for money to be exchanged. I shudder to think of what he'd make of me selling rights to his diaries. But we have to eat."

"I know you want to keep his name in front of the public, but surely his books sell briskly enough."

"That's what I once thought, too. But it seems Mr. Fields paid for my husband's postage stamps, cigars, brandy, biscuits, train fares, and even our dog. Those and other expenses were taken as advances out of sales, but apparently not enough books sold to pay them back." Mrs. Hawthorne's voice was low as she explained that copyright laws meant they never got a cent for novels sold in Europe. "Your mother suggested I take in boarders as she did, but I can't bear the thought of strangers in the house. I had no choice but to accept the offer to publish parts of my husband's diaries and letters."

May tried to keep her face even, but she was shocked to learn of the family's debt. Julian's carelessness about money had been annoying before, but was worse as she realized there was none to waste. She said, "Maybe there's something Una could do."

"We didn't bring up our girls to earn a living."

The way I do, May thought. She returned to the tower room, where she pushed back memories of playing cards, swimming, skating, kissing behind doors or between houses, and hopes for a pretty proposal. She tried to concentrate on copying sentences in her best handwriting. She came across some pages where she recognized the story Julian had told about the schoolteacher who'd left her bonnet and shoes and walked into the Concord River. May read about lanterns reflecting in black water as one man rowed the *Pond Lily*, while two others poked hay rakes through the weeds and water. Eventually an oar struck a bruised, bloated body that they pulled to the surface, brought back to land, lifted onto a bier of boards and fence rails, and carried to the house to be laid out on the kitchen table. At the funeral, Mr. Hawthorne wrote that people said the young woman "had refined herself out of the sphere of her natural connections."

May shut the old diary and wept. Was that all that could be said about someone who died alone, who'd wanted more than what she'd had, and been told she wanted too much? Was that what everyone was told? What if her mother, who kept them safe and taught them to be good, had claimed leather diaries instead of cardboard and lectured before the public instead of just to her girls in the parlor? What if Mrs. Hawthorne had demanded places for her pictures on walls? May heard the music box playing downstairs, the same strains rattling, chiming, echoing within tin and wood.

❦

SITTING NEAR HER FATHER'S APPLE TREES, MAY PAINTED rowboat-shaped leaves whose colors changed with the light. Breaking a way through blank paper was hard, with each mark as much a chance for failure as success. Sometimes she thought she needed long stretches of quiet time in order to paint well, but then she remembered that serenity often came during, not before, putting her brush on paper. She heard Freddy call,

"Auntie May! Mama said I could play for ten minutes before my nap. Let's play horses!"

She lifted the little boy onto a low, curved bough, handed him imaginary reins, then helped him down. He sat before a rock, tapping it with a stick.

When Anna came out with her baby in her arms to fetch Freddy, May asked, "Is he pretending to write? Being like his Aunt Louisa?"

"Or a bookkeeper like his father. I don't like to see him playing that."

"You're proud of John."

"Of course. He works hard and earns an honest living." Anna paused. "I know it's wicked to sound discontented when I have so much, but I wish John worked in an office where he had a chance of moving up. I can't help wanting more for my boys. Can't you see Freddy preaching from a pulpit?"

"He's three years old."

Anna curved her hand over the baby's head. "I love this age, when it seems you know everything about them."

"You're a good mother, Anna."

"That's all I ever wanted to be. I'm not talking about you or Louisa, but some women who don't have children can get selfish."

"Who are you talking about?"

"I should have known you'd take it wrong. I only meant that it's impossible to really know what love is until you hold a baby who depends upon you for everything."

After Anna brought her boys inside, May returned to her watercolor. Gradually, one wash made the next evident and necessary. She forgot everything but what was close. Then she heard footsteps. She glanced up and saw Julian's blue-specked eyes framed by wavy dark hair. His shoulders pulled at the broadcloth of his shirt, a sight that turned her belly tender before remembering her resolve to end whatever was between them.

He threw one arm around her waist, kissed the bottom of her ear, and waved a kite. "I made this from an old shirt of my father's. I can show Freddy how to fly it."

"What a bonny idea! I think he's sleeping now, or pretending to, and not to be disturbed."

"How I hated naps at his age. Staring up at the ceiling when it was light outside. Of course, now naps seem delightful."

"Freddy is still talking about how you took him sledding behind our houses." May handed him her sketchpad and asked, "What do you think?"

"Lovely. But isn't a tree enough without painting it?"

"There are more to trees than leaves, branches, and trunks."

"Next you'll be telling me the woods are transcendent."

"No." May hated the way that word appeared like a sign, wrecking the view.

"I stopped at the river. The water lilies are out." Julian set the kite by a stone and handed her a ball of string. "Tell Freddy I'll come back soon. May I see you tomorrow before dawn?"

There seemed no harm in one last small adventure. Early the next morning, May's narrow bedroom was dark, the gods and goddesses she'd drawn on the walls hidden, when a tug on the string she'd wrapped around her ankle woke her. She unknotted the string that dangled through an open window, slid out of bed, took off her nightgown, and slipped on a white frock. She held up the hem as she tiptoed downstairs, then ran across the dewy clover.

She and Julian held hands, guiding each other around blackberry and huckleberry bushes and over roots and rocks, which were hard to see in the dim light from stars and a waxing moon. They hiked through a meadow of wild strawberries and honeysuckle. A kerosene lamp flickered in the window of a farmhouse.

Soon she heard the slow river and rushes and horsetails blowing in the breeze. She smelled moss and stone. Water caught and reflected moonlight, so it wasn't hard to find the rowboat kept by the Old Manse. Julian held her arm to steady her as she climbed in, but the boat tipped, then settled. Their knees touched as they faced each other on narrow seats. He picked up the oars and rowed with smooth strokes through water that quietly swirled and foamed.

Hoping her added effort would help them reach the lilies before sunlight touched them, she moved next to him, rocking the boat as she grabbed an oar. The pale moon fell in the west. Mist rose, and pink streaked the blue-black horizon. By a big, smooth rock where the river split, the water slowed down enough to let lilies and pickerelweed grow. Their oars caught wide, flat leaves. Lily buds, rounded as closed fists, bobbed on the water's surface. As sunlight slowly spread, dim colors appeared, but the spot around the river bend stayed in shadows. Leaving her oar in its lock, May bent over to fold a closed, slippery bud in her hand. It wasn't shut tightly, but like gently folded fingers, and it fit perfectly in her palm. She let it slip away as Julian rowed into the midst of the lily pads.

At last, sunlight touched the water. All around them, petals unfurled. The river turned gold and white. She reached out again and grasped a slick stem, which slipped from her hand. The rowboat wobbled as she stretched further, and still further. The boat teetered, and water splashed in. She lost her balance. The wooden boat tipped. Water flooded and filled it, spilling May and Julian into the river. They thrashed among the flowers, sputtering, kicking, shrieking, and laughing. He caught the boat and dragged it closer. She felt her dress press against the curve of her breasts as she raised the lily over her head.

"I hope you like it." Standing waist-deep in the water, Julian's soaked shirt outlined his broad chest.

"I want to paint it."

They waded to land and moored the boat. Butterflies fluttered over red trumpetweed. May lifted her white dress, now streaked with mud, to her knees and wrung it. As she climbed past willow trees, she stumbled into a puddle and laughed. Julian embraced her from behind, turned her around, and kissed her. His warm mouth was as wet as their clothes. She kissed him hard, like someone who hadn't known she was thirsty until she was offered water. She dropped the lily. The space between her breasts seemed to widen and reach. She placed her palm on the side of his face.

His hand slid from the small of her back to a softer curve, which made something open between her legs. The air smelled of his skin and sweet ferns and wild peppermint. He pulled her toward him and pushed his hands under her dress. His fingers spread across her thighs. Her palms curved over his hips. Her breath heaved through her chest. She wanted him to unbutton her dress and touch all of her body, which felt long and soft and good. But she grabbed his wrists and pulled her damp dress back down over her legs.

"May, don't you want more?"

"Of course I do, but . . ." Her broken breath made her voice burst out. "I'm not ready to have children."

"Some of the fellows at school told me what to do." He put his hand over her breast.

"It's not just that. We have to think about the future."

"You want to wait until we're married?"

Her face burned, partly with excitement, partly anger. She'd been foolish to expect words in a rose garden. But couldn't he at least get on his knee and pose words that didn't sound like they came on a lark? "Do you call that a proposal?"

"Marry me," he whispered, undoing a button behind her collar. He slipped out another button with one hand and tugged up her dress with his other.

Wind sighed through the pines and touched her throat and wrists. She said, "Julian, we can't risk this."

"I thought you liked babies."

"Of course I do. But they stop everything else for women. And you know you're not ready to be a father."

"That may be just what I have a talent for. We could rent a little cottage. Plant a garden. Maybe keep bees and sell honey and candlesticks and huckleberry pies."

This was like her own daydreams, but coming from his

mouth, she heard its foolishness. "That's hardly a living."

"The bookshop at the college put up some of the illuminations I copied from medieval manuscripts. Maybe I'll sell more."

"You're not that young anymore. It's time to think ahead."

"You mean you're not that young anymore."

"I meant you're not a boy, conjuring a future as a vagabond. Julian, you need some means of supporting a family one day." May flushed. She didn't mean to talk about this, or anything. She pressed her lips on his.

He stepped back. "You didn't answer me. Do you want to get married?"

"You don't mean it. You're just lonely."

"Aren't you?"

"It's not a reason to get married. Not now, while you're deciding if you want to be an artist or a beekeeper or a baker for all I know."

"You don't take me seriously."

"I do." She felt a tug through her throat, thinking how she hated when Louisa hinted that she lacked character because she didn't see things just the way she did. "I know you don't want to be stuck in a dark office. I understand. But we can't live like field hands, at least not when we have children."

"Then I'll look for a job somewhere else. Some of the fellows are going to New York to make their fortunes."

"For goodness sake, who lives there?"

"I don't suppose everyone can trace their roots back to patriots and ship captains, and there's no history of tea spilled in the harbor. But there's been a lot of building going on since the war. I can use a saw and hammer."

"You change your mind all the time about what you'll do. We need . . ."

"Money, I know, that's what you care about. Do you know what that feels like? To be always told to wait?"

"Julian, your mother told me that your family is in debt. That Mr. Fields has paid for everything."

"I suppose something is owed him, but income from the books is bound to pay him back. Things always turn out."

"I won't see my children go hungry, or ashamed of their clothes or their home." She struggled to keep her voice even. "You don't want that either. Why, your parents gave you an excellent education in Europe."

"I'd rather have been with other fellows, making slingshots and shooting marbles instead of listening to my father recite Shakespeare or my mother insist we sketch Roman ruins."

"I just saw the sketches she did there. It's a shame she didn't paint more."

"That would have been grand. Then I'd have two parents shut behind closed doors."

"And someone should have pulled your father from his room."

"My mother wasn't earnest about art. Surely you aren't either."

"You assume that because we're women."

"There's never been a female Michelangelo or Rembrandt."

How had they begun arguing about art? May touched his arm and saw the blue leave his eyes as they clouded. His cheeks crumpled. His chest shook. She thought he might cry, but his voice burst out in anger. "I used to think you were different from your family, but you're not. Your mother has to right every wrong, feed every stranger. Your father can't let an apple just be an apple. No one can be just enough, and you're the same."

"I'm not like them."

"You want to paint lilies prettier than they really are. You can't leave a plain wall alone. You want to make everything better than it is. You tell me I'm too young, too aimless. And it's not just me. I expect you'll find something wrong with every man you meet, even one who promises to sweep you off to Europe. You don't know how to love."

"I do!" Hadn't she loved him, and rowing, and the way the lilies made the water pale? But maybe because she didn't plead more, he spun around and headed toward the woods.

She stood by the empty rowboat at the spot where a young woman had left behind her shoes and bonnet. May picked up the water lily, which was already wilting. She'd never be as foolish as the woman who'd waded too far, but she shouldn't have pulled the flower from the water. The pearly shine of its bloom was magnificent, but she loved more the beauty of what didn't stay still, but opened and closed, and was impossible to hold.

8

ART ANATOMY

As fall arrived, May tried to put aside thoughts of Julian even as she copied letters and diaries in his house. The work let her afford art anatomy classes, which were held every Wednesday. She liked each better than the one before, though she worried that her interest in art, choosing the distance a painter needed, always gauging perspectives, had doomed her romance with Julian. Was squinting and stepping back a dangerous habit? But learning about bones and muscles would improve her ability at painting portraits, something she might make a living at. Could she one day even earn enough to travel to Europe, without depending on a man?

On a day when the milkweed leaves had turned yellow, she wore her favorite dress and a hat with a velvet bandeau and an egret feather. The train from Concord arrived well before her class. Remembering the sculpture of a dying gladiator she'd admired in Alice's house, May decided to see one of Dr. Rimmer's recently erected sculptures. She strode past Boston Common, where veterans, one with a missing arm, another with a bandaged head, sat by faded blue caps holding a few coins. Nursemaids wheeled carriages and held the collars of little boys getting too close to the pond while tossing bread to swans. May turned down Commonwealth Avenue and stopped at the statue of Alexander Hamilton. The founding father was shown in a windblown cloak and with muscular calves below breeches that buttoned below the knees. His stance was bold, his mouth determined, his chin lifted high, looking proud but, May thought, too much alone, until a pigeon lighted on the granite shoulder.

She continued past a department store, an art gallery, and a shop displaying tins of paints with postage-stamp-sized blocks of colors and pristine tubes of blues and reds, too dear for her to buy more than a small tube at a time. She could almost taste the lemon yellow, imagine the rich scent of burnt sienna. Passing an antique store, the stuffed owl in the window made her wish she could paint from such a model, not just remember glimpses from a dark tree. But the owl was expensive, too.

May entered a room in the Art Studio Building. She greeted Alice, Charlotte, and Anne Whitney, who was perhaps the most dedicated student and the only one older than May. They looked through the sketches of bones, muscles, and organs they'd done in earlier classes. Alice said, "I can't wait until we draw a real person, but the model won't come until after New Year's. Dr. Rimmer will have us sculpt before we paint. To master three dimensions before we attempt two."

At the sound of heavy steps, everyone stopped talking. May pushed a chair close to the skeleton that hung from a hook by the blackboard. Dr. Rimmer took off a rumpled black overcoat with a green sheen around the buttonholes and collar. His stained wool vest, which was high-buttoned in the old German style, was tight over his round belly. Wiry gray hair puffed over his ears. Without a word, he picked up some chalk, faced the blackboard, and began drawing parts of an ear. May copied examples of the helix, tragus, concha, and auditory passage. She savored the vaguely forbidden quality of it all, discovering what was usually reserved for those in the medical profession. She wished he'd stick with unfamiliar terms and maps of the body, but Dr. Rimmer sometimes digressed to topics such as selling art.

"The judges who decide what gets in the Paris Salon miss a lot about what makes great art, but work shown there gets seen by those who can afford to buy it. So an artist can feed his children and keep working," he said. "At least Europeans care about art. Boston calls itself the Athens of America, but there's not even an art museum open to the public."

"There's talk of building one," Anne said.

"They like to talk. Gilbert Stuart refused to show his pictures here because they were always so poorly lit. Mr. Copley moved to England."

As the weeks passed, some young ladies stopped attending. Dr. Rimmer looked unsurprised as he called names from a book and heard no response. He murmured, "They send excuses. Family. Someone is engaged. Or uninspired. Everyone is uninspired."

The remaining students continued to copy bones and muscles until January, when they learned how to construct an armature, bending wires around a steel rod and attaching small wooden crosses to hold clay and make tabletop models.

Dr. Rimmer grimaced at these maquettes. "There are hundreds of ways to show someone standing, not just one! With a shoulder raised, one foot in front of the other, perhaps at a slant. Consider the shapes of the hands, which can tell as much as a face. Each bent finger offers a chance for a new expression."

At the end of one afternoon's work, May, Alice, and Charlotte headed down the hall, hearing the soft thudding of ballet students practicing glissades and jetés. Alice complained, "He never praises anyone. You always were so encouraging, May. I wish you'd teach again."

"He admires Anne Whitney's work."

"I'd hate to be such a bluestocking," Alice said. "Her hair falls from her combs, and I don't believe she bothers with lacing and stays."

"She's talented." May tightened her cloak as they stepped into a bitter wind. "Not everyone marries."

"Especially since the war, which took so many good men. But Miss Whitney chooses not to. It's strange." Alice shrugged as they walked down a narrow, curving street. "She wants to go to Rome and carve marble. I'd rather see Paris."

"I hope you get there. Will your father travel with you?" May asked.

"He has so much business to tend to. And . . . he isn't well. But he's anxious that I broaden my vision and perhaps meet someone, which was the greatest desire of my mother, may she rest in peace," Alice said.

May took her hand. "I hope it's nothing grave with your father."

"I don't think so. He says I might go to Europe with the proper companion. Someone with a bit more experience. Perhaps my favorite art teacher."

May's heart beat hard, though she cringed to think that she was considered old enough to be some sort of chaperone. "I'm not sure I'd be suitable."

"My aunt might come, too, to keep me out of trouble, making sure any suitors aren't swindlers or such."

"I could see that you got into just enough trouble." May squeezed her hand.

⬦

IN THE GLOAMING, MAY TRUDGED THROUGH THE SNOW before her house and opened the door. Freddy flung himself at her as if she'd been gone longer than half a morning and an afternoon. He, his mother, and his little brother had recently settled back here. Anna had said that she could bear how the thin walls of their city lodgings let in cold winds, and the renters downstairs who rapped with a broom on the ceiling, as if that would quiet a baby, but a recent fever left her hard of hearing. And after the pipes froze, she couldn't get water for her children.

"Where were you?" Freddy asked.

"You know I went to the city, chipmunk," May said.

"I'm not a chipmunk!"

"Of course you're not, my little skunk."

"I'm not a skunk!"

"Are you a little bear?"

"No! I'm a boy. You're silly, Auntie May."

"Yes." As she sat in a chair by the fire, he scrambled onto her lap. He slid off when Anna screamed from upstairs.

"Wait here," May said, and she sprang up the steps.

Anna stood by the crib, tears streaming down her face. She said, "The baby won't stop crying. I fed him. I changed him. I rocked him. I tried everything, and I'm so tired!"

"Of course you are." May felt like crying, too, but she saw that Freddy had crept upstairs and stood quietly in the corner. Even in the dim moonlight, she could see fear in the way he stood too still. She picked up the wailing baby. "Anna, why don't you read to Freddy while I bathe Johnny? That may help."

May stripped off the baby's damp gown and diapers and dropped them in a pail filled with soiled garments. She brought the baby down to the parlor, where she warmed water over the fire, then poured it in a basin. He stopped crying, though he looked alarmed as she dipped him in the water. She patted him dry, put on clean clothes, and brought him back to Anna.

Freddy tugged his mother's sleeve. "I want to go outside."

"No!" Anna snapped. Then she spoke more gently. "It's dark and cold."

"You said I could play!"

"That was hours ago."

"There's a full moon," May said. "I'll take him. Anna, maybe you'll get some peace."

After she gently twisted and tugged Freddy's arms and feet into a jacket and boots, he gave her a fluttery hug. May helped him dig a snow fort. He jumped from a pile of snow into a soft patch under the elm, opening his arms wide, like that of a bird or an angel.

❧

A FEBRUARY BLIZZARD KEPT MAY FROM EVEN OPENING the door into gales of sleet and snow, never mind getting to the road. She supposed the trains weren't running, and she tried to console herself that class must have been canceled, though she wished she could continue working on the painting of a model they'd finally begun. A few days later, Mother was plagued by dyspepsia and lightheadedness. On the following Wednesday, May considered wrapping her in a shawl by the hearth, since she could manage to get to the fire and keep it up. But once Mother was on her feet, she couldn't be trusted to keep from tending to chores. Even worse, May had found Mother rummaging among flour bins for a doll and in the linen cupboard for red slippers she'd worn as a child. May stayed, though her throat ached with thoughts of what she was missing while she made the house fragrant with cinnamon, nutmeg, and ginger. She couldn't help wishing someone wanted a painting more than gingerbread.

A few days later, the cold Anna had recently caught grew worse. May held the baby in one arm while making Freddy an F-shaped flapjack. Another began to burn. She told him stories and took him sledding behind the house. A neighbor boy joined them, and May asked him inside to warm up by the hearth. They built a castle, fort, and depot out of books, but Freddy refused to let the boy use his little wooden train. Hearing shrieks, Anna came in to scold him.

When the boys were playing quietly again, May went into the kitchen and told Anna, "He's four years old. He has the rest of his life to think about other people first."

"Don't lecture me." Anna said. "You'll understand when you're a mother."

⟨⟨⟨⟩⟩

THE FOLLOWING WEDNESDAY, ANNA COUGHED, RUBBED her forehead, and said, "I can hardly stand, never mind dash after a toddler and care for a baby, too."

"I'm sorry, but you'll have to manage this one day," May said. "I've waited so long to work with a model. She could start another pose before I get to finish my painting."

"I need you!" Anna's gray eyes widened. "Goodness, I'll pose for you."

"Sitting still is harder than you think. I'm sorry. People miss a lot in one class, and some think they'll never catch up and don't return. I'll get back as soon as I can."

When May got off the train in Boston, snow and sleet began to fall. As she headed down a street, a dog darted in front of a horse and carriage. The horse shied and bolted. Passersby rushing to get out of the way knocked May onto the slippery sidewalk. She twisted her ankle and landed hard on one hip. Boys chased the dog. Men yelled at the driver. As May stood up, someone accidentally pushed her onto a frozen-over puddle, which broke under her weight. Her boot got soaked through. Her ankle stung from the cold and a possible strain.

She hobbled forward, managing to hold up her weight, step gingerly over icy patches and around slush, and make it to the Art Studio Building. The train schedule forced her to arrive early, so even after having walked more slowly than usual, Room 55 was empty when she entered. She took off her cloak and wide-brimmed hat. She sat by the stove to shake snow from her boots, pull them off, and rub her twisted ankle and toes that had turned the colors of bruises.

But when she put her boots back on, she felt better standing in front of her partly finished painting. The model's shoulders looked too limp to hold up her arms, but the color of the mouth was a satisfactory shade of rose. May was pleased with the way she'd straightened her turned-up nose. Dr. Rimmer lectured about the need to observe with accuracy, even when truth didn't flatter, but she believed few others held such a position. Who wouldn't prefer her skin to look unblemished and unwrinkled?

She tied on her blue smock and squeezed modest dabs of paint onto her palette: Chinese white, Cerulean blue, and a mere hint of crimson for the skin. She glanced out the window, eager for company now. She stepped over to the skeleton and studied the sockets where the eyes and nose had been. When she touched a hand, the wired-together bones clattered. Heading back to her easel, she saw something glitter in the wire wastebasket. She bent down and scooped up two crumpled paint tubes. Both were mostly empty, but one held enough scarlet paint to tint several small faces. She unscrewed the cap, smelled its exquisitely sharp scent, then spun around.

Dr. Rimmer watched from the doorway.

May clutched the salvaged treasures, lifted her chin, and strode to her easel, hoping he didn't notice how she blushed. She wasn't stealing or even begging. She had simply saved what someone else had thrown away. As Alice and Anne passed through the door, she called hello, thinking that a gentleman would have pretended not to see her sifting through the trash. A nice man would have turned away.

She kept her face turned from him as she complimented Charlotte on the quills in her bonnet, mixed paint for the shadows on the model's neck, and greeted the young woman who settled into her pose.

As the students painted, Dr. Rimmer moved around the room, commenting. "Do you see only one color in her hair, Miss? Observe. Her skin is darker near the top of her forehead and the tip of her chin. Her nose is bigger." He took the brush from a girl's hand and rubbed out a line. "Every stroke must mean something. We don't paint just skin, hair, and cloth, but the human spirit. Paint her as a Madonna, Athena, or a noble idea such as Liberty."

May tried to think of the model as a saint, goddess, or symbol, but instead she found herself wondering what she'd eaten for lunch and if she were tired. Who did she go home to? May stepped back, feeling her chest tighten as Dr. Rimmer examined her canvas. Before stepping away, he said, "Keep working. *Travaillez.*"

May heard the students around her stir, reacting to the

absence of criticism, which might be the grandest compliment of the day.

Dr. Rimmer scolded Charlotte. "Do you remember nothing I taught you about bones and muscle? They are your alphabet, for you to write the opera of the face."

"I'm trying." Charlotte's cheek muscles looked strained.

"You're all spoiled." Dr. Rimmer shook his head. "How can I expect you to see when you've never lived? How can you express feeling when you've never known need?"

Tears fell down Charlotte's face.

"If you can't bear a few honest words, go home and embroider handkerchiefs," he said. "I teach to help you recognize meaning, not add to falsity, but why do I even say such things? None of you have suffered enough to be able make art. None of you know real work."

May let out a breath. She thought of how she'd sewed undergarments for aunts and strangers until her fingers burned from the needle. She'd spent mornings stacking alphabet blocks with toddlers. Maybe Charlotte had never worked as a seamstress or a teacher, but wasn't it work, too, to smile and be silent while men told you it was wrong to yearn for more than a husband and children—as if such were easy to come by? How many of the women here had gotten slush in their boots, wore gloves that were too thin to keep out the chill, and kept on, never minding the cold? Wasn't it work to refuse a sister's plea for help, knowing that such requests would be repeated, while her own desires could get lost? How many had mothers or sisters who weren't well, who might never be well, or hearts broken by men who didn't survive the war or other disasters? Weren't keeping such secrets a struggle, too?

"I'm afraid you don't know American women." May looked directly at her teacher, then glanced down, remembering he was American, though he wore Germanic vests and uttered French phrases. "Just because we don't wear black crêpe doesn't mean we haven't known hardships."

Dr. Rimmer stared at her.

She willed him to say anything, but when he stayed silent, she gathered her things and hurried into the hall. She heard footsteps behind her and stopped at the top of the stairs to put on her cloak and broad-brimmed hat.

"You mustn't go." Dr. Rimmer caught up and stood beside her. "Of all the young ladies in class, I think you might have a chance to become an artist."

"I haven't even finished a painting here." Her ankle throbbed.

"I didn't say you *are* an artist. I said it was possible. Talent doesn't need canvas to be spotted. I saw it in how embarrassed you looked holding crushed tubes of paint, but by how you stiffened your shoulders and got to work. You have more studying to do, but that capacity to be seen, then to keep on despite shame, shows me someone who can paint."

"Am I to thank you for those words?"

"If you know poverty, show it. You're hardly alone."

"People look to art for a better world."

"Art must not lie." He reached toward her. Perhaps to get a better view of her eyes, he lifted her hat brim, his hand brushing her hair.

She stepped back.

His gaze trailed from her eyes, over her mouth, down her throat, to her chest. He said, "But you must pledge yourself to it. I've seen this chance in a few others, but then they leave, they marry. They forget what they once loved. They have children, and no time to devote to their vision."

She let her eyelids fall, willing him to stop talking, which made her aware of how much she wanted everything, how that was impossible, and that he was right. One had to make choices between being loved and making art, telling the truth or turning from it. She heard dresses rustle from down the hall and expected some students were listening. Despite the pain in her ankle, she swiftly strode down the stairs, past the ballet and sculpting studios, and onto the sidewalk. She crossed into the Common on her way to the train station. Children so swaddled they looked like soft toys lumbered near the frozen pond. May turned from the clatter and scraping of skates, passing the spot where she'd once waved a handbill, begging people to listen to her father. Her eyes burned at the thought of that hopeful little girl who should never have been sent out alone.

She boarded the train. Dr. Rimmer's words and silences filled her as she looked through smoke-stained windows. Had he touched her? Had she stepped back? She couldn't find words for everything that had happened in that room and hallway. All she knew was that she couldn't go back.

9

LANDSCAPES

ven with a shawl swathed around her head and neck and gloves under her wool mittens, May shivered while sketching crackling ice on the river, dried cattails, the curved bridge, a squirrel on a dead limb, and vast sky. A memory of Dr. Rimmer's voice rose between her pencil and the frozen river. *Choose*, she heard. Was it his fingertips brushing her hair or the prophecy that she could become an artist, though it would bring terrible loneliness, that made her hand tremble? She kept moving her pencil until her thoughts and heartbeat slowed to meet the pace of her eyes and hand. The strength of the stones and exposed roots felt like hers as she drew them. Perhaps it was just as well that she concentrated on pictures of Concord for the book she'd proposed. But she couldn't help wishing someone noticed that she didn't take the train into Boston the following week or the next. By the time the roads became muddy and orioles built nests, even Mother seemed to have forgotten she'd ever taken classes.

May couldn't bother her with the story of why she'd stopped, or even risk that she wouldn't understand, for lately she sometimes seemed confused about not only the day, but the decade. May wouldn't tell Anna, who might blame her for being alone in the hall with him, saying too much, wearing her hair unpinned, wanting to make art, anything. She hoped she could confide in Louisa when she returned from Europe.

But even after Louisa had been home a few days, she hadn't finished talking about water cures, old palaces, mountains, and how she wished that she'd never seen Charles Dickens in London, wearing scads of diamond rings and a fur coat. As Louisa said that monarchy wasn't as pretty as she'd imagined when they were girls, May guessed she made more of the disappointments to keep her from becoming jealous. It didn't work. She was glad when Mother changed the subject to how it was a pity that Father wasn't here, as he'd already left to give his conversations. There seemed to be more interest in them this year, as if having President Johnson in office had increased people's appetite for idealistic words. Mother mentioned a recent rash of burglaries that made Mr. Emerson reluctant to leave the silver cream pitcher. "He's relieved his son returned to college, after going West and seeing a buffalo. But it's a shame Julian was asked to leave Harvard."

"Oh!" May cried, then tried to quell her surprise. "His mother must be upset."

"She tried to convince the president to give him another chance but was told they'd already given him so many. So she's decided to use the money earned from the collection of letters to move them all to Germany. People say they can live more cheaply there, though I don't understand how," Mother said.

"You didn't know any of this?" Louisa asked May.

"I no longer waste time with Julian." Her dismay that he was going to Europe mixed with her fury that she wasn't. Everyone got to go but her. Alice's hope that they might go together seemed to have vanished with her father's illness. May said, "I've been drawing Concord scenes."

"And portraits? Mother wrote about your anatomy classes."

"I stopped taking them."

"You must learn to finish things."

"I finish plenty! I've been drawing since I was twelve years old!"

"But with all your heart? You divide yourself."

"I don't!" May left Louisa with Mother.

The two of them spent much of the next week whispering together. Louisa went to Boston for a few days, and when she returned, she said that she'd taken a job overseeing *Merry's Museum*, a children's magazine. Louisa packed to move back to the city without a word about how May had spent the past year looking out for Mother and helping out with Anna's children. She said, "I'm surprised how confused Mother gets. Maybe the time away makes me notice how much she talks about her father's good deeds and her family's pew in King's Chapel. Yesterday she left the teakettle on the stove so long that the bottom burned. The whole house could have set on fire."

"But it didn't." May's chest grew warm. If Louisa wasn't going to stay to help, she shouldn't act so concerned.

❧

MAY FINISHED PICTURES OF THE OLD NORTH BRIDGE, the Old Manse, their home and the rustic summerhouse that Father had built in their yard. She included a small figure in some sketches, like those she'd seen on ancient Chinese scrolls. She showed a boat crossing Walden Pond steered by a man with his back to shore and two girls sitting outside the Hawthorne's house. Her ink lines were as strong and precise as an oar slicing water, the right steps on the right path. At some point, one must put down the oars, take off one's shoes, wipe ink from the nib of a pen. The finished details gave the work power, but a sense of something missing made her ache to pick up her pen again. These sketches weren't yet good enough to show Mr. and Mrs. Fields.

When Father returned in fall, May asked if she could use the old shed behind the house as a studio where she could paint and offer classes. He not only agreed, but suggested attaching it to the house, so it would be near a hearth when the weather turned cold. He and a neighbor took the shed off its foundation, put it on wagon wheels, and rolled it to a space between his study and the kitchen. May scrubbed and whitewashed the walls, sanded the floor, and washed the high windows. Father sawed through the bookshelf in his study to make a second door, so May wouldn't have to leave the house to go to work. She told everyone this door shouldn't be opened by anyone but her. This seemed difficult for Mother to grasp, when, after all, she sometimes had only a short, simple question. And Anna's boys missed her. May loved them so terribly much.

That winter, she bought a bucket of clay and a bag of dry plaster. She sculpted a bas-relief of Charlotte Corday, a figure of Diana, and a plaster bust of Father, who was patient while she measured his nose, the spaces between his forehead and chin, and between his eyes. She wished she had more clay, so she could try several expressions and compare them, rather than have to try one after another. She liked clay's cool, slick feel but gave up on more attempts at sculpting. It was hard enough for a woman to make her mark in any art, never mind one that called for messy clay and expensive stone. Even the finished work took up more space than a painting, calling for shelves or even floors or land.

She drew silhouettes of visitors on the walls as examples to her students. Alice and Charlotte came from Boston to join some local girls, including Rose and Kate Peckham. May lectured about composition and demonstrated how to crosshatch or change the pressure of their hands to shade. As they worked, they complained, confided, and gossiped. Alice mentioned that her father wasn't as hale as usual and that she'd heard that Dr. Rimmer had left to teach in New York. May felt a pinch, now that the possibility of returning to his classes was gone. Of course it had always been so. She examined Kate's drawing and said, "You could be more diligent in this corner. Press harder with your pencil. Show some conviction."

"I knew it was terrible," Kate said.

"I didn't say that. You're just starting."

"Nothing will come of it."

"It shall if you keep at it. Slow down. Art isn't a race."

The students were happiest when she showed them how

she coated a piece of wood with a thick layer of black tempera, then painted an open-throated lily on a stylized vine. She left no signs of dirt, petals that drooped, buds shriveled or not yet unfurled, or leaves nibbled by insects. She painted only perfectly opened blooms. She suspected that Dr. Rimmer would call her flower panels mere decoration, but was it a crime to please? Maybe a small one. It might take more talent to draw something as it was, to show something others didn't see as beautiful, until an artist peeled away layers to point it out.

Early in fall, Alice stopped coming to class. It hardly seemed possible that there should be more tragedy in her family, but the girls whispered that her father was gravely ill. May still had more students than could comfortably fit in the room, especially since some insisted on wearing crinolines or hoops that hampered them from reaching the easels. But May thought she should look for more students and offer more classes. She remembered talking with Judge French on the train to Boston. He'd mentioned that his son who'd started at the new Institute of Technology across the river didn't find it suited him any more than farming, but last winter, he'd shaped some realistic lions from snow and recently carved a turnip into a reasonable likeness of a dog. When Judge French asked her to stop by and give him a bit of advice, she'd instead suggested the name of a shop where he could buy clay. She'd had enough of boys spoiled by their parents. Then she'd seen him in town, a tall, handsome lad. She suspected that if he enrolled in her classes, every young lady in Concord might develop an interest in art.

One afternoon, she wound green ribbon, which brought out the red sheen of her hair, around her hat. She filled a basket with clay wrapped in damp rags to keep it soft, sculpting tools, wire, and metal tubes, all of which soon felt heavy. She stopped at the Emersons' house and asked to borrow Dolly. She rode sidesaddle through town and past meadows of redtop grass and timothy, which turned the landscape beige and gold. Piles of potatoes looked forgotten on the edges of fields. Pumpkins seemed to have stopped in mid-tumble among dried vines. Sunflowers sagged under the weight of their own seeds.

She stopped by a picket fence before a white farmhouse, lashed the horse to a granite post, knocked on the green door, and asked if Daniel was home. Mrs. French eyed May's fashionable hat and loose hair, then offered to look. She returned with a tall young man whose dark brown hair swept over eyes as shiny and dark as molasses.

"I hear you have a knack for carving squashes," May said.

"You know how fathers are." Daniel's mouth reminded her of Julian's, the kind that easily turned up. "They think any little accomplishment is a sign of genius. After you told him about the shop in Boston, he bought me some clay. I molded a few things that didn't turn out too well. The only thing I let dry was a deer I rather liked."

"May I see it, Mr. French?"

"Of course. And please call me Dan."

"Miss Alcott makes me sound like my sister. You can call me May."

Dan led her past clucking chickens and apple trees to the barn. He tugged open the high, wide doors. As May's eyes adjusted to the dim light, she saw several buckets of clay, far more than she'd ever bought at once. A small sculpted deer stood on a windowsill. The fawn's eyes were wide, its ears alert, as if fear and trust were crossing. The delicate legs smoothly joined the body. She thought there should be something for her to criticize, but she didn't see it. She asked, "Where did you find the model?"

"I went hunting with a friend." His eyes lost their shine. "Once. I'll never carry a rifle again."

She turned it over and saw he'd etched "Daniel Chester French" in tiny script across the belly. Though he had modest manners, he seemed to be proud, too. "What else have you done?"

"I tried making a clay bust of my father, but it collapsed."

"What did you use for an armature?"

"What's that?"

"Then there is something I can teach you. Just as a skull supports flesh, clay needs something hard to hold it up. I hope you'll sign up for my classes, but we can start now if you have some wood scraps around here. And we'll need a hammer, saw, and pliers."

While Dan gathered the tools and wood, May peeled off her white gloves and took out the wires and tubes she'd bought at the plumbing supply shop. She pushed up her sleeves, then sawed a square of wood. "You have to be a bit of a carpenter to be a sculptor."

She wielded pliers to twist a thin pipe around an iron tube she set on the wooden base. She wrapped wire around scraps of wood to make crosses, which she fastened to the metal pipes. "The clay will stick to these, instead of slipping off the smooth pipes. Keep adding water, but not too much. Splash on a little and knead it in. I expect your father's head is about the size of yours." She took out calipers to determine the lengths between his nose, forehead, chin, and the back of his head. "You should measure the spaces between his eyes and the distance between his chin and hairline. His nose, mouth, and everything you can think of."

She rolled a small slab of clay into a nose, pressed an orangewood stick to make an eye socket, then scraped away clay to shape brows. Dan looked eager to hold these tools, and she let him coil, pinch and prod the clay.

"After you finish this bust, I'll show you how to mix plaster to make a mold and then a permanent cast."

"Capital! And then I want to learn how to make statues like those I saw in the Athenæum."

"Wouldn't we all?" She laughed, remembering her own ambition and innocence when starting out. "But why not? Unfortunately, there's no art school in Boston where even men can work from unclothed models, not like there is in Paris."

"Have you been there?"

"Not yet." She couldn't bear to say simply, *No.* After the clay head was roughly shaped, she said, "I'll leave you to work on the details. Keep the orangewood sticks. A small gift to celebrate the start of a grand career."

She packed her tools and rinsed her hands at the well while Dan saddled the horse. Long shadows darkened the ground. The slightly chilly air smelled of wild grapes, drying leaves, and cornstalks. She returned the horse to the Emersons' barn and walked the rest of the way home. Rose petals had fallen, leaving prickly stems and knobby centers the color of dried blood.

Goldenrod had turned brittle. Only hardy asters bothered with purple and blue. She felt melancholy at the memory of how Dan moved his hands as if they were almost attached to his sight and had a right to any direction, as if he believed he'd get every shape correct in the end. Such faith might be part of his talent and maybe came in part from his being a young man. He didn't need the murmurs May offered her students, a sort of music that drowned critical voices that ran through their minds, assurance they were making progress, which most found as necessary as advice on craft. Dan's confidence might come from having a father who bought him sacks of clay, asked a neighbor to offer instruction, and expressed interest in what he did. May knew it wasn't every girl whose parents would let her draw on the walls or help her make a studio from an old shed. She was grateful. But Dan had something women didn't have. One day, if he chose, he could take classes with Dr. Rimmer without worrying that he would touch his hair, spoiling everything.

⌘

MAY RETURNED TO WORK ON HER DRAWINGS OF houses, the Concord River, and the bridge. Her moving eyes uncovered grace within the lines of rooftops and strength in the curves of branches. She worked until there seemed no traces of her clenched hand, but unlike the hands of a cook or house cleaner, also invisible, she left something lasting.

One afternoon, she summoned her courage and put everything into her cardboard portfolio. At the townhouse on Charles Street, she gave her *carte de visite* to a maid, who ushered her to the second floor, where she waited among tall mahogany bookcases. A butler practiced in noiselessness opened doors and laid out china and silverware. Another young man almost silently moved logs in the fireplace. Mrs. Fields bustled in, wearing a plum-colored gown and matching slippers. While pouring tea, she asked about May's classes.

"You should come." May lifted a heavy silver spoon and a delicate china cup.

"I wish I had the time, or talent. I'm eager to see what you've brought."

May untied the blue ribbon from her portfolio and took out her drawings.

Mrs. Fields exclaimed at one after another. "For those who haven't visited Concord, how truly soul-enriching it will be for them to glimpse where Mr. Emerson and Mr. Thoreau gathered their thoughts. Mr. Hawthorne, may he rest in peace, would like this drawing of his home. His genius was that he celebrated humble origins."

"Then you think these can make up a collection?"

"Of course I must consult with my husband."

"I can leave these with you. And draw others if you choose."

May pressed her hands together to keep from clapping. After bidding her good-bye, she wanted to skip past shops with windows holding baskets of rolls speckled with cornmeal and shiny squares of gingerbread. Others displayed lace parasols and pearl-buttoned gloves. She passed the Childs and Jenks gallery, where people paid twenty-five cents admission. Maybe one day her work could be displayed there!

May turned onto Washington Street and raced up the steps into the *Merry's Museum* office. Louisa was alone in a room that smelled of ink and stacks of papers. May cried, "It looks like Mr. Fields will publish a volume of my drawings!" She twirled around. Why not be merry? At last she had something to show her sister.

"Congratulations!" Louisa stood to hug her.

"It's a dream come true. Maybe it's time we forgive Mr. Fields for turning down your story about the girl who went out to service."

"I meant to put that behind me, and I sent him a collection of fairy tales. He lost the manuscript."

"Lu, that's terrible!"

"There are other editors." Louisa tugged down the sleeves of her plaid dress, smearing ink on the white cuffs. "In fact, one paid a call recently. Mr. Niles remembered meeting you years ago at a dinner, and he asks to give you regards. It seems he's moving on from books without words. He told me that books for boys such as *Tom Brown's School Days* and *Hans Brinker and the Silver Skates* are selling nicely, but there are few novels with girls at the center. Apparently he admires my stories in the magazine and thinks I might be just the person who could write about regular girls with some good lessons. Parents these days don't have the time to teach their children the way they used to. Mr. Niles said that if the book did well, they'd want more, like a series Horatio Alger writes called *Ragged Dick*."

"You must write what you please."

"He offered a thousand dollars."

"Gracious!" May realized Mrs. Fields hadn't said anything

about payment. She was also trying to forget what Louisa had said about her lost manuscript. "That must be more money than Father *ever* made, and for something you haven't even written yet."

"That's the problem. I can't write the book he wants. I liked climbing trees, forgot my manners, and could never keep my stockings straight. I know nothing about being a girl."

"Don't be silly. You could even write about us."

"A stranger family never lived."

"You must leave out Father and all the times we were hungry. We had good times, too. Think of the picnics in summer and skating in winter."

"I could make things turn out any way I wanted. But I don't have time. It turns out that I not only read manuscripts and correct grammar and punctuation here, but I must write most of the poems, articles, and stories myself." Louisa swept a stack of papers into a carpetbag.

They headed out the door, crossed a few streets, and strode along the pebbled paths of the Public Garden. Children pressed their faces against wire fences, looking for the deer among the trees. Some fished in the frog pond, dangling strings with pins in the water. Ducks swaggered toward breadcrumbs. May wanted to talk about her sketches of houses, but the turn in her luck made her feel generous, and instead she spoke of Louisa's chance. "Did you ever dream of being offered a thousand dollars?"

"Or Mr. Niles said I might instead take a percentage on the profits. I could gamble."

"Why not?"

"He hinted that if I wrote the novel he wants, he might publish some of Father's transcendental writing."

"Then it's settled." May couldn't imagine Louisa resisting the chance to please Father, who'd been trying for years to get his musings into print.

"I could write about the vain younger sister who always tried to get her way."

"The artist who is as determined as her sister to succeed, and who quotes Michelangelo: 'Genius is infinite patience.'"

"Didn't Mother say that?"

"One or the other. And write about sweet, motherly Anna, and the tomboy who was bound to be a famous author. Write about Beth."

"I'd like people to know her." Louisa smiled, then shook her head. "It would be the dullest thing I ever wrote."

10

THE MISSING PORTRAIT

After Louisa decided to leave her editorial job and work on the book, May helped her pack and move back to Concord. May also helped her friend Edith crate wedding presents and books for her move to an elegant home. But only when Mrs. Hawthorne asked her to help sort through things to be sent to Europe, stored, or given away did May worry that people might be starting to think of her as a kindly spinster. She was closer to thirty than to twenty-five, a dangerous age for an unmarried woman. She'd recently seen Mrs. Fields and been assured that her Concord drawings would be compiled into a book certain to be wanted by every literary person in Massachusetts. She was proud, but if she had to choose between artistic glory and a happy family all her own, as she'd been told so many times she must, she wouldn't have picked quite the life she had now.

As she helped empty and fill trunks, Mrs. Hawthorne talked

about her eagerness to see Raphael's *Madonna and Child* and hear Wagner at the opera house in Dresden. She told May that the engineering school there offered free tuition, and Julian would learn to design buildings, bridges, and roads. May supposed he'd look for a countess or baroness or whatever they had in Germany. Or an heiress, a pretty expatriate. May told herself she didn't care.

After sealing some boxes, Mrs. Hawthorne gave her the Swiss music box. May would have preferred her old tin of paints from Italy, with its dried, cracking *cremisi* and *azzurro* colors, which she suspected had been thrown away. The furniture and rugs were being left for the renters, along with the red sled and the green rocking horse. May asked if she could have the old russet boots from the trunk that had once been in the garret.

The next day, she gave these to Louisa, saying, "Maybe they'll inspire you. Remind you of the princesses and pirates in your old plays."

"Mr. Niles says Roberts Brothers wants a book about ordinary girls," Louisa said.

She began spending most of the day at the half-moon shaped desk, looking out at the road or turning her head to the view of larch trees growing between their yard and the rambling house next door, which she was using for her book's setting.

When everyone sat in the parlor one evening, Mother asked, "When will we hear your story about the four girls?"

"I can read some tonight," Louisa said. "They're not children, but little women."

"Little? They must be closer to six feet than five, if they're like us," May said.

"I mean they haven't yet reached the age when they find out their dreams will never come true," Louisa replied.

"Dreams do change, but can one ever stop hoping? Look at you, gambling on a percentage of what this novel will make. And what if I'd given up? We both have books coming out." May smiled.

"May must illustrate yours, Louisa." Mother picked up a small red hat she was knitting.

"I have my Concord scenes to draw and students to tend to. Drawing people isn't my best talent," May said.

"I cherish that crayon portrait you made of me."

"I wish you'd put that away, Mother. I drew that when I was a girl."

Mother told Louisa, "She's devoted to teaching, like her father. That matters more than art. The girls adore her."

May's cheeks burned, hearing herself praised for what had never been her ambition. She said, "Perhaps I might show Mr. Niles some sketches. If someone's going to illustrate these girls, there's no reason it shouldn't be me."

Louisa nodded, then began reading from her novel featuring a family that stayed in one spacious if humble house instead of moving about once a year, the way the Alcotts had. The oldest sister, Meg, was kind, brave, and bent on finding a good man, just like Anna had been. The next oldest, Jo, was an ambitious writer. The third was as sweet as Beth had been on her best days. The vain youngest sister busied herself with what Louisa called mud pies or pots of paints. May remembered coveting pickled limes, and she did primp, but was that so terrible? Louisa liked a decent gown as much as she did.

"Do you really think that's me?" May asked.

"There's a line between truth and fiction," Louisa said.

"Shouldn't that line be a little thicker? You're Jo instead of Lu. You switched the letters of my name so I'm Amy instead of May. And you changed months for last names, using March instead of May."

She was annoyed enough that when Louisa read aloud on following nights, she let her sister's voice fade in and out, concentrating on the picture taking shape under her hands. She was pleased with the composition of the girls around the mother, which would be used as a frontispiece, but everyone's arms looked too long. She started a new sketch, with the sisters standing farther apart, but now the heads looked out of proportion. She found it hardest to sketch the youngest sister's face, and she solved that by having her burrow it on the mother's lap. She enshrouded Beth's body in a jacket, hid the oldest sister's body behind a chair, and drew the writer gazing off at nothing.

One evening, her hand tightened on her pen as Louisa read an episode in which the youngest sister shoved a manuscript into the fireplace. May cried, "I would never burn your work! I was the one who encouraged you to write this novel!"

"I told you, it's a story."

"Even if you didn't use the scrambled version of my name, don't you think people will recognize the niminy-piminy chit with her wretched attempts to burn images on wood with a hot poker?"

"I'll make it up to you."

The next night, Louisa read about the writer, still furious

about her burned manuscript, skating away from her sister on thin ice. The ice shattered. Amy fell into the river and almost drowned but was rescued by the boy next door. May's hands turned as cold. "Is this supposed to be an apology?"

"I write about what I see and invent things, too. People do that every day."

"I know what fiction is. I expect I could have been a nuisance back when we were growing up, though all I wanted was to be like you. To go off and make my fortune, with hardly a look back."

"I was always looking back. But if you really want the truth, I did think you were spoiled. Intent on impressing everyone, with pretty clothes and manners."

"I didn't want to impress you. I wanted you to know me."

"We're sisters. Of course I know you."

May told herself it was foolish to worry, when this book seemed unlikely to be any more successful than a painting of girls washing clothes in tin tubs. But she stayed away on the following evenings when Louisa read aloud. She knew enough to draw Jo with her skirt billowing as she skated, hiding her hands in a muff that matched her hat. She illustrated the oldest sister standing before a long mirror for a chapter called "Vanity Fair," and she drew Beth running into the arms of her father when he came home from the war.

Louisa looked them over and asked, "Where's the portrait of you?"

"You mean the affected goose? Readers see enough of her in the frontispiece."

Just before her birthday, Louisa brought her stack of papers and May's pen-and-ink drawings to her publisher. They were quickly approved, but Louisa had to wait two months for the cloth-covered books. May liked seeing "illustrated by May Alcott" on the cover, though naturally the lettering was in smaller and plainer type than the author's name. She found some fault with the engraver's work, but the book sold so well that a few months later, Louisa was asked to write a second section.

"It's not enough that the oldest one got engaged. Mr. Niles tells me readers want all the girls to marry, as if there aren't other perfectly good ways to end a story," Louisa said over breakfast one morning. "I understand a writer should please the public, but why not teach something, too? There's nothing wrong with life as a single woman."

May interrupted. "I suppose they'll want more illustrations?"

"There won't be time. I promised to write this section quickly."

It seemed peculiar that a book twice the original length should suffice with only four illustrations, but perhaps it was just as well, for May was busy that spring. A few weeks after the full edition of *Little Women* was published, May came home one day to find Louisa and Mother exclaiming as they looked through a stack of letters.

"Mr. Niles forwarded these from readers," Louisa said. "I'm stunned by how many say they want to be Jo. I thought they'd adore Beth most or sweet Meg. Of course, some prefer glamorous, artistic Amy."

"He clipped reviews claiming our girl to be a genius," Mother said.

"That's not their exact wording," Louisa said.

"Don't be so modest. We know how proud you are," May said.

"It's all vanity and bad for the soul." Louisa spoke lightly and nodded at Mother. "It's the better lot to raise a family than to write about one."

May turned her face. Everyone knew she had done neither.

A few nights later, May brought Louisa's book to her chamber. She stayed up late, skipping the chapters she'd heard Louisa read aloud and skimming others, looking for the parts about Amy. She finished the book and slammed it shut. She'd thought being portrayed as a girl with a muddled vocabulary who cared too much about what the neighbors thought was embarrassing, but this second section, in which the youngest sister married the dashing boy next door, was worse. Did Louisa think she wouldn't care that she'd engaged her paper girl to a fellow who'd really left May? She'd set the proposal in Europe, where she'd never been. Worst of all, this girl gave up making art, saying, "I want to be great, or nothing."

May strode into Louisa's bedroom, yanked the pillow out from under her head, then threw it against the wall. "How dare you write about a boy who wastes his talents and his family's money, then marries the youngest sister! How dare you have a girl who's even a little like me marry a man as jolly and lazy as one I wish I'd never met."

"May, be quiet. You'll wake up Mother." Louisa pushed her hair off her face and sat up.

"Why shouldn't she wake up? And it will be my fault. You've shown that everything is. I knew you had little use for art, but I didn't know you thought so little of me, too, that I'd put aside work I love because it isn't getting enough attention. Even 'a commonplace dauber' has the right to look for beauty."

"You stopped lessons with Dr. Rimmer."

"You know nothing about that!" And it was too late to tell her, though it made a schism, like splitting ice, between them. "I don't claim to be a genius, but I don't see why not being one should stop me from making art. Imagine if I'd written about a woman who'd never write great literature."

"Then I'd see myself as I was."

"Don't be ridiculous." May took a breath. What had she done to make her sister lash out at her like this? Or if she hadn't meant to hurt her, was it worse that she'd given such little thought to how she would read it? This portrait of a woman like her who'd gone to Europe seemed to ruin her real chances, as if someone in a fairy tale had wasted wishes. No, she hadn't been tricked. Did the book make her face the truth that she'd see few rivers but the one in her town? She'd never row across a lake with a view of the Alps; she'd never see the particular texture and angles left by Michelangelo's paintbrush.

⟨≈⟩

SETTLED BY A SILVER TEAPOT AND LOOKING PAST THE green drapes to the view of the Charles River, May listened to Mrs. Fields express delight with her drawings. She said, "My husband wants a label for each house or site. Perhaps with some quotes from local poets and philosophers. And now that your sister is becoming well known, we hope she will write the preface."

"Louisa knows nothing about art!" May sat back in her chair.

"And I'm afraid you know little about the marketplace. A famous name sells books. Just a few lines from her could make a difference."

May supposed she couldn't argue, though she was in no mood to beg Louisa for any sort of favor, even just a paragraph she might dash off. But maybe it was for the best. Louisa would have to look at what she'd accomplished. And while she might never understand what pictures meant to May, wouldn't she be bound to respect something soon to be enclosed between covers? May couldn't forget the portrait in Louisa's book, but she also couldn't help feeling pleased at the thought of a little praise from her sister, even if it was on paper instead of face-to-face.

Louisa agreed to write a paragraph, which she promised to drop off at Mr. Fields's office when she was in the city on errands. A week later, May meant to see the preface and the photographs of her sketches, but when she left her card with the maid, she was told that Mrs. Fields was away for the week. May knew she might go to Mr. Fields's office, but it seemed so impersonal, or masculine, with its smell of cigars and papers piled so high that she thought it wasn't a wonder that Louisa's fairy tales had gotten lost.

She decided to wait to see the sample book and walked to Alice's home. She hadn't visited her since her father's funeral. Sitting in a parlor, May thought that the Copley portraits in gilt frames and the silver dish of calling cards couldn't keep out grief. Alice told her about being thankful for being with her father at the end. May hesitated, knowing it might be ill mannered to ask, but she wanted to know. "Did you see anything surprising?"

"He was at peace."

"Nothing rising afterward? Some kind of mist? I've heard that can happen."

"I was praying. I had my eyes closed. Anyway, plans are already underway for me to move to New York to live with my aunt and uncle. They were appointed guardians."

"I'll miss you!"

"And I'm sorry I can't return to your classes." Alice paused. "I still want to go to Europe."

"You mustn't consider such things now."

"My relatives think of nothing but my future. And theirs, too, with my family's money under their charge. Some cousins have moved to Rome where there's a neighborhood of Americans, all from good families. My aunts would make introductions once I'm out of mourning."

"I'm glad you have something to look forward to," May said.

She tried to push down her own selfish disappointment that her hopes for travel were dashed. During the following days, she reminded herself that she was lucky to have a book going to press. And drawing the rough stem of a geranium or the shadows on a stone gave her regular reminders of a day's ordinary graces. But these were hard to remember on evenings when Louisa complained about the mail she received from adoring girls, some with requests for pictures of her. Louisa said that these were a bother to fulfill, for she'd found that if she sent one, all the other girls in her school requested them.

"Some write back for more, I suppose to sell them," she said. "I don't like people to think I put on airs and don't remember what it's like to be poor, but it's not just pictures people want. Someone just wrote to ask that I buy him a house. I'm just finally managing to pay off the loans on ours."

May understood that such requests must be vexing, but even if fame didn't bring an end to loneliness, surely it at least nudged one further from it. She became busy planning a party to celebrate her book publication, buying a bolt of sapphire blue silk and a pair of elegant boots with c-shaped heels. When a wide, flat package addressed to her arrived one afternoon, May screamed. She wanted to remember this moment forever. While Mother looked for Louisa, May ran upstairs to brush her hair, run some ecru lace through it, and put on her new boots. Ready now, she tore the brown paper to reveal a book almost as large as a tea tray. The title on the violet cloth was printed in gold. She opened the book to a page with her name and the title written in Gothic lettering woven through a wreath of flowers and grapes she'd drawn.

She turned the pleasantly hefty pages to each of her drawings, then flipped back the pages to read the preface. Her face stiffened as she read Louisa's words calling the book the work of a student, having no artistic merit, valuable only because it referenced important places in the artist's birthplace. May let the book fall on her lap. "How could you call me a student? And the book worthwhile only for the places it depicts?"

"What's wrong with being called a student? You've referred to yourself that way, wanting to go to Rome or Paris to learn from professionals," Louisa said.

"I've been working for years! And I'm a teacher, too, with pupils who look up to me."

"I thought you'd be pleased that I called it a labor of love."

"Which it is, but more. Don't you think there can be room in a family for two famous people?"

"I never courted glory. I don't think of posterity, but write to earn a living. And to make people see what is possible for an Alcott."

"Girls!" Mother squeezed both of their arms. "This is a happy day."

May pulled away. As she turned, the delicate heel of her boot cracked.

❦

A FEW WEEKS LATER, SHE FINISHED SEWING A DRESS she'd designed referring to a magazine picture showing Paris fashions. She brought her boot with the collapsed heel to the cobbler, hired a fellow to tune the piano, baked three kinds of pie, and set out the green-and-white china cups and plates. Just before guests arrived, she laid out a few copies of *Concord Sketches*, ignoring her temptation to slice out the preface.

May welcomed the entire Emerson family. Edith had left her baby at home with the servants and brought camellias from her greenhouse. Dan French, who told her he was continuing to sculpt, and his father offered congratulations. Most of May's students were there. Some had brought beaux, brothers, and cousins, so there were plenty of gentlemen who held the doors as if May didn't open them herself dozens of times a day. Alice couldn't manage the trip from New York City, but May had hardly expected her to come all that way.

A light rain drummed on the windows and slate roof, mixing with the sound of a fiddle brought by a neighbor. May would have wished for sun, but at least the overcast sky meant a forgiving light was cast on the worn furniture. Soon there was dancing as well as soft, satisfying exclamations as May put *Concord Sketches* into guests' hands. She turned the wide pages past the preface right to the drawings. She poured a glass of Mr. Bull's grape wine for John, who watched his boys play among stacked books they pretended were bridges and castles.

Hearing a knock on the front door, May opened it to greet Mr. Niles, who had more gray in his dark hair and more droop in his mustache than when she'd last seen him. She said, "How kind of you to come!"

"I wouldn't miss the chance to congratulate you. And Mr. Fields for his good luck to have you as an author, or I suppose I should say artist." As Mr. Niles stepped inside and stamped his feet on the mat, he looked around and said, "It's rather like the parlor in your sister's book."

"Perhaps a bit." Only that morning she'd been glad that the geraniums had bloomed and been pleased with the effect of a velvet swathe she'd arranged behind the bust she'd made of Father. But now it took all her strength to keep from apologizing for the humble furnishings. "I'm afraid the weather kept Mr. and Mrs. Fields home."

"A wise decision. I left looking more dapper, but I had to help the groom dig the carriage wheels out of the mud. And where is your hardworking sister? Back at her desk?"

"In the kitchen." May wondered if she was keeping out of the way so no one would gush about her book instead of May's. Or was she bored or even jealous? Was that why she'd written so cruelly in the first place?

"People are already asking for a sequel," Mr. Niles said.

"Why, the ink is hardly dry."

"And we've sold twenty-five thousand copies. We're planning a gala to celebrate its first anniversary."

She nodded. "I must see to other guests. But let me introduce you to my mother. Where did she go?" She checked the kitchen, then ran upstairs. After looking through all the rooms, she glanced through a window and saw Mother on her knees under the elm tree. May ran downstairs, out through the rain, and kneeled beside her.

"Where are my lilies of the valley?" Mother asked. "Remember how I wore them in my hair at my wedding?"

"They'll come back." May heard the rain patter on the leaves above her, falling more softly on the ground.

THE GALA

*M*ay checked her reflection, adjusted her jet earbobs, and practiced her smile in a room where maids helped ladies arrange their hair and brushed dust from their hems. The townhouse was spacious, but she'd felt crowded as she passed guests including some of the most eminent families in Boston, all expensively if not fashionably dressed, in rooms scented with lilies and beeswax dripping from candelabras. It seemed as if everyone, or at least their wives or daughters, had read Louisa's book. The event celebrating its first anniversary had even lured Alice back to Massachusetts.

"Isn't this wonderful?" she said. "New York isn't such a backwater as we've been told, but it's still difficult to meet the proper sort of gentlemen. Oh, May, how thrilling for you to be in a book."

"I told you, I'm not. Most everything is made up."

"You'll do better than Julian, but I'm glad Louisa had the youngest sister marry the dashing neighbor and have a baby. Even if I can't understand why she hinted that their poor little girl might die."

"I should go make sure she doesn't glare at admirers." May found it hard not to feel annoyed that Alice seemed giddy to be here, while she hadn't come for May's own smaller celebration.

"I wanted to ask you about . . ." Alice reached for her wrist.

"We'll talk later." May headed toward Louisa, whose high-collared black dress would be all right for church, but not a gala, and certainly not one given in her honor. As usual, she wore her brown hair parted in the middle and pinned above her neck. She'd refused to see Madame Canagalli, the Italian hairdresser favored by the city's elite, saying, "People come to see what success looks like and feel better when it looks ordinary."

But no one seemed disappointed. Many snuck peeks at the family, too, as if trying to decide if their mother was as wise as the one in *Little Women* and whether Anna could be as good-tempered as the oldest sister. May supposed they thought of her as the girl so jealous of a sister that she'd shove her life's work into the fire, and so careless of her own life's work that she'd swap it for a young man she didn't love with her whole heart. One lady told May, "It seems Louisa, with her way with words, is following in your father's footsteps. How extraordinary to have two famous people in one family."

May supposed she meant that three renowned people in a family would be impossible. She accepted a glass of sparkling wine she carried past a grand piano, a harp, and ladies holding tiny bouquets that swayed as they danced, flashing color and fragrance. Father stooped over a table laden with sliced chicken sandwiches, creamed oysters, and iced cakes. He explained the benefits of whole grains to maids who silently poured Madeira wine, though not to the rims of the crystal glasses. This was Boston. May wasn't surprised that the cream puffs were sliced in half.

She sat between Mother and Anna, who'd left her ear trumpet at home. When people approached, she did little but nod and try to look agreeable.

"I used to know Boston, but this isn't the same city." Mother's gray-brown eyes widened. "My grandfather was a minister here."

May squeezed her hand and leaned toward Anna, speaking with her mouth near her ear. "Stop fretting about the boys. They'll be fine for one night."

"This is the first time we've left them with someone who isn't family. And John doesn't get out much."

"Like you. Is he all right?" May had noticed how he increasingly depended on his cane, which he must have left with the cloaks. Strangers were apt to ask if he'd injured his leg in the war, and May expected he found it easier to lean on a wall than to watch sympathy fade from faces as he explained that his legs had hurt so severely and for so long that he'd never fought.

"He works hard and doesn't complain. We don't live in style, but we're happy."

"Like the young women in Louisa's book."

"It's a good story. Though I'm afraid Lu doesn't know much about being a mother."

"Perhaps you'll write the real story. Father always said your sentences were the finest."

"He liked my penmanship. Besides, that was years ago. Now one sister is a published author. Another brings art to our town. And what have I done?"

"Father says your children are your masterpieces, and there could be nothing finer." May looked up as a girl hurried toward her with a book, saying, "Please, Miss Alcott, may I have your autograph?"

"I believe you're looking for the author." May pointed her mother-of-pearl fan toward Louisa.

"Then you must be Amy. Didn't you marry Laurie?"

"No." May's voice was louder than it should have been. "No, I haven't married anyone."

The girl backed away. May sighed. She hadn't meant to frighten the poor child. As Louisa, Father, and Aunt Bond claimed chairs next to theirs, Mother whispered, "Where are we?"

"Boston," May said.

"Everything's changed," Mother said. "Boys ride their horses so fast, it's a danger just to cross the streets. There are warehouses where there were once homes and churches."

Anna told Aunt Bond, "This may become just like *Uncle Tom's Cabin*, with Uncle Tom coffee cups and little Eva lamps. Louisa gets stacks of letters from girls asking for another book about the March sisters."

"Why, soon I may be known as the father of Louisa May Alcott," Father said.

Everyone laughed politely.

"It's too bad, dear, about your illustrations." Aunt Bond put her wrinkled hand on May's wrist. "I'm glad I have my first edition."

"I tried to keep her pictures, but editors don't bother about what authors think. They care only about sales," Louisa said.

"Publishing is all about favors. They have an artist they owe work to, who might be somebody's friend. There's no loyalty to excellence," Father said. "People laughed at Michelangelo, too."

"Father, they were right. The girls did look swollen," May said. "And engravers changed the quality of the lines."

"But to call your command of anatomy slipshod," Aunt Bond said. "What was it, that the heads were too big? Or too small? What a shame."

"Aunt Bond, will you be attending the new concert series in the Athenæum?" Anna tried to change the subject.

"The Athenæum isn't what it once was. The new pictures are so dark that I can hardly tell who is who," Aunt Bond replied.

"A review is just one man's opinion. And critics are always jealous," Louisa said. "I'm sorry that your illustrations weren't put in the reprints. You know I tried to . . ."

"It doesn't matter." The last thing May wanted was pity. She was glad to see Mr. Niles coming toward them.

Louisa introduced Mr. Niles to Aunt Bond, who said, "You're my niece's editor? We were just saying how our May . . ."

"How we appreciate your work," May interrupted.

"But we won't talk business." Mr. Niles extended his white-gloved hand to Louisa. A perfect half-inch of cuff showed from under the sleeves of his swallowtail coat. "Success becomes you."

"All I want of success is that it make me a better person." Louisa tightened her lips.

"Poverty is the philosopher's crown," Father said.

Violinists lowered their bows. Dozens of white-gloved hands clapping made a padded noise. A new piece began, and feet swept, scuffed, and swished over the floor, which had springs installed underneath to add bounce to the dancers' steps.

Mr. Niles asked Louisa, "Would the guest of honor care to dance?"

"I'm afraid I must stand here and write my name," she replied, as a girl thrust a copy of *Little Women* toward her.

"Yes, the duties of celebrity." He turned to May. "Might I have the honor?"

"I'm not a celebrity, and I have no duties." She dipped her right knee and curved her fingers for him to take.

"I would have thought a belle such as you had her dance card filled." Mr. Niles's smooth pink fingernails and pearl cuff links contrasted with his dark coat and black, silver-streaked hair.

"I always leave a space for the best-dressed man in the hall."

He offered her his elbow, shook his handkerchief, set it on her half-bare shoulder, and put his left hand on top. As they waltzed, she let her fan tap the space between his shoulder blades. She smelled soap, the cream-colored gardenia in his lapel, and something waxy in his moustache. As they glided into a pas de basque, she thought his arms seemed strong for a literary man. But while he could execute a perfect glissade and chassé, he didn't try to tug her closer than was proper.

"I'm afraid your sister is enjoying none of this," he said.

"She'd be happier writing in her room."

"But these days, an author must also meet the public."

"We're very proud of her."

"So family loyalty isn't part of the fiction?"

"You read Louisa's book?"

"Not every word, though my assistant did. Generally, I prefer more action. My favorite scene was when the hot-headed writer skates away while her pretty younger sister falls through the ice."

"Not a word of it is true." When the music stopped, she thanked him and said, "That girl is clawing the hem of Louisa's skirt. I'd better help out, before she steps on her fingers."

As she headed toward Louisa, Alice grabbed her arm and pulled her from the dance floor.

"Haven't you met any eligible men?" May asked.

"I came here to talk to you. May, my aunt said I may finally go to Europe, but I can't travel alone. They're all watchful that I don't get swindled, but I need a friend who might guide me. My aunt says we might provide for your expenses."

"To go to Europe! Your family would pay for the voyage?"

"And the inns and travel while we're there."

May shrieked and hugged her. The violins in the next room got louder.

"There is a condition." Alice stepped out of her arms. "Your sister must come, too. If we traveled with someone so renowned, we might be given rooms with views and the liveliest dinner tables."

"Louisa is awfully busy now." May felt her heart thump. "She's already been to Europe and didn't have much good to say about it when she returned."

"She's too polite to trumpet her adventures to you. May, I'm an orphan now and must listen to elders willing to guide me. My guardians insist that I must make the trip worthwhile, and they think that Louisa might be a way for me to meet the best people."

"You mean the wealthiest people."

"Don't raise your eyebrows. You want a well-to-do suitor as much as I do."

"I don't call such people 'best.' What about love?"

"I understand some marry people with lesser fortunes, but I've never been that kind of romantic. And don't think New York has made me craven. I'm not thinking only of myself, but must look out for my family, too."

"I'll talk to Louisa." May gave her a quick hug, then walked away, telling herself that all that mattered was that she might finally cross the sea. If they left soon, she might see the spring Salon in Paris and arrive before her birthday. For a few more months, she could honestly tell people that she was in her twenties.

She broke into a group of girls surrounding Louisa. "Pardon us, but I need a word with my sister." As May whisked her to a quieter corner, Louisa said, "Thank you for rescuing me. A gentleman told me that his wife had read my book, expecting me to be flattered. Because his wife apparently can't speak for herself? Because he can't be bothered to pick up my novel himself? Maybe he's right. I wanted to write something worthy." Louisa glanced at Father, who'd pulled some papers from his pocket and seemed in danger of delivering a poem.

"Everybody else loves your book. You didn't write it for Father," May said.

"I write everything for him. At least everything I put my name on."

"Then that's your mistake. Maybe you should take a pseudonym more often. You've achieved your dream, and you've never looked so miserable. You have silk dresses and fame . . ."

"I hate how people speak of mine as 'sudden' when I've worked for twenty years."

"You must simply say 'Thank you,' the way Mother taught us. And try to be happy."

"I craved fame so much that I never prized what I had. A writer has to observe others. It's easier when they're not staring back."

"Then we must fix that. Let's go to Europe and meet people who've never heard of *Little Women* and don't expect the author to be a genius or a saint. You can be yourself, or invisible, if you choose. Alice asked me to go with her! She'll pay my expenses. All I have to do is lecture to her on the differences between Renaissance and Medieval Madonnas."

"I'm so happy for you!" Louisa threw her arms around her.

"You should come, too. I don't think Alice would mind." May thought it wise to conceal that this was required, which might only alarm or annoy Louisa.

"I've already been," Louisa said.

"As a nurse, who couldn't go where she pleased."

"We can't go to Europe when Mother is so—not herself."

"We'll write to her. We'll describe everything, and she'll enjoy it as much as if she were with us."

"Her health could worsen, and it would take weeks or even more in the middle of winter to make plans to sail back. And we must think of Father."

"He'll live to be one hundred."

"It's the healthiest people who surprise us."

"Didn't your doctor order rest? You'll do that better away from home, with me looking out that you don't overdo."

"I suppose you want to go to Germany."

"To see Julian? No, that's over." May thought of how his mother had written to hers that the girls were taking piano lessons with Clara Schumann, a most talented woman as well as a mother of eight, and Julian was doing very well in his engineering classes. May suspected he spent more time in cafés with tankards of *bier* than he did in lecture halls. She looked past Louisa to an oil painting of a girl holding a baby lamb signed with a name that looked French. "I have dreams besides romance. I'm not that girl you made up, who gives up art because she's not a genius."

"May, you're talented, but . . ."

"Don't say it. No one ever tells you that you can't rival Shakespeare or Dickens."

"I hear that all the time."

"From someone besides yourself? Lu, isn't it time to rest on your laurels, as you never have before?"

"I have been tired. My doctor says I should stop writing for a while. A real vacation might finally cure me from whatever I got in the hospital during the war. You don't think Alice would mind if an old lady tagged along?"

"The eminent author? I'm sure I could persuade her."

"I'm not only worried about Alice," Louisa said. "I'm not sorry I wrote my book, but I'm sorry I hurt you."

"We can leave that behind us."

"Yes. I won't write about you again."

May turned as John limped toward them. He said, "Anna is getting your mother to the door. I was asked to deliver their good-byes."

Louisa turned, spotted them, and hurried toward them. John apologized for interrupting, then said, "But I'm glad for a moment with you. I couldn't find one at your fête, when you were surrounded by admirers. I wanted to give you something to celebrate your book." He took a small box from his pocket. "Anna and I wanted you to know how proud we are. And grateful for all you do for our boys."

"Thank you." May opened the box. The silver locket held a picture of Mother, which May lifted to her lips. "No one could work harder."

"Except maybe her girls."

May nodded, though that wasn't how she wanted to be remembered. She hugged John, then watched him return to Anna. His fingertips were gentle on the small of her back, which was wider than it had been when they were first married.

THE GRAND TOUR

*W*ind-filled sails snapped. Ropes thrummed. The *LaFayette* set out across the Atlantic. While Louisa, Alice, and others went below deck, May stayed by the rail, waving her handkerchief at John, who'd escorted them to the harbor. She'd said her farewells to everyone else back in Concord: kissing her parents, tucking tiny presents into her nephews' jacket pockets, and telling Anna it must be her turn to tour Europe next.

Now May watched John leave the wharves, passing a woman pushing a cart of lemons she'd been peddling to ward off seasickness. A boy turned with books he'd had on sale for the voyage, waving a copy of *An Old-Fashioned Girl*, Louisa's latest novel, which had sold so briskly that she could not only afford to take this trip in luxury, but left plenty of money with the family. *That must give her some comfort*, May thought. She'd chided Louisa for worrying, but she, too, felt pangs at the thought of being so far from home for a year. Most of these thoughts disappeared as she watched the world around her turn blue with sea and sky.

After the sun set, May made her way down the narrow stairs to the berth where Louisa lay in the lower bunk bed, wrapped in a red blanket. May picked up an invitation from the captain. "He's hoping the esteemed penwoman will share his table at dinner. Aren't you going to get ready?"

"I can't look at food," Louisa moaned. "I wish the ship would stop rolling. You can go in my place."

May felt queasy, too, but she opened the trunk that balanced on top of Louisa's and rummaged for a looking glass tucked away with her rolled and pinned clothing, guidebooks, a curling stick, a foot warmer, her portfolio, and the four bottles of champagne that Ellen had given her. May set some smelling salts and dried ginger near Louisa's pillow. "How did women manage to fit in these berths when wide skirts were the fashion?"

"At least hoops would help them float in case of shipwreck." Louisa buried her face in the pillow.

"I'll bring you back a roll." May lurched while climbing the stairs to the dining hall, which boasted rosewood paneling, crimson drapes, and ornate mirrors. The captain stood at the head of a table, which had rims around the edges to keep china from sliding off when the ship pitched. May offered Louisa's regrets and introduced herself. He signaled to a servant who was collecting place cards printed with the names of others who must have felt seasick, too, and gave May the seat beside him.

During the ten-day voyage, Louisa and Alice generally stayed below deck, nibbling crackers and sucking oranges. May read and sketched near the prow, enjoying a horizon that was entirely blue while listening to waves splash the hull and sailors sing while hoisting sails. On starlit evenings, she walked around the deck with the captain, whose white hair and beard contrasted becomingly with his tanned, weathered face. He told her about rumors of a war that might keep tourists out of Paris.

In the morning, May passed on the news to Louisa. "It has something to do with the Germans."

"We must root for them. They helped us during our war, while the French sided with the South."

May was sorry not to go straight to Paris, but she wouldn't waste time on disappointment. After the ship docked, she dashed around the harbor and found a ramshackle calèche pulled by two gray horses. She negotiated with the driver in flawed French but a confident tone. As he loaded the trunks, Louisa murmured about his flushed complexion and the bottle poking out of his pocket. She and Alice stepped inside the carriage, but despite their protests that it would be windy, dangerous, and unconventional, May climbed up by the driver. She didn't want the sounds, sights, and smells of France to be blocked by a windowpane.

As they bumped along Brittany's dirt roads, the driver loudly recited poetry, claimed to be Victor Hugo's best friend, and asserted that English ladies were divine, but cold. When he reached for her hand, May told him that American ladies were cold, too. She watched peasants tie up vines or carry baskets of leafy greens on their heads. Windmills spun on hilltops. Boys climbing cherry trees shouted greetings to the mademoiselle atop the carriage. She waved back.

In the village of Dinan, they booked two rooms in a boarding house with a view of blooming linden trees and an old stone church with a picturesque steeple. The world seemed waiting to be painted. After drinking bowls of hot chocolate the next morning, May and Alice set out with campstools, paints, and easels to paint the church. When children left school for lunch, some stopped to look at May's canvas, voicing strong views on colors. May wished she could paint the little girls with braids under round caps, wearing blue dresses and wooden shoes, who followed a nun.

She liked painting *en plein air*, but she didn't want to give up on portraits. Their landlady, who wore a linen cap with crisp folds and peaks and a white apron over an ankle-length blue gown, said she was too busy to pose, but she offered her son. Gaston sat for May wearing a bright shirt, buckled shoes, primrose-colored gloves, and a Breton hat with dangling ribbons and flowers. He was dark haired and wide shouldered. One afternoon, he attempted to show off by trotting away on his horse, but when he returned, May borrowed both his beribboned hat and horse. She galloped farther and faster than he had.

May painted every day, but Alice more often accompanied Louisa strolling around the village, where women led cattle, tilled the soil around cabbages, tended grapevines, swept the stone streets, and mended cartwheels. Women ran almost all the shops and stalls in the marketplace, minding babies, chickens, ducks, sheep, and cows, sometimes all at once. Louisa said she was glad to spend time in such a place, and where no one had heard of the Alcotts. She even grew optimistic about her health after meeting a British doctor on holiday, who suggested that her pain might be caused by the calomel she'd taken to cure the typhoid pneumonia she'd contracted as a nurse. Apparently the medicine contained mercury, which never left the body and slowly spread its poison.

Louisa took the iodine of potash he prescribed, and her color grew brighter and her voice regained more of its lilt. One afternoon, while she and May picnicked on black bread, sharp cheese, and strawberries nestled in cabbage leaves, she said, "I'm glad you suggested this trip. Alice has been a good friend to you. And kind to put up with an invalid like me."

"She adores you." May wished she could tell her that Alice had insisted on her coming, and not the other way around, but confession seemed risky while sharing a small room in a foreign country. She satisfied herself that her lie had been worth it, if only for the doctor's advice.

After two months in Brittany, May said good-bye to Gaston, who was leaving to help defend Paris. More than all the talk she'd heard, the fact that a young man whom she'd seen do little but loaf was wanted by the military made her realize that the war wouldn't end as soon as she'd hoped.

"Empress Eugènie refuses to accept Chancellor Bismarck's apologies. And I expect the armies have new weapons they're anxious to try out," Louisa said, stroking an orange cat that often visited their room. "I'm sorry you won't get to your museums."

"I suppose we'll have to go straight to Rome, and see Paris on our way back."

"Alice wants to see her relatives in Rome, but I hoped we could go through Switzerland, and stay a while at Lake Geneva," Louisa said.

"Where you staged the proposal in *Little Women?*" May asked.

"We pledged to forget about that book," Louisa replied. "My doctor friend says the mountain air and juniper berry tea will do wonders for me."

"We'll be introduced to other Americans, perhaps suitors. The people here aren't the sort we came to meet," Alice said.

Along the way, they stopped at other villages, including one where they toured a great cathedral and May bought a pair of exquisite French boots. They rode a train past fields of poppies, honeysuckle, lavender, and wheat. In a *pensione* in Vevey, May was greeted as if she were the lady, while Alice, who wore her shabbiest clothes for traveling, was assumed to be a servant, and Louisa a prim duenna.

At a long dinner table, they joined Americans and tourists and refugees from Paris and Strasbourg. Before long, rumors circulated that Louisa was some kind of American duchess, but only a few recognized her name. A girl asked her to write a verse in her memory book. Her mother spoke of being glad to give *Little Women* to her without having to fold over pages not intended for young eyes. Louisa couldn't seem to keep away from the Americans, but May spent her time beating a Russian baron at croquet and pitching horseshoes with a troubadour or sketching him playing his guitar. She waltzed with the owner of a copper mine and a young Spaniard with titles, blue eyes, and a shaven head. She got the impression that he was likely to return to Spain to wreak havoc or be executed, but that was all right. She expected nothing from the flirtations and was just as happy strapping on a rucksack and hiking in the mountains, drawing edelweiss or goats and chamois grazing near chalets.

❧

ONE EVENING, SETTLING IN THEIR ROOM WITH WINE and apricots, Louisa remarked on how good Alice was to keep her company while May was sketching.

"I know I said that Alice would be willing for you to come with us to Europe, but the truth is, she insisted on your presence," May confessed.

"I wondered when you would tell me."

"You knew?"

"She mentioned it on one of our walks. Couldn't you have just told me you needed me to come along?"

"I'm sorry. I was wrong to lie. I hate to ask for so much, and be beholden. I suppose it's how you felt owing money to Mr. Fields. I don't mean to envy you, but it's hard when you have so much of what I want. Even strangers love you."

"Gawking isn't love."

"All that attention must feel like a hand on your shoulder, assuring you that you've done good." May imagined that hand was as comforting as her sisters brushing her hair all those years ago.

"Applause always ends. Then it's me, pen, and paper."

"That used to be enough."

"Which is what I miss. I might never have written if I didn't need to prove an Alcott could pay her bills. Poverty, people's lack of faith in me, all the things that stood in my way kept me working, too. Here I am the renowned author I dreamed about when we were children, but the fantasy seemed better back when we played dress-up. You don't know how lucky you are to be unburdened by fame."

"You mean no one expects anything of me. That's a curse, too."

"I mean you can paint whatever you want with no one waiting to judge it. People can't wait to compare whatever I write next with *Little Women*, and find it wanting."

"You forget that though I'm not the famous sister, I'm not quite anonymous either. People think they know me because they read your book. We have to move ahead. You wouldn't want those old days back, being poor. I remember your old stories about Italian cads with gold rings and vials of poison. Why don't you write again about palaces with towers and trapdoors?"

"You forget I'm a proper children's author now, renowned for my morals."

"I don't forget anything. Lu, you're rich and famous. You can do whatever you want. Why don't you try something new? Maybe the story of a woman who does work she loves and finds romance, too."

"No one will believe that."

⌘

AROUND THE LONG TABLES IN THE DINING ROOM, guests gossiped about cheating carriage drivers and garlicky stews in Spain, the short beds in Germany, and the fires of twigs and vines that never truly warmed Italian hotels. Some French men complained about the revolution and the coffee.

"There are troubles in Rome, too," murmured a lady.

"But Rome is where we mean to go next!" May put down her fork.

"There's always some sort of uprising in Rome," Louisa said. "We'll hope for the best, and that the mail gets through better than it does here. I know the trains must be used to transport soldiers, but you'd think there would be a place for a few mail sacks."

They began their journey south a few weeks later, stopping at an inn close to the Italian Alps. At dinner, an Englishman mentioned that the view from the St. Bernard pass was one of the finest in the world.

"I've been reading about the army Julius Caesar sent there—"

May interrupted Alice, before she had a chance to get to Napoleon's troops. "How grand to climb one of these mountains!"

"There's a full moon tonight, so tomorrow you could leave before dawn and make the climb in a day," the Englishman said. "Or some stay in a hostel at the peak where monks train big dogs to rescue mountaineers."

"The weather doesn't look promising. Showers here in the valley can mean storms above, where there's no place to hide from rain or snow," the innkeeper said.

"I don't mind getting wet," May said.

"There's more risk than getting wet. A dark sky makes it hard to see the edges of precipices," the innkeeper warned.

"May, you can't go!" Alice said.

"I'll be careful. I'd love to get my first sight of Italy from high above," May said.

She arranged for a guide named Maurice. The next day, she woke well before sunrise, pulled on her boots, put a waterproof over her dress and pea jacket, and grabbed her umbrella and satchel. Rain fell as she and Maurice rode a carriage through the valley, under the light of a full moon. The rain pelted harder after the sun rose, when, having reached the hiking trail, May and Maurice left the carriage. They hiked up increasingly steep slopes as rain flooded the river by the narrow path, washing away much of the banking. May slogged through torrents of water and deep mud. Her dress sagged as she stumbled through the thick fog, sometimes feeling with her feet for the edge of the trail. Once she lost her footing and fell, but she caught herself before sliding over the edge.

Maurice made the sign of the cross and said, "I've never been above the forests in such a storm. God willing we don't get struck by lightning."

Thunder crashed. Cold water rose to their knees. May felt exhausted from bracing against the current, bearing the weight of her drenched clothing and satchel. At last they reached a hut near the steep slope before the summit. Other wet hikers huddled, cursed, cried, and prayed in the small refuge above the tree line. May was shivering, but she insisted that if she and Maurice were going to be soaked, they might as well be moving. Heading back down would be even more slippery and dangerous.

Soon it grew so dark that she could see her feet only when

lightning flashed. Hailstones beat down on her head and shoulders. She was scared but was also determined. She kept climbing, though her muscles burned and it was hard to breathe in the heavy rain and the thin air.

At last they reached the peak. Monks carrying lanterns hurried out in the rain to usher them into the hostel, where May was offered a loan of spare dry clothes. She was too tall to fit any of the skirts they had on hand, but she overlapped several, leaving buttons undone, until the layered skirts reached a proper length. She fastened her velvet jacket and went downstairs for hot soup, crusty bread, and red wine. After supper, she sat by a great open fire as a handsome priest regaled her with tales of terrible winters and just-barely-rescued travelers. St. Bernard dogs dozed by their feet, making a brown-and-white carpet, as he played a piano that he said had been a gift from the Prince of Wales.

It was late when May retreated to her room. She slept soundly, and she woke while it was still dark to the sound of chanting prayers. The patter of rain on the roof had stopped. She put on her borrowed clothes and soaked boots and found a roll and flask of coffee left by her door. She pocketed the roll, hurried to the chapel for a quick but sincere prayer of gratitude, then walked out to the barren peak.

As the sun rose, seven big, beautiful dogs bounded up, licked her hands, and sniffed her clothes, doing their job of checking to see if she was hurt. May watched thickening sunlight turn the mountains gold, pink, then stunningly white. Clouds drifted below her. Mist rose over cliffs and caverns and a faraway lake. Yesterday's rainfall still splashed over rocks and paths. She could now see that one wrong step could have ended her life.

She hid her face in a dog's shaggy coat, then reached in her pocket for the pale brown roll she'd tucked away. She gave some to the dog and ate the rest. Her feet were cold in her soaked boots. Her neck felt chilled where it was touched by her hair that hadn't yet dried. But even the ache in her legs reminded her that she'd said she could make it here, where she could see the country where she'd be going. One valley in Italy looked small enough to hold in her hand.

ᴀ3

ROSES AND RAIN

*M*ay, Louisa, and Alice bundled in blankets in a carriage pulled by horses trotting in and out of chasms, through stone tunnels, over rickety bridges, and along narrow, winding roads. May caught her breath at the sights of waterfalls cascading off ice. Wooden crosses marked sharp corners where carriages must have toppled into gorges. They stopped and stayed for a while in a town where May and Louisa shared a room with a view of a park and the back of a stage. They watched an opera from their window, while sipping Frascati and singing along. They traveled to Milan, where May found *The Last Supper* disappointingly dark, then to Florence, where Michelangelo's *David* made her certain the trip had been worthwhile.

Late in fall, they took a train to Rome. A chilly rain fell over grape vines twisting around cypress trees, fig and olive groves, ancient aqueducts, and the crumbling wall. The train clattered to a halt at a depot under construction. May tramped through mud to find a horse and carriage to take them to the Hotel Washington. Here she was again taken for the lady, but as she signed her sister's name into the register, the staff turned to fuss over Louisa's cloak, express concern over her fatigue, and fetch a basket brimming with invitations. May expected her celebrity won them a room with a view of a fountain with Triton circled by dolphins. She admired the god of the sea's muscular chest but preferred Bernini's nearby statue of a seashell, with water falling from the mouths of bees.

The next day, Louisa insisted they go right to the embassy, where mail was supposed to be held, but the day was fine, and May wouldn't let her stay inside poring over letters from Massachusetts. Streets scented with cut stone, sausages, and roasting chestnuts bustled with people speaking a musical language. Donkey carts filled with oranges and eggs rattled by old palaces divided into new apartments. Bakers carried baskets of fragrant bread on their heads. Women wearing loose, soft blouses and red or green skirts bent over ancient fountains to wash clothes, which they hung on clotheslines strung between open windows and ancient columns.

During the following days, Louisa often settled by the grate to read Dickens or write tales about scoundrels and women who wore masks, while May and Alice set out with umbrellas past houses painted yellow, orange, pink, and red. Oxen pulled carts loaded with marble to sculpture studios. The scarlet jackets of officers and red robes of Cardinals made bright spots among the dark horses and pale stone. Some men stared boldly at May's

loose, light hair and called to her, "*Oh, bellissima, bellissima.*"
May and Alice looked in the windows of milliners and furriers
on the elegant Corso and stopped in a pawnshop on a side
street, where May bought a dagger and Alice a pistol to slip
under their belts, since people at the hotel warned of *banditti.*

They admired marble statues of gods, goddesses, saints,
emperors, and warriors that perched on rooftops or amid
fountains. They stopped in churches, where they drew back
leather curtains to find masterpieces even in humble chapels,
and they tried to figure out how Fra Angelico made the dusky
rose on Mary's cheekbones fade to ivory, and whether she was
more beautiful than the rounder Madonnas painted by Raphael.
They toured St. Peter's, where May declared all the art was
stupendissimo. They climbed the wide winding stairs to look out
at bright roofs and distant hills.

On the way back to her room, May stopped at a farmer's
stall for some cream to bring to the cat Louisa had befriended.
She found her curled up with a Dickens novel and what looked
like a new stack of mail. May propped her umbrella to dry,
poured the cream in a saucer, heard the cat pounce, and added
olive wood to the small fireplace. She ate a roll Louisa had
thriftily brought back from the dining table and an orange so
sweet and tart that it prickled her tongue. She picked up a letter
from Mother and read that a mole had invaded Father's
vegetable garden, Dan French was still sculpting, and everywhere Father went, he found people reading *Little Women.*
May couldn't help wishing for a single mention of *Concord
Sketches.*

She put down the letter and picked up one from Anna,

who wrote about Johnny's impressive vocabulary and how Freddy had loose teeth, and no one had the nerve to yank them. Anna worried about her husband, who was plagued not only by his legs, but now suffered from neuralgia, too.

"A stack of letters must have been held up somewhere. Mother says that Mrs. Hawthorne wrote that Julian is spending a great deal of time with a young lady."

"He's always smitten with some pretty fräulein or another. Whom I expect is rich. I suppose you've heard from Mr. Niles."

"He informs me I was the highest paid author in 1870. He sends you his regards."

"It's kind of him to remember me."

"I expect it's more than courtesy. I thought you found him dashing."

"His curled moustache is fashionable, but I can't abide wax. It would be like kissing a candlestick."

Louisa shook her head. "He keeps asking me to write a sequel, so girls can find out what happens to Jo and her sisters now that they're married off. Nothing, really. I'm done writing about them."

"You're rich enough now to write whatever you want."

"Perhaps, if I'm careful and nothing unexpected happens. But something always does."

"You've spent enough time on mail. Let's go to the Vatican museum this evening. The stone looks entirely different in torchlight. The statues seem alive."

"I've seen enough. It's no wonder there are revolutions here, when the priests are taken care of but there are few schools for those black-haired children you admire, and their poor mothers scrape for food. And Rome is colder and rainier than I expected."

"It's almost winter, and the roses are still in bloom. What does it matter that they're wet?"

"I've met a few interesting people here in the hotel. Did I tell you George Healy insists on painting my portrait, at no charge for the honor?"

"That *is* a privilege. His reputation is great. But you must venture out. Let's go to the Forum tomorrow."

"We'd catch our death of cold out there. Or Roman fever."

"If it rains, we'll hire a cab and go to St. Peter's. Alice is moving in with her relatives in a few days. They're just a few streets away, where Americans stay without having to learn a word of Italian or develop a taste for garlic, but she'd like an excursion with you."

❧

AFTER A BREAKFAST OF *CAFFE LATTE*, APPLES, AND figs, May, Louisa, and Alice rode a carriage over a bridge adorned with stone angels, so exquisitely carved that May thought they might soar over the river. Stepping out in the vast courtyard, they passed beggars holding out thin hands, monks in brown robes chanting, and vendors selling sweet drinks, small papal flags, and inkwells shaped like the cathedral. The women climbed the wide steps, passed through the massive bronze doors, and looked up at the high, domed ceiling. Bronze lamps burned in alcoves crowded with sculpted saints, elaborate gold crosses, and silver chalices. Men perched on campstools painted copies of frescoes. Their hands were red from the cold, while their feet rested on clay pots filled with glowing coals.

"All the pictures stacked over each other makes me miss our plain New England churches," Louisa said.

"Come see the *Pietà.*" May drew her and Alice past paintings darkened by centuries of smoke from candles and incense. They stopped before the sculpture of a mother holding her dying son. Its gleaming marble curved like real flesh and cloth.

"Michelangelo was just twenty-four when he sculpted it." Alice waved her red guidebook. "Later, the pope asked him to paint the apostles, but instead of twelve men, he painted three hundred and fourteen people on his ceiling. We should go to the Sistine Chapel next."

"Haven't you already been?" Louisa asked.

"No one sees anything of worth on the first look. Maybe I finally understand Father's talk of transcendence. Michelangelo shows there's something beyond stone," May said.

"We can know that without being in a church filled with enough gold to feed all the beggars on the streets for eternity," Louisa said.

As they left the basilica, May thought she would never choose a plain ceiling when she could have a painted one. And why shouldn't the floors and walls be covered with decorations, too? But while she was irritated about all the time Louisa spent in their room and the way Alice was always quoting from her guidebook, she felt more like a tourist than an artist, seeing everything as if from the outside. She hadn't drawn since they'd been in Rome. Was Louisa's old prophecy coming true: did all the magnificent art make clear the weaknesses in her own?

Surely her own attempts must have been worthwhile. Maybe she needed to be around more living artists. She thought she'd visit Anne Whitney, who was living here with her companion, making a good reputation for works in both marble and bronze. But first May had to help Alice move from the hotel into her relatives' suites. Then Louisa said that she found the sounds of the water constantly splashing around Triton annoying, and they'd save money in a smaller room in the back of the hotel. Their new view was of a shadowed courtyard and an ancient chapel. At street-level, the smell of horses was strong. But May reminded herself that what was important was for her to draw. On the next sunny day, she asked Louisa to go with her to the Forum, where she would sketch the broken temples.

They stopped to collect the mail, then continued through a neighborhood where grindstones in marble shops spun chunks into tiny spheres. Women sat on doorsteps beside clay pots of geraniums and rosemary, keeping an eye on children playing tag. Models milled around a statue of a half-sunken boat at the bottom of the Spanish Steps. Boys dressed in goatskins stood near a white-bearded man who May supposed might be shown as Moses, Jupiter, or God. Several young women called, "*Buongiorno, signorina,*" and held up their *bambini,* in hope of being asked to pose as Virgin Mary. May was pleased that they seemed to recognize that she was an artist, perhaps because she wasn't strolling with a man.

Arriving at the Forum, she studied the way cypress trees cast shadows on temple ruins. Birds nested in the broken, moss-covered stone. Cats scouted for mice. May and Louisa sat on a stone, where Louisa unwound a string that held together a thin and tattered envelope that May knew must be from Mother, who was conscientious that the cost of postage was based on weight. May sketched the narrow trees and pale pillars, though her gaze sometimes shifted to couples strolling under parasols and boys in ragged jackets drawing circles in the dirt and shooting marbles. A mother helped a little girl balance on a stone altar, which might have once held silver chalices and pomegranates offered to goddesses.

Louisa refolded the thin paper. "Mother says Mrs. Hawthorne wrote her that Julian got married."

"It's not possible!" May put down her pencil.

"Didn't you refuse his offer to marry?"

"I'm just surprised. He's so young."

"He must be in his mid-twenties. Lots of people get married then. She says her grandparents own a glassworks in Maryland. I expect she's rich."

"And young and pretty."

"You can't expect him to pine for you forever."

"I just never thought he'd marry before I did." May's chest ached, not just from the words but also from the sympathy she saw in Louisa's eyes. May supposed this woman didn't paint and didn't yearn for anything but Julian. She asked, "Louisa, what if I can only recognize love when it disappears?"

"We're all like that."

"We Alcotts?"

"Artists and writers. We only see the meaning or shape of things when they're over."

"That's horrible."

"It's a choice."

May remembered feeling outraged when Julian's mother spoke about stopping painting because her husband's genius mattered more. She'd always known Julian didn't have such genius, but now she'd stopped painting for no reason at all.

∽

ONLY A FEW DAYS LATER, MAY RETURNED TO THEIR room to find it smoky. Crumpled balls of paper, some half-blackened, smoldered by the grate. Louisa, who'd been bent over, straightened her back and handed May a black-bordered letter.

"Who is it now? Please. Not Mother." May shut her eyes.

"Those poor children," Louisa murmured.

"Not Anna's boys?" When Louisa didn't answer, May opened her eyes and read: *Our dear John passed over. May heaven rejoice, though we grieve.* May's hands felt as bony as those she'd seen of saints and prophets. "He's too young. People don't die from pain in their legs."

"It wasn't that, but they think pneumonia. He died within a week."

"They should have sent a telegram. The funeral must already be over."

"We couldn't have arrived back in time. Those poor boys."

"Thank goodness Anna has them. What a comfort they'll be."

"She'll have to be both mother and father."

May cried, thinking of John lifting her valise at the wharf

while trying to balance on his cane. Anna must have put away all except her black dresses. She would have combed her boys' hair and reminded them to be polite to neighbors who stopped by to offer halting words and trays of fresh rolls. May wished she'd been there to open her arms, which might have given Anna a moment's relief from looking brave for her boys.

"He was dying, and what did I do? I should have been there instead of here, writing worthless stories about criminals and ladies of the night." Louisa stood, grabbed the poker, and shoved papers under the flames. The cat's shoulders hunched high.

"Don't! It's your work." May grabbed the poker, but the pages were already curling, turning to ash.

"I must work now, anyway," Louisa said. "I'm going to write that sequel Mr. Niles has been asking for. He promised me it will make at least as much money, maybe even more. I can give it to Anna for her boys."

"Lu, you know John. He surely guessed, more than we did, that he might not live to see his sons grow up. I'm sure he left his family provided for."

"Anna's children deserve the best schools. And college."

"Freddy still likes nursery rhymes. Johnny has barely learned the alphabet."

"People should look ahead."

"And what about Anna? She grieves now, but she's as strong as Mother, who raised us while earning a living. Father used to say Anna was the finest writer of us all. Death brings some kind of gift. Perhaps hers is a chance to earn a living with her pen."

"I must be the boys' father now. I'll write to Mr. Niles, ask for an advance to send her, and give him the sequel he wants. " Louisa picked up a sheet of paper.

May felt furious at the sight of that perfectly white paper, the way Louisa had everything figured out. "You're going to write about those sisters?"

"Of course they've grown now. I recently had an idea. Jo and her husband can run a school for boys, who will get in a lot of scrapes."

"That Jo will set right?"

"Yes. Maybe the oldest sister's dear husband will pass over, and the children will attend her school."

"Where they'll get better care with their aunt than with their mother? I thought you weren't going to write about that family again."

"You, I mean Amy, will hardly appear. And I'll make it all right. Her baby will grow up a to be a pretty little girl. Maybe her mother will pick up paints again."

"You're not directing a theater. I don't need your script."

"I thought you'd like to read about someone who is both an artist and a mother."

"No woman does that!" Maybe that was what hurt most. She'd been wanting something that was impossible. May's face felt thick with tears under her skin—for John, for Anna and the boys, for herself. She could hardly fuss about a book when her dear brother-in-law had died and her oldest sister must cope. Her own concerns couldn't compare to that. She couldn't protest when Louisa was doing so much good, even more than her duty. This wasn't like when she'd been sent away to her aunt's house when Beth had been dying. She'd stayed away from John all by herself. There was no one to blame, but anger stayed with her during the following days. She wished Louisa hadn't burned her stories, but she envied her that moment, hearing flames gust higher and louder, and her sense of purpose. Even if Louisa didn't love the book she felt bound to write, she had something to do.

She was always busy now. May also missed the company of Alice, who was increasingly preoccupied with a young man introduced to her by her aunt, the nephew of the owner of a textile mill. May stuck a pin set with jet beads in the wide brim of her topaz-colored hat and met Alice in a piazza, where convent girls walked in two straight lines. Women sold fresh fish packed in snow brought down from the Alban hills.

"What does Milton think of your painting?" May asked.

"We've never talked about it."

"Alice!"

"The truth is, it's a relief to stop sketching. Don't say you've never imagined that! I might enjoy art more now that I'm not always comparing others' work with mine."

"You don't mean you're giving it up?"

"Giving up what? Questions and ridicule? Some people want to play the piano in concert halls, but most are content with parlors. I'll consider it a blessing if I can teach my children the joys of line and color someday."

"Children? Has Milton spoken to you of marriage?"

"I expect he'll first want to speak to my guardian in New York. We're going back with my cousins after the ice breaks in the harbors." Alice took a breath. "It seems though his uncle has a fortune, he does not. He knows I have an inheritance."

"Do you love him?"

"I believe what I feel could turn into that."

"Make sure he acts tenderly toward you." May squeezed her hand.

"He does. We read Miss Browning's poetry together."

At first, May questioned Alice's choice, but as the days passed, she thought how it might be a relief to stop trying to be someone who she was perhaps never destined to be. How could May protest giving up art when she'd hardly taken out her paints in Italy? Was it because there were few painters among plenty of men with marble dust in their hair and studios that resounded with the crack of mallets on chisels, the ring of chisels on stone? The paintings in the churches and museums were gorgeous, but none seemed to speak to her, none whispered that she, too, might one day leave a mark. Instead, the art that had survived for centuries seemed like signs that she could never paint anything worth sharing such a wall.

May supposed that few people achieved their dreams. Was life about learning to accept that with some grace? Giving up wasn't a crime, at least so long as one didn't pretend it didn't matter. She was glad that she hadn't burned the breadboard she'd imprinted with an impression of Raphael. It wasn't very good, but she liked the girl she'd been, insisting on art in the kitchen.

Maybe she was just weary from traveling. She could no longer muster the effort to make whoever was sitting by her at the hotel table feel important during conversations about the trials of living abroad, the cheating and thefts, the brawls and poverty of Italians, and, more recently, peoples' eagerness to see the book Louisa was now writing. May found a nearby trattoria that let her bring dinners to her room if the dishes were returned the next day. The *minestrata* with plates of grated Parmesan, *lasagne*, *ravioli*, or *risotto* with cheese and saffron were more delicious than the hotel's overcooked beef and under-cooked potatoes.

As they ate one evening, Louisa said, "I finished posing for Mr. Healy. Have you stopped to see the portrait?"

"Yes. It's impressive. But he makes you appear too gaunt and old."

"That's how I look. You see me the way you remember."

"I see you the way you should be remembered. But I'm glad if you're pleased. Personally, I'm tired of Americans. They're not why we came to Rome."

"You're right. Mr. Healy begged to paint my portrait at no charge, he said for the honor, but then he asked me to read a novel his daughter wrote, and perhaps put in a few words to my editor." Louisa's cheeks sank as she pressed her lips together. "Sometimes I just wish people would ask directly for what they want."

"It's hardly polite to say, 'Give me something.'"

"All I want now is to go home. Mother needs us. And I miss her. Don't you?"

"I miss everyone." But she wasn't sure that meant she was homesick. "I want to go back through France. We won't do anyone any good by missing Paris in the spring."

"Don't you read the newspapers? The French surrendered to Germany, but the terms were so harsh that citizens rose against the empire. The Communards are said to run around with kerosene and matches, burning down the Tuileries, the Palais de Justice, Notre-Dame, and the Louvre."

"Not the Louvre! Why would anyone burn art?"

"I suppose there are too many paintings of kings and popes. In any event, as soon as spring comes, we must go straight to London."

May turned, pushed back the curtains, and looked out as a monk knelt on the stone steps of a church. The curve of his back, his deep stillness, reminded her of the devotion she'd once felt when her painting went well. He shifted, adjusting his brown robe, revealing patches on the soles of his sandals. May's throat ached. She supposed he hadn't thought anyone would ever see the bottoms of his sandals. He'd probably repaired them himself, but she hoped someone had cautioned him about blisters and helped with needle and thread.

14

R E F L E C T I O N S

*M*r. Niles took May's valise as she stepped down from the train in London. When he reached for Louisa's manuscript, she tightened her arms around the box. He instructed a driver to bring their luggage to an inn, then led them to a carriage with shiny black doors and velvet-covered seats. Looking dapper in a dove gray overcoat that matched the color of his hair, a small ruby pin in his leaf-green cravat, and checkered trousers, he shouted over the noise of whistles, bells, and horses' hooves on cobblestones. "We've already taken orders for fifty thousand copies of *Little Men*."

May turned from the window, where she'd been trying to peer through the yellow-gray fog, to hug Louisa.

She straightened the box on her lap. "Not a soul has seen it yet."

"Your books don't have to be seen to sell, Miss Alcott. I'll read your manuscript tonight, and if everything seems in order, in the morning, I'll bring it to the printer, who has the type out and ready to set. I'm arranging a British copyright so you won't be cheated on sales overseas. Things will move quickly with you here to sign the papers."

"We hoped to sail home straight away," Louisa said.

"It won't take more than a fortnight, and we should have your books in hand by then. While we wait, I'd be honored to show you around the city." He turned to May. "I arranged for tickets to several art exhibitions."

That week, he escorted them around Westminster Abbey, the Tower of London, and Madame Tussaud's Waxworks Show. After looking around an art gallery, they strolled up Regent Street, looking in windows. May said, "Louisa, we must get new gowns. I noticed bustles in Rome, but still more here. We shouldn't be seen with flattened silhouettes."

"It's a ridiculous fashion. And you have enough dresses."

"Queen Elizabeth had five hundred," May said. "I think twenty-eight would be good, one for most days of the month. Or a single gown designed by Worth."

"They say his stitches are so small they can't be seen even under a magnifying glass," Mr. Niles said.

May admired perfume bottles artfully arranged in a window beside a display of wrinkled, elbow-length *mousquetaire* gloves. "They're just like ones I saw in a picture of Sarah Bernhardt taken in Paris. It's a shame we can't get there. Louisa tells me it's not safe for tourists yet."

"She's right. The plague is everywhere, and bombs are still hidden," Mr. Niles replied.

"I heard they won't even allow petrol in the city, though I expect much is exaggerated," Louisa said.

"I expect so, Miss Alcott. But some agencies are advertising trips to see the ruins of the Tuileries, promising souvenirs of blackened stones and charred timber. They spread talk so people will go see for themselves, and then the cab drivers rob them. But there will be no Salon des Beaux-Arts this spring. Its halls have been turned into a hospital for the time being."

"No Salon!" May cried, then, feeling embarrassed as she'd been when urging Alice to keep painting, she realized they hadn't yet been to the National Gallery. She suggested they go. Now when crossing the street, Mr. Niles looped his arm through hers, instead of Louisa's. May felt no warmth through the cloth, but she didn't mind being the object of a bit of jealousy. She was surprised Louisa didn't seem to see he was more intrigued by women's fashions than the bodies underneath.

Inside the museum, May stepped lightly past Hogarth etchings and paintings in elaborate frames that hung above and below each other. She stopped for the first time in front of a Dutch painting in which slanting light seemed palpable. A young woman was shown mending, something May had often done in life, but until now, she had never seen needle and thread in a painting. She also admired a Madonna and child painted by Pieter Brueghel. Unlike most of the nativity portraits she'd seen in Italy, Mary and Jesus had no halos, and they didn't demand the whole canvas. Instead, they were surrounded by peasants and princes who weren't young and handsome and didn't claim any more glory than the people around them.

But as they entered a gallery of paintings by Turner, May breathed deeply, as she had when first on the ship and watching the world turn almost entirely blue. She'd been viewing paintings with strokes so perfectly blended that she couldn't detect a single hair from a paintbrush gone awry, but here was someone who didn't bother to pretend he hadn't used paint, who hadn't been afraid to let it splash or scatter. In one watercolor, she saw traces of a hand that lifted as well as pressed down, revealing a river as being like mist or memory. Blue and yellow shimmered like a real river in sunlight. Had she ever really seen water at all? She raised her hand toward the painting.

"Put down your arm before someone thinks you're trying to steal that," Louisa said. "Though I don't know why they would. How can anyone tell which side goes up?"

"I believe John Ruskin made those decisions after the artist bequeathed his hundreds of paintings to the nation, requesting that they all be kept here, in one place," Mr. Niles said.

"Artists' and writers' wills seldom keep the living from doing as they please," Louisa said.

"Where are the rest?" May asked.

A short woman with brown hair and a deep voice turned from a nearby painting. "I beg your pardon, but I couldn't help but overhear your admiration for our nation's genius. Some watercolors are stored upstairs."

"Thank you." Louisa nodded curtly, then tugged May's arm. "We should get to the next wing before the museum closes."

"Go ahead. I'll stay here."

"But you haven't seen everything," Mr. Niles said.

"I've seen almost nothing. That's why I wish to stay." May moved toward a painting of a sun rising over a meadow. The sky seemed as lively as the land. The pinks and yellows made her tongue feel soft. "Mr. Niles, would you escort my sister to the Renaissance gallery? Let's meet at the entryway just before closing."

"Ladies in London don't stroll alone." He glanced at the woman whose faded dress was frayed at the cuffs, then back to May. "Or speak to strangers."

"Artists recognize each other. We're like a family."

Louisa smiled at Mr. Niles. "I never thought I'd miss the Italians, but let's see if we might find a Correggio or two. I can appreciate a beheading or something with some gore."

May joined the young woman in front of a watercolor of torrential rains and heavy snow. The woman said, "No one can paint weather the way Turner could. They say he lashed himself to a ship's mast during a blizzard so he could view the storm without being blown overboard."

"It's as if he just let beauty move though him. Are you a painter?"

"Yes, though I make my living with my needle. I'm Jane Hughes."

"I'm May Alcott. I've worked as a seamstress, too."

"Professionals can get special passes to copy Turner's paintings, which are kept in drawers to protect them from fading in the sunlight."

"Do you think I could see them?" May reached for her hand before remembering they'd just met.

"Can you bring some of your work to show the director

tomorrow? If it's approved, you may get permission to copy and sell those in the shop. I'll meet you when the museum opens."

The following day, May packed watercolors and pen-and-ink drawings of the French countryside, Lake Geneva, and the Alps, as well as her portrait of the Breton landlady's son. She brought these to the long steps of the museum, where she met Jane Hughes and a thin man with inexpertly cut hair, whom she introduced as another artist, Mr. Ramsey. As they looked over her work, they both gasped in a satisfying way and pointed out the strengths of her composition and color choices. Their enthusiasm not only made May instantly believe these were friends, but also buoyed her courage to show the paintings to the director. He looked briefly but intently, nodded, and wrote her name on a pass.

May climbed the stairs to the second floor of the museum in a sort of trance. A caretaker let her into a room that was quiet except for the soft rippling of water as the artists around a long table rinsed their brushes. The men looked prim with their high-buttoned collars, though caution stopped at their wrists. They angled their hands, using the whole of their brushes, not just the points, to spread paint lavishly. Some slanted the paper, letting colors ripple into each other. After May explained that she'd come back to work soon, but today just wanted to look, the caretaker opened a wide drawer and lifted a painting. Holding it between his palms, keeping it level to the floor, as if it were a tray of jewels that might fall if tilted, he offered the painting to May. She willed her hands not to tremble. She looked until she felt she must move or her pounding heart would break. She passed back the watercolor and thanked the caretaker, who said, "We're open every Tuesday and Thursday morning."

May dashed down the stairs and threw open the door. Rain clattered on the stone steps, brisk and precise as British speech. She snapped open her umbrella and strode through puddles, smiling at strangers, wanting to wave her treasured pass. Instead, brimming with confidence, she stopped in a gallery, shook her umbrella by the door, stamped her black tasseled boots, and brushed water from her emerald walking dress. The front room was filled with the biggest paintings, which she knew got the best prices because they depicted stories from the Bible, history, or myths, or at least suggested a narrative meant to stir hearts, such as that of a hungry child, a repentant fallen woman, or the tragic death of a mother. May preferred the smaller paintings hung on the pale green walls of a side room. A blue bowl of lemons, a vase of unfurling tulips, a brown rabbit that made her feel like she was looking out a window, rather than listening to a sermon.

She asked to see the manager and was led to a room where a gentleman looked over her work, sliding out a painting of the stone church in Brittany and one of her Alpine landscapes. He said, "Charming, with the little donkeys."

"I believe they're goats."

"I've never been good with animals, but I know distinguished art from bad. From your accent, I presume you're American."

"Is that a problem?"

"On the contrary. I hear they don't buy much art at home

but like to bring back souvenirs from Europe. When they're painted by their countrymen, they can show they're patriots as well as travelers of means. But they want pictures of places beloved of sightseers. Could you bring in some views of Westminster Abbey, the Houses of Parliament, Big Ben, done in your fine pen-and-ink style?"

⬥

RETURNING TO THE INN, MAY QUICKLY CHANGED into her evening dress, but she was still late meeting Louisa and Mr. Niles in a room where a waiter unfolded their linen serviettes, turned over their glasses, and poured water under chandeliers with dangling crystals. After greetings, May described her triumph. "I'll get to see works few others see in the room of Turner paintings."

"Splendid." Louisa lifted her glass.

"Yes, indeed. And I have good news, too." Mr. Niles ordered oysters, *Soupe à la Reine*, and roast beef. He turned back to Louisa and gave her a bound copy of *Little Men*. "It just came from the printer."

They passed the book back and forth, then May held it to her nose. Its scent mingled with beef, hothouse roses, and warm beeswax from the candles.

"You might read it as well as smell it. Anyway, now we can go home," Louisa said.

"So soon?" May asked.

"We've been away almost a year."

"Then what difference would a few more weeks make?

You could write in England as well as Massachusetts. Think of Dickens and Shakespeare!" May said.

"I'll check schedules." Mr. Niles reached into a leather satchel by his feet. "And I brought you more mail."

The way, May thought, to avoid an argument and win her sister's heart.

When they returned to their room, Louisa pored over Mother's letters. May opened her small watercolor box, filled a cup with water from a pitcher, and began sketching a river.

Louisa commented as she read. "I was afraid of this. The housekeepers I persuaded Mother to engage don't suit. One makes the tea too strong. Another cooks soup that's always too salty."

"There's Father, and now Anna has moved in for good."

"You know we can't count on Father to remember whether he's eaten breakfast, never mind to fix Mother tea and toast. She says she misses the way you put the house all in apple pie order. And poor Anna has been too long with no sisters to ease her burdens. Mother doesn't spell things out, but it seems the fatherless boys get into more than mischief, and Anna is too grief-stricken to set them straight."

"I think of her every day, but really, what can we do?"

"Our duty. We've been selfish long enough."

May squeezed the water from her paintbrush, set it down, and lightly tugged her silver locket. With one sister now a widow caring for two little boys and another who was saving the family from financial ruin, she had little chance of seeming anything but frivolous. Perhaps time out of Massachusetts had made the word *selfish* seem less of a weapon, worn down, like a blunted blade. She said, "It's as if I traveled this far just to see these Turner watercolors. Even if I can't paint something as amazing as his rivers, if I stayed here, I might makes copies for tourists. My new friend, Mr. Ramsey, says he earns a living that way. Turner himself started out as a copyist. If I can't manage that, I can teach or sew."

"It's not just the paintings, is it, that's keeping you here? I suppose you could do worse than Mr. Niles."

"Goodness. He's attentive, but when he takes my arm, it's with no sense that he's a man and I a single lady."

"Would you have him grope?"

"There's something between leering and good manners. A gentleman shouldn't sneak looks into a bodice, but there's nothing wrong with a glance across a throat."

"He spends half the year on the continent."

"I may be thirty, but desire doesn't stop."

Louisa blushed, then said, "I understand. I really do. When I was in Europe the last time with Miss Weld, at our inn by Lake Geneva, I met a boy who was recovering from an illness he got while helping the Polish rebellion. He played the violin quite sweetly. We talked about Goethe and rowed on the lake. But I knew it could never be serious. He might have been twenty-one. I could have been his mother."

"Perhaps if you gave birth at thirteen. You never saw him again after you left Switzerland? Did you look for him when we were there?"

"I saw him once in France after I left Miss Weld and before I sailed home. We had one perfect day. And night."

"Louisa!"

"We didn't do anything indecent. But in Paris, you can stay out until dawn, and we did. We went to the theater, then a café by the Seine, where gas lamps reflected in the river. We climbed a hill in Montmartre to watch the sun rise over the city. We walked back past flower stalls, smelling fresh bread women carried from bakeries, hearing street sweepers yell at cats. Then I told him I was going home."

"Because he was young?"

"Not just that. I couldn't believe he could care."

"Oh, my poor owl." May realized that it had always been Anna and Beth, and not Louisa, who'd bestowed her with confidence while brushing her hair. She poured water into a china bowl she set over the gas lamp to warm, then settled by Louisa, put her hands in the bowl, and gently, one by one, washed her fingers, which relaxed under her touch. She patted dry her hands and rubbed in rosewater-scented lotion.

"Mother got married at your age," Louisa said.

"She'd known Father for a while. I missed my hour. But here is a place where I might be able to make a living with my brush."

Louisa held her gaze, then said, "I'll leave you with money enough to stay through summer. You can come back before the harbors start to freeze over."

"Thank you!" May threw her arms around her.

"I'd just sooner you ask me for help than a stranger. I look forward to seeing our family. And to writing a forty-dollar check. I wanted to pay off the house debts first, but with this new windfall, I can finally send Mr. Fields the money I owe." Louisa picked up the paintbrush May had left by the cup of water, smoothed the splayed hairs, dipped the brush in a spot of carmine, and ran it over a scrap of paper. Her stroke left only a faint trace, but she regarded the wobbly line as if it were a small masterpiece. "You were right: I might have smiled for that portrait Mr. Healy did back in Rome. I hope you'll paint a better one."

WATERCOLORS

*M*ay's new friend, Jane, mentioned a room available in the Bedford Square boarding house where she lived. It smelled of beef, cabbage, and onions from the kitchen, but it was clean and reasonably priced. The neighborhood was lively with shoeshine boys, girls selling bunches of lilacs or lavender, butchers wearing blue aprons and straw hats, chalk artists drawing on the pavement, boys shuffling with scrapers and pans behind horses, and an old woman in a ragged shawl selling baked potatoes from a pushcart filled with hot coals.

"Bloomsbury is hardly a proper place for a lady," said Mr. Niles, who'd stopped with Louisa before accompanying her to the train.

"Some people may be down on their luck, that's all." May didn't mention the women with rouged cheeks and painted eyes who lingered in doorways at night. "Lu, you needn't tell Mother that Jane and I are the only ladies in the boarding house. And all Father needs to know is that I'm near the big library."

The National Gallery was also just a short walk away. Twice a week, May sat at the table as if she'd been invited to a feast. The caretaker's keys jangled as he slipped a painting from one of the wide drawers and propped it on a small easel. A fire crackled in the hearth to keep the humid air from damaging the paintings. May loved wielding a paintbrush that was wider than any she'd yet owned. It took practice to loosen her grip and broaden her stroke, to earn the confidence to lift her brush and believe in what a few strokes, or their absence, could show. Jane and Mr. Ramsey showed her how to stipple, putting bits of color in patterns, letting some of the white of the paper shimmer through, and to spread thin layers of pigments, which they let dry before adding another, to make the surfaces luminescent as real sky or water.

After the museum closed, May, Jane, and Mr. Ramsey ate egg sandwiches and talked about John Ruskin, the famed art critic who had written *Modern Painters*. They debated his theories about the moods and symbolism of color and argued over his advice to remove the black paint, perhaps even brown madder or burnt sienna, from their tins. Jane spoke of setting aside money to take classes in fall and urged May to join her.

"I'm afraid I must leave London by then."

"You can't go back to America without seeing Paris," Jane protested. "There are still reports of guillotines and fires, but that's bound to be over by next spring, when the Salon will be held again."

"No one knows what the French will do. They cry *Vive la République* one day, then beg for an emperor the next," Mr. Ramsey said.

"The *Venus de Milo* was found in the cellar of the Prefecture of Police, hidden behind documents stacked before a wall. A broken water pipe saved it from fire. I'd love to see that. And imagine setting up an easel in the Louvre," Jane said.

"People can paint in the museum?" May asked.

"Even ladies. And some life-drawing classes are open, though they cost three times as much as classes for men. The French believe American girls have money."

"It's hardly fair, but the classes would be worth it," May said.

"Yes. The teachers often are on the Salon jury, and they like to see their names printed beside their students' in the *programme*."

"But even some of the most celebrated artists are turned down. We tried last year. And were rejected." Mr. Ramsey slipped out a green card marked "*refusé*" from his billfold.

"Mercy, why do you carry around that horrid thing?" Jane asked.

"I'm told we should expect to collect at least a dozen before our paintings get in. The card reminds me that I must try again."

May dreamed of such a chance as she spent her days making copies. She was elated when some were put up for sale in the museum shop, and she found she could set higher prices as the winter passed. When the room in the National Gallery was closed, she often perched on a campstool in Westminster Abbey and sketched arches, chapels, cloisters, tattered banners, and the slant of sun through stained glass. She didn't love making short, stiff strokes as much as she liked copying Turner's watercolors, but she was proud to have this work shown in the Dudley Gallery. They also displayed her still lifes of antique books, silver candlesticks, and spotless apples she planned to submit to the Salon.

But her life wasn't all work. While she was careful with her money, she didn't want to be mistaken for one of the British women who seemed forever in waterproofs and round-toed boots. Happily, Mr. Niles enjoyed accompanying her to Oxford Street shops and advising on scarlet heels, a velvet hat circled with pink tea roses, and a beaded purse. He seemed to appreciate how her silk gowns set off his jacket with a velvet collar and narrow trousers with stripes up the side, though he glanced at handsome young men as furtively as she did. They attended a flower show, saw plays at Covent Garden, watched horses jump hedges in Hyde Park, and visited the zoo, where she sketched caged bears and rode a camel. Sometimes they just shared dinners, where she liked hearing his American accent as he replied to her accounts of news from home. Dan French had won the art prize at the Cattle Show and sent baskets of strawberries to the Alcotts in appreciation of his first teacher. Sadly, Mrs. Hawthorne had passed over, with Una by her side. She never got to see her first grandchild. May didn't tell him that Julian, his wife, and their baby moved to New York, where he was designing bridges.

But May forgot about Julian and everything else on learning that Turner copies made by both her and Jane had been selected for a watercolor show that would be attended by the members who'd selected what would be shown as well as prominent art critics.

"John Ruskin! No one is more respected. What an opportunity," Mr. Ramsey said.

"For humiliation," Jane said.

"Louisa points out that a critic is just one man," May said.

"Your sister is famous enough to say such things."

"She wasn't born with privilege." May lifted her chin, the way Louisa did when people suggested things came easily to her.

"If Mr. Ruskin calls something art, then it is, according to those who matter. And if he says it's not, then that's the end of a career," Mr. Ramsey said. "I don't say he's not knowledgeable. Better him than Queen Victoria, who thinks a good painting is a painting of a deer."

The evening of the show's opening, May looked over watercolors that were romantic or realistic, conservative or innovative in technique. She watched Mr. Ruskin move toward a painting, step back, then forward again, training his eyes on the work. She walked toward her copy of Turner, which she thought was as close as she'd yet come to showing water in conversation with wind and sky.

"What will we do if his review is scathing? It would have been better if our work hadn't gotten in," Jane said.

"Don't be foolish," May said, though her stomach ached. She was glad to be distracted by the approach of Mr. Niles. She was pleased she could ask him here, though it couldn't repay him for the excursions he'd treated her to. As they looked at paintings, he said, "We donated books for a bazaar at the Music Hall in Boston to benefit *The Woman's Journal.*"

"I didn't know Roberts Brothers supported women's suffrage."

"We don't, but we like to keep our most famous author happy. I suppose she'll be happier still when you return. It won't be long now?"

"No." May missed everyone, but she wished a return to Massachusetts didn't mean she'd never come back to Europe. She secretly thought that if her painting was accepted by the Salon, she might not only go to Paris to see it, but stay on a while to paint.

As people made way for the critics who headed to the main gallery, May joined Jane and Mr. Ramsey. Mr. Ruskin stepped behind a podium, spoke about the genius of Turner, then took out a piece of paper. "Those who honor his legacy with diligence and talent include . . ." He read a few names, which blurred together, until May heard her own.

Jane and Mr. Ramsey didn't have to hold up her elbows. She wasn't going to faint. But she felt her knees give, as pleasure pulsed through her, warming her face and hands.

After the men stopped speaking, May accepted congratulations from friends. Then she and Jane headed home, taking long strides, speaking of all the people who'd seen their work that night. Near the boarding house, a woman wearing a crushed hat and ragged cloak held out her hand. May fumbled with her purse, then dropped four pence on her palm. The woman nodded her thanks, with a glance that acknowledged the slim line between their fates, between good luck and bad, past and present. *Does your father know where you are?* It didn't seem so long ago that May had been a girl waving handbills at people who hadn't seemed to see her, or pretended they didn't. Now she remembered how despite her shame at being seen as poor, the sky had seemed to brighten and lift, as if asking her to paint it. Maybe her work as an artist had started then.

·16

THE BRİDGE

*L*eaves had fallen from brambles that looped over the rustic fence. May passed boys playing leapfrog and girls rolling hoops toward the house next door, then walked up the path to home. Mother embraced her and wouldn't let go even when Anna and Louisa squeezed in to make a place for themselves. Father was slightly stooped. Anna's boys, who now had lean faces and wore long trousers, accepted May's kisses with shy, beautiful grins. May hoped Anna would at least choose lavender or gray rather than follow Queen Victoria's or Mrs. Lincoln's fashion of interminably wearing black crêpe.

Everyone settled in the parlor, where May tried to sound modest while explaining the importance of Mr. Ruskin's praise. She decided not to mention the green *refusé* card she carried, even though she craved hearing protests that such was unfair. The conversation soon turned from art to how the Damens' carriage harness had been stolen, and now Mrs. Damen had to be wheeled to church in a wheelbarrow. Ellen Emerson had bought a donkey, which was proving to be a nuisance around town, running into clotheslines and trampling gardens. Mother showed May around the house and yard, pointing out things Louisa had bought: a new rocking chair, soapstone sink, and furnace. She'd even bought a horse and a wicker cart.

When May went into town on errands, neighbors greeted her warmly, but when they asked, "How was your trip?" most waited only a moment, as if her time overseas could fit in a sentence. Some old friends showed off newborns, toddlers, and even children old enough to be in school. May bounced babies on her lap, admiring their soft fat fingers and letting them touch her coral earrings. She envied the way these mothers could wake every morning with a purpose as visible as their children's bodies, instead of wondering how to fill blank paper. Still, hearing some speak in fast, shrill voices, as if they expected to be interrupted, made May miss artists who talked about ways to suggest the movements of water or faces, the different qualities of blues and greens.

She was glad to see Dan French, who said that he was busy making dozens of clay maquettes, trying to decide whether his statue of a minuteman, which he was sculpting to commemorate the first battle of the Revolution, would look best sitting, standing, or striding. May was glad to learn that one of her former students, pretty, plump Rose Peckham, still painted. She told May about the art museum under construction in Boston. "It's supposed to open in time to celebrate the hundred-year celebration of the nation."

"I suppose it takes time to carve all those fig leaves."

Rose begged May to teach classes again. Her studio looked smaller than she remembered, so one evening, she put on her blue bonnet with its ostrich plume and attended the selectmen's meeting, where she got permission to use the unoccupied second floor of the old Mason's Hall. Rose and Dan helped her haul out boxes of trash and termite-ridden furniture, sweep the wide-planked floors, and scrub the windows. May tacked up her Turner copies and drawings of Westminster Abbey. She borrowed anatomical casts from the School of Technology and art books from the Emersons, slipping in her copy of John Ruskin's *The Elements of Drawing*. She ordered watercolor paper almost as thick as linen, rolls of canvas, and bags of dry plaster, and painted a sign for the Concord Art Academy.

Rose and more than a dozen other young women enrolled. May used her notes from Dr. Rimmer's class to talk about the shapes of skulls and hands. She set up still lifes, though she was tired of painting flowers bright as if just plunged in water and landscapes that suggested the world was always sunny. She brought strips of wood, a saw, nails, and canvas that smelled like sails. She taught them how to build a frame and stretch canvas over it. More often, they used watercolors. She demonstrated how to soak the paper and apply glazes and scumbles, layering pale colors and transparent washes to give the effect of light. Only Rose worked with much dedication. May thought too many wasted time without understanding how fleeting it could be, and they hardly listened when she urged them to tour galleries.

"My father said he might send me to Paris to study, but

how would I ever find a safe place to live or the right school?" Rose asked.

"Paris is the only place a woman can study the figure. But let's get back to what's under our hands." May didn't want to talk about Europe. She'd recently visited Dan in the barn his father had helped him convert to a studio, where he'd propped up a mirror and a copy of the Apollo Belvedere, which Mr. Emerson had arranged for him to borrow from the Athenæum. He'd soon cast his statue of a Revolutionary soldier in bronze, but he'd told May he wouldn't be at the town's centennial celebration when it would be unveiled. He'd met a fellow whose father sculpted in Florence and had invited him to join them in Italy.

❧

IN THE MIDDLE OF APRIL, SNOW FELL AS MAY HUNG A flag in the window, though yesterday bluebirds had flown over the yard. She, her parents, Anna, and her boys dressed warmly and walked past many horses and buggies on their way to the Old North Bridge. There, new ice had formed on the river's edge. Townspeople wearing colonial costumes or century-old clothes scavenged from attics stamped their feet to stay warm. Men decked in three-cornered hats and breeches brushed snow from the benches and a podium. One told May that the Middlesex Hotel was full and the train from Boston was running extra service.

The snow stopped, but the sky remained gray as May looked for Louisa, who must still be with a few other eminent women escorting the wives of President Grant and some Cabinet members. May found places for Mother and Father in front of the speakers' platform and took a seat beside Daniel French's family. She congratulated them on his statue, which was now draped with flags so that all she could see was the granite pedestal.

"Have you heard anything from Dan?" she asked.

"He's discovering sculpture in Italy such as he never dreamed of. And congratulations are due to you, too. We heard you won first place at the Cattle Show," Judge French said.

May had been pleased with the eight-dollar prize. She moved over as Louisa crowded in beside her on the bench, leaned toward her, and whispered, "When I asked Judge Hoar where the ladies and I should sit, he replied, 'Anywhere in Concord, Miss Alcott, except on this platform.'"

May looked at Carrie's father sitting in front with male orators, poets, and politicians. After prayers, some tunes by the Marine Band, and a long meditation on memory, glory, and liberty, the platform seemed to settle into the wet earth. President Grant looked nervous. As gentlemen kept on praising ancestors, Judge French slipped a newspaper under his vest and murmured, "Perhaps more will die of the cold here today than did in the battle we're commemorating."

After more than two hours of speeches, Mr. Emerson pulled the cords attached to the flags, revealing the Minuteman statue. Everyone stood and cheered for the seven-foot-tall statue of a handsome man holding a musket with one hand, while stepping away from a plow. He was about Dan's age and wore a shirt with an open collar and pushed-up sleeves, breeches, and knee-high boots. May thought the soldier in tight trousers looked a bit more like someone sauntering up to a belle rather than heading into battle, though the face was noble.

Some people headed to the Old Manse, which its owners had opened to serve hot meals to out-of-town visitors. Special guests headed into the Cattle Show Building. May greeted friends, then she and Louisa walked to the river.

"It was good of you to give Anna your seat for the dinner," May said. She watched Anna keep an arm around Mother's waist as they navigated the uneven ground. Her boys were throwing rocks into the water and stomping on thin ice. Father was trying to get through a crowd of men around President Grant, probably to offer advice.

"There will be more speeches. Anna will be more patient since she can hardly hear them," Louisa said.

"The rum punch may help."

"I've had enough of men who think they can mark the beginning of our nation's freedom and not invite a single woman to speak." Louisa shook her head. "No taxation without representation, they say. Rubbish. We still don't have the vote, and I pay the highest taxes in town."

"Things will change." May linked her arm through Louisa's as they walked past leafless elder bushes to the river's edge.

"Before the war, we were told that slavery must be abolished before women could get the vote. It's been ten years since we trounced the South, and the old promises are forgotten."

"I thought you were tired of speeches." May glanced back toward the statue. "I expect Dan was right to avoid the ceremony."

"They might have mentioned his first teacher."

"Dan is always gracious about thanking me, but everyone knows teachers don't get publicly honored."

"Especially when they're women. Mr. Emerson might at least have asked to see your sketches before they gave Dan the commission."

"I was in Europe when the competition was announced. And I'm not a sculptor."

"Dan had never done such a big statue either, had he? I dare say they'd have asked you if you were a man."

"Art isn't easy for men either. Dan told me the commission only paid for the clay. He got nothing for his work." May heard Freddie and Johnny shriek as they dipped their hands into the cold water, piling up rocks to dam puddles. She said, "Do you think they'll become engineers, like Julian? Building roads and bridges?"

"They can be anything." Louisa looked at her. "I know you always wanted children."

"No one can have everything. You told me that years ago."

"Back when I was young enough to think I knew something. May, did you ever give your answer to the world?"

"What?"

"A long time ago, you told me that sometimes a view speaks to you, and you painted to answer back."

"I'm only now finding the right language." May watched a blackbird dart past the yellow willow branches. Small waves swiftly changed from blue to green to gold. "I still see the beauty here, but I can't paint it."

"I understand. Sometimes I think I love home more when I'm away."

May looked back at the statue. "Dan's sculpture is grand, but what I admire most is that he didn't need to hear the applause. He chose to work instead."

"You're like that, too. Far more than the girl I foolishly wrote about in my book, the one who stopped making art. I admire the way you never gave up."

"And now one of my students may be the genius. I hardly spoke more than a few words to Dan, but I can't help feeling a bit proud. A teacher's greatest reward is to see her students go beyond her."

"Perhaps. But you were meant for something besides coaxing work from others."

May shook her head. "Do you want to go rowing soon? There's a boat kept at the old Manse they let anyone borrow. In another few months, we can even see the water lilies."

"I want to see them, but I suppose you'd rather be in Paris. Rose told me she's been begging her teacher to go with her. I don't want people saying how the Peckham girl goes where you haven't been. Why should I have wealth if I can't help my sister?"

"What? Go to Paris?"

"You might learn enough in a year to show everyone what a woman can do."

"And an Alcott?"

"You must show everyone that a woman from our little town can put a painting in that big art show you always talk about."

"My work might not get in. I sent something to the Salon when I was in England, and it was refused."

"You don't think I'd be impressed by a single rejection?

Don't you remember all the editors who turned down my work? I'll provide enough money for you to stay a year, if you're careful."

"Thank you!" May threw her arms around her. "I don't know how I'll ever repay you, but I'll try. You'll see your sacrifices were worthwhile."

"You don't have to pay me back."

"But I want to give something. When I sell a great painting, I'll buy you a ticket to visit. You could look for that Polish revolutionary of yours. And it could be like it was years ago in Boston. You writing. Me at an easel."

"Was it ever like that, the way you remember?"

May wondered if she could see more clearly in memory, paint this river as she couldn't paint it while hearing the skim of ice crack, the small waves ripple. "I love it here, but I've never felt I quite belong."

"I've felt that, too. But I can see it, the beauty you showed me. The dazzle of broken ice. The boys' round shoulders, the round rocks."

May hoped that classes in the capital of art might show her how to paint so people could not only see but hear and smell the river, understand its currents, mud, and the long, hidden roots of lilies. "And you made your mark, as I hope I can in Paris. You wrote a book that let readers see themselves, or who they want to be."

"I thought you hated my book."

"I didn't like being painted as an affected niminy-piminy chit. I don't see those sisters as you do, but you got a lot right, too. We loved each other."

Louisa looked at her, then away. "I'd like to come. But right now someone needs to stay with Mother. She doesn't want a stranger to watch her. I still hear about the one who pulled the cords under the bed so they were either too taut or too loose. She never could fold the newspapers just the way Mother likes."

May felt her chest tighten, then loosen, at the thought of Mother recently asking when her baby, Abbie May, was coming home. May didn't like to leave her, but she thought love must be more than loyalty. She said, "I'm grateful for everything you do. Mother never thought she'd have a soapstone sink or furnace."

"She says it makes the parlor too hot. She misses the way we all used to gather around the hearth."

"And you helped Father publish some of his writings."

"You understand that Marmee isn't well, don't you? When she was so ill a few months ago, she had me make a list of where things should go. We all know you want the green-and-white china."

"The only thing I care about is her diaries."

"Anna and I want those, too. Maybe you can copy them as you did with Mr. Hawthorne's."

"I didn't mean the diaries should go to me." They were the one thing Mother prized that she'd kept, perhaps because she couldn't sell them as she had old wedding presents and inherited treasures. May didn't want to read them, expecting they were full of stories of how much she'd given up. But one day, she wanted to hold them. She said, "More than anyone, she made us strong and want to keep working. But why are we talking about this? She'll be all right. And so will you."

"I wasn't thinking about myself. But it's true that ever since the war, I brood that my life will be cut short. Maybe I'm wrong. You and I will grow old together. But if I don't, will you be with me when my time comes?"

"Don't talk like that. Nothing is going to happen."

"I've been blessed with more time than I thought I'd have. But someday, I want to know I won't be alone."

"I'll be with you." May straightened Louisa's bonnet and pushed back a wisp of her hair that had fallen from its pins. She watched the water ripple in lines that would never be exactly the same, with a murmur that seemed unchanging. Promises were made, promises were broken. The river flowed on.

THE CITY OF LIGHT

$\mathcal{M}$ay and her friend Rose walked up the steep streets of Montmartre. People wearing ragged clothes lined up with tin pails in front of cafés with red awnings, while cooks ladled soup made from leftovers. Women leaned over wrought iron balconies on yellow houses, calling to friends returning from markets with baskets of black radishes, carrots, and romaine lettuce tied with wisps of straw. Newsboys sorted morning papers. Street sweepers yelled at cats. May smelled leeks, tobacco, horses, and the long loaves of bread women tucked under their arms.

She and Rose stopped at a crèmerie for warm rolls and bowls of milky coffee. They'd found a respected art school and a nearby apartment a few months ago, and by now, May ordered without pausing over French words. As they walked to the studio, May savored both the sense of just living her life, forgetting she was in Paris, and the spells of feeling tremendously lucky to live among people who cherished art, food, and fashion.

She and Rose entered the atelier, which was in an old warehouse with tall windows. They took off their hats and gloves, greeting women who were mostly American and British, with one Spanish, one Swiss, and one who was French. They chatted about the weekend, gave each other advice about paints and perspective, and laughed at the caricatures of the instructor that one girl drew in the margins of her sketchbook. All twenty students were single and younger than May, except Fanny Osbourne, a handsome woman about her age who'd left a husband in California.

Monsieur Krug, the artist in charge of the studio, usually came in to check their progress only on Tuesday and Friday mornings. A monitor had overseen the drawings from plaster casts they made in fall, and after the first snows, which swiftly melted on buildings and streets, he directed a model. Now he bent over, making chalk marks on the floor to note the placement of easels, so that if they were nudged aside, each student could find the angle from which she began, and not accuse the model of changing her pose. May didn't expect any of these women would speak harshly, but she'd heard the men's classes were rowdier.

May tacked paper to her easel, which today stood right in front of the model's platform, a position granted by Monsieur Krug as a reward for what he considered one of the best sketches last week. He'd also honored her by hanging some of her work on the wall. May was delighted, but such acknowledgment wasn't enough. Her whole body felt tight with determination to get work into that spring's Salon.

As a graceful, dark-skinned young woman stepped out from behind a screen, Fanny whispered, "I heard she's from northern Africa." A hush fell as the model took off her robe. May swung her arm wide as if she were swimming, sketching shoulders, arms, breasts, hips, and legs. Such a drawing would be kept within these walls. Though women could submit work to the Salon, they were forbidden to display nudes, leaving such to men who named the paintings after goddesses or subjects like liberty or purity.

The following day, May daubed paint on her palette, primed the biggest canvas she'd ever used, and began a portrait. She chose to paint the model as she looked before she disrobed, so that she could display it in public. Her hair was tucked under a gold scarf that picked up the earth tones of her skin. May painted the chemise slipping over one shoulder, as the woman glanced to the side. She put much of her face in shadows, which she found as compelling as the features. She meant to leave something out, to suggest what might never be known, but remained hidden between the glances of the artist and the person who posed.

She finished the portrait by February, when everyone began concentrating on work they could send to the Salon jury. She painted a stuffed owl she'd bought at a flea market and set on a stack of leather-bound books. Each precise stroke briefly turned her panic about passing time into patience. She was finally satisfied with *les petites taches*, the small brushstrokes she blended until they were glossy. She coated the surface with lacquer so it would look as if it had been found in an old church, stained by centuries of candle smoke and incense.

Monsieur Krug found this work impressive, but the next week, May began another still life of yellow, green, and red apples, a jug, and a bottle on a polished table. Unlike Turner, who showed backgrounds as intriguing as what was placed in front, May kept the wall behind the objects evenly dark. And hearing *le Maître*'s footsteps, she hastily mixed Prussian blue with sienna to deepen the colors. Smocks and silk dresses rustled as the women stepped aside to make a path between the easels. Monsieur Krug stopped in front of the portrait Rose was painting of May, wearing her blue dress with a frill around the pointed neckline and a matching plumed hat, tilted stylishly down. He said, "*Pas mal.*"

He briefly commented on other work before turning his eyes to May's still life. "*Bien fait!*"

The words warmed her cheeks, but as Monsieur Krug turned to another canvas, she said, "*Pardon, Monsieur.* Surely there's more I can do. Do you have any suggestions?" The lessons were pricey, and she wanted more than a word or two.

In his heavily accented English, he said, "Perhaps the bottles and bowl could be darker. Unless you aspire to be a student of, what do they call themselves? *Les Impressionnistes, les Indépendants?* Independent of what, all rules of perspective? All admirers? Then you could make those apples as yellow as you please, or why not orange? Why bother spending years studying nature?"

"*Merci, Monsieur.*"

"Patrons want what's enduring, not some impression of

the moment. Hundreds of years of art can't be wrong."

"*Merci.*" She felt annoyed by the way the artist's eyelids drooped, suggesting that he thought it beneath himself to be teaching, particularly a class of women. But his paintings regularly appeared in the Salon. If being listed as one of his students helped win her a place, she shouldn't complain about his meager advice.

Soon after the rounds ended, most students scrubbed their hands, untied each other's smocks, and pinned on hats. Some were met by maids or footmen who escorted them home to the more fashionable sections of Paris. But May kept working, and she insisted that Rose stay, too. They rinsed their brushes only when the sun began to set, then headed home on streets crowded with men wearing berets, cravats loosely tied over open collars, paint-stained jackets, and wide trousers. Many painters lived in this hilly neighborhood on the outskirts of Paris. The light was better than on the narrow streets of the Left Bank and the rents cheaper than on the Chaussée d'Antin, where wealthier artists lived. They passed stalls where men gambled at wheels of fortune or tossed balls at clay statues of politicians. A pigeon darted from a blue slate roof to a catalpa tree. As boys lit gas lamps, May pulled her cloak closer. She averted her eyes from a box by the door of a convent, where she'd heard infants were sometimes placed, for the nuns to find them homes.

During the following weeks, she thought about which painting to submit, while Rose worked on the portrait of her, making her chin shorter, her eyes longer, and her nose slimmer. May liked the shimmer of her blue dress, but she felt taken aback by the wistful, determined, and perhaps melancholy eyes. She hadn't known that anyone saw the loneliness, which sometimes weighed on her shoulders. She still wore her hair down most days, though it was darker than it had been, and she noticed fine lines around her mouth and eyes. But May thought she'd aged more from a growing, heavy impatience. She'd lost her old need to make determination look pretty. She was still kind when she commented on her friends' work, but she had less time for niceties, went more directly to the truth. Instead of signing her name in the corner, she twined together *M* and *A*, in red script, thin as embroidery thread.

⤜∽∝⤏

ON A MORNING IN MARCH, MAY AND ROSE LINGERED AT the round wooden table covered with a jar of jam, a tin box with tablets of paint, a hair-curling stick, dominoes, and an antique dagger May had bought at a flea market to use in a still life someday, but which meanwhile she used to open letters or pierce bread to make toast over the grate. The atelier was closed today, as both Monsieur Krug and the man who monitored planned to join other artists watching thousands of submissions arrive for the Salon jury. May was sending the painting she called *Fruit and Bottles*, while Rose had chosen her portrait of May, though she was now having second thoughts.

"Even if our paintings don't get in, we'll have a chance to look at other fine art. Most painters have to collect a dozen refusals." May was trying to prepare herself, as much as Rose, for a possible rejection.

"How can we wait six weeks to find out our fates?" Rose asked. "I can't stop thinking about those men pointing umbrellas or walking sticks at our paintings, saying *Oui* or *Non*! I heard that last year, one artist sent a note with his canvas, saying that if it was refused, they should look for his body in the Seine."

"Only a dramatic Frenchman would throw himself in the river." May got up from the overturned potato box, went to the window, and glanced down to the street. Horses hauled wagons filled with art toward the Palais de l'Industrie, where members of the jury would mark the backs of paintings: "*a*" for *admis* or "*r*" for *refusé*. She said, "Let's go watch the paintings arrive."

"We can't. The streets will be mobbed," Rose said.

"Why should men have all the fun?" May took out her poplin walking suit with its braid trim on the shoulders and cuffs.

"You can't go alone," Rose said.

"I'll ask Mary Cassatt."

"She won't go. She's too dignified."

"I'll find out." May had met this artist from Philadelphia, who she guessed was a few years older than she was, soon after she arrived in Paris. She often attended the Thursday-evening soirees at the apartment Mary shared with her parents and older sister.

May hurried down the stairs, pulling on gloves the color of pale lemons. She walked past houses with lace-covered windows and balconies jammed with pots of geraniums. Round tables and wrought iron chairs had been set in front of cafés and pâtisseries, where customers lingered over croissants and espresso.

May liked seeing Parisians idling in full view. If someone in Boston wanted to daydream or gossip, the last thing she'd want was for someone to catch her at it.

She reached the Cassatt apartment, where a maid led her into the parlor with red-and-gold striped wallpaper, mahogany tables, and chintz-covered chairs. Mary, her mother, and her sister, Lydia, all wore loose morning dresses.

"I was about to get ready to work, but it's hard to concentrate knowing that thousands of paintings are about to be judged." Mary had a pointed chin and sharp dark eyes. The way she pressed her lips together at the ends of sentences and her thin patience for small talk reminded May of Louisa.

"What did you send?" she asked.

"She sent an oil painting of me! She did a pastel in almost the same pose. Mary, may I show her?" Lydia asked. When her sister nodded, Lydia left the room and quickly returned with a picture of a woman leaning forward in a theater box, wearing a ball gown the color of butter and sugar beaten together for a cake. The pastel strokes seemed hasty, even slapdash, though May was charmed by their energy. She said, "What a superb portrait."

"I thank the model." Mary nodded at Lydia, whose skin didn't glow as much as that of the woman in the picture. Her hair was more brown than red.

"I look forward to seeing it after you finish blending the pastels," May said.

"It *is* finished," Mary said.

"Of course. I'm sorry. Pastels make it hard to tell. I've never been good with them."

"You must try again. I leave mine in the sunlight to warm them. Once they get soft, you can layer one color over another."

"You don't think it's too bright?" Mrs. Cassatt's eyes were as dark and sharp as her daughter's, though the rest of her was soft and wider.

"My mother thinks I should paint as I've done in years past. Women playing mandolins, toreadors, or Spanish dancers against dusky backgrounds. Probably the Salon jury likes those more, too."

"Your work will get in! It's been chosen before," May said.

"Yes, and been turned down, too. One year *yes*, the next *no*, which was more discouraging after my acceptance. I retreated to Switzerland. With the Alps outside my window, I couldn't *not* paint." Mary shook her head. "I darkened the background of my rejected painting, and it got in the next year."

"Where are our manners? Won't you have tea?" Mrs. Cassatt asked.

May smiled, then looked at Mary. "Actually, I came to see if you'd come with me to watch art being delivered."

"Won't there be an awful lot of bohemians out today?" Mrs. Cassatt pressed her lips together.

"Mother, they're preparing for an art show, not a revolution." Mary turned to May. "Should I ask our driver to hitch up the horses, or do you want to walk?"

"A carriage would have an even harder time than we would getting through the crowds. Do you have suitable shoes?"

"I'm not sure I could do without my gowns and hats made in Paris, but I order my shoes from England."

Mary changed into a tailored gown cinched at her waist, with enough room in the fashionably slim skirt to take reasonably wide steps. As they headed up the street, she said, "I'm glad to leave before my mother started citing all the dangers of being out among such riffraff."

"She didn't really protest your going."

"She didn't have to. I've had thirty-two years to study the way she sets her mouth when she disapproves."

May was surprised by the way she bluntly stated her age. She'd assumed Mary was older than her, not four years younger, because of her prior successes at exhibitions. Or perhaps she shaved off a few years, the way May sometimes did.

"At least living with your family, you know when to worry or not. Louisa writes that my mother isn't well."

"You've told me your sister exaggerates her maladies."

"She writes as if Mother's every stomachache will be her last one. But I miss her. As she's confined, I hope my letters with details of life here bring her some pleasure."

"I'm certain they do. Why doesn't your sister come visit?"

"Her health is poor, too. And she gets seasick."

"It's a terrible curse. I told my parents I couldn't bear another voyage, and if they wanted to see me, they'd have to come here, where I have a better chance of selling work. I was surprised when they did, but my father retired, and he likes the horse races. My mother and sister enjoy the opera and ballet."

"None of those would entice Louisa. Neither would art."

"My father once said he'd rather see me dead than be an artist, but now that I've made some money at it, he's softened. He pays for our home, while my paintings must cover art supplies and a studio. I told them I wanted to spare them the smells of paint and solvents, but really, I'm not sure I could paint with them in the next room."

"I used to hate suppertime, when everyone would report their good works, and all I had to say was how I'd spent the afternoon with a paintbrush. Even to me it sounded small."

"But it's not. I'm lucky to save money on models, as Lydia wants to be of use, and not being well she is limited in what she can do. Even my mother agreed to pose reading *Le Figaro*. I'm not sure what to do with these, and I'm having trouble earning money with portraits. One woman said I made her look old. She *was* old! Which doesn't mean I didn't find beauty, just not the sort she wanted. Others are insulted because I pay as much attention to a teacup, bonnet, book, dog, or fan as I do a face. Such things make a composition come alive. But how did you bewitch me into speaking so much about myself? How is your class?"

"Monsieur Krug rarely comes, though he sends in other artists to assess."

"That's how most *cours* are run here. One can learn more copying in the Louvre, but the younger ladies say they're too busy studying from casts of the antique or from models."

May remembered arriving in Paris and spending days walking through halls full of paintings and sculptures, standing nearly breathless before the *Venus de Milo*. Sometimes she'd set up a rented easel and tried to copy the delicate mouths painted by Michelangelo, or the pink and peach tones of Titian. She didn't go as often once foot-warmers were offered along with the easels, around the time when they'd begun painting from life in class. She said, "When you're paying for classes, it feels wrong to miss a day at the atelier."

Mary pressed her lips together, the way her mother had when they planned to go out. "The Louvre is one place women can talk with other artists, including men. We can't do that at the cafés or brasseries without damaging our reputations. I met Monsieur Degas in front of a painting."

"You've mentioned him before," May said as they crossed a bridge. On the other side of the Seine, the wider roads were crowded with carriages driven by men wearing red waistcoats and top hats brushed to gleam. More buggies crowded the Champs-Élysées. They passed galleries and shops displaying jewelry and perfume bottles on damask-covered stands.

"We speak only about art or the group, which he dislikes calling a group, that he is part of. Some mean to insult with the name *Impressionist*, criticizing the work as hasty sketches, but some are adopting the name," Mary said. "Why shouldn't the impressions of fleeting moments be captured? They work fast to catch the light and keep traces of their hands in the brushstrokes."

"Isn't art about getting the details right?"

"Let beholders imagine their own details."

"Are you courting?"

"Monsieur Degas? No! He's about ten years older, set in his ways, cross, and outspoken. Of course, I have a temper, too."

"My sister says she regrets her anger, but I wonder if she'd write so much without it."

Mary smiled. "Sometimes Monsieur Degas finds fault with my work, and I vow I'll never talk to him again. Then I pass one of his paintings in a shop window and must visit him. He sees the world as I do."

May had glimpsed him through the window of the Café Nouvelle Athènes, a bearded, round-shouldered man wearing salt-and-pepper tweeds and a scarf wrapped around his neck. She understood that Mary might find it hard to admit she was drawn to him. "Perhaps he'll escort you to the Salon."

"Perhaps, as a friend," Mary said. "Neither of us are besotted, though I rather prefer older men, who understand more."

"But young men are beautiful."

"Then you don't care for Mr. Houghton? He smiles at you at our soirees."

"The widower? I expect he has his sights on any breathing woman who might look after his seven children. My escort will also be a friend, from London. Mr. Ramsey has decided that whether or not his work gets in, it's time to see the exhibition."

"Monsieur Degas isn't submitting anything to the Salon this year. He's just showing with his group, the way they did last year. It was magnificent."

"You went to the Impressionist exhibit?"

"Stepping in was like entering a lush garden. There were no pecking strokes, just great splashes of color. But few sold."

They passed the charred and roofless Tuileries Palace, where clipped boxwood lined crushed stone paths and sentries made sure that no one entered with a dog, which might leave a mess, or carrying a package, which might contain an explosive. Just beyond was the Louvre, with rows of arched windows, turrets, and many palatial rooms. May said, "Your painting will be accepted into the Salon. And someday, perhaps in this museum, too."

"Thank you for your faith."

They stepped more carefully as the wide streets grew crowded with packed omnibuses, each pulled by three horses. Long-haired men wearing floppy ties over wrinkled shirts and wide corduroy trousers crowded the top decks. Some held paintings large enough to catch the wind. In front of the Palais de l'Industrie, men carried paintings overhead or cradled marble busts like babies in their arms. As deliverymen climbed the stone steps, boys and men balanced on fences and yelled praise or insults.

May held Mary's arm, murmuring, "*Pardon,*" as she made a way to a bench with room for them at one end. She hoisted her skirt, bent her knees, and stepped up, pulling on Mary's arm. They had a good view of the crowd and paintings of the exodus from Egypt, Gauls entering Rome, crownings, and beheadings.

"Some artists rush to do the themes that won prizes the year before," Mary said.

"My humble bowl of fruit can't stand out among all the grand ideas."

"Noble ideas can get wearisome. One can hope, but we shouldn't expect fairness. The juries are fickle, not known for honesty or even knowing anything about art."

"I don't suppose it helps us that all are men."

"I've heard that when one votes for a woman, the others jeer, 'Is she pretty?' We have more opportunities here than at home, but still the *Académie des Beaux-Arts* is closed to women, and their students are the only ones eligible for some of the important prizes."

Six men carried a large painting of a nude Venus rising from a seashell. As other men called, "Ooh, la la," the earnest carriers turned the painting to face the other side. This exposed the work to a new group of men, who hooted. When someone brought in a painting of an angel, several men flapped their arms. Another pressed his hands together as if in prayer. Men mooed at a picture of cows. They barked at a picture of dogs.

Deliverymen took more paintings from handcarts and wagons. They set marble sculptures on trolleys they trundled to the back entrance.

"That's a crime against art!"

"*Non! C'est très belle!*"

"A horror!" A man straddling a lamppost shouted.

Another shook his fist at a still life. "Throw that in the garbage!"

May said, "For all the talk of freedom there is in Massachusetts, I never knew what it was until I came here."

Mary shouted, "*C'est magnifique!*"

May laughed to hear her dignified friend raise her voice. Then her face heated as she followed Mary's gaze to a man lifting her still life of bottles and fruit from a cart. He stashed it under his arm along with several others and hurried up the steps. May's painting with all its careful strokes disappeared from view.

Mary cried, "*Vive Mademoiselle Alcott!*"

May grabbed her hand, which felt as thin and hard as her sister's. She thought of how her brushwork had grown steadier, how her vision had widened since she'd been here. She'd enjoyed the sounds of her sweeping brush, the accomplishment of mixing a color to just the shade she wanted or making a shadow the right shape. But she still wanted her painting to be chosen for the Salon. She wanted her work to be seen.

⬤

DURING THE SIX WEEKS BETWEEN JURY DAY AND THE announcements of decisions, May worked on more still lifes. On weekends, she went to the Louvre or for carriage rides in the Bois de Boulogne with the Cassatt sisters. She arrived home late one afternoon to find Rose holding a pale green *refusé* card, printed with, "Please come to collect your work at the Palais."

"I never thought I'd get in. Not really," Rose said.

"I'm sorry. That portrait should have been accepted." May hugged her, feeling her heart beat hard as she let go and glanced at the table, which held Camembert cheese, *vin ordinaire*, and *macarons*. She asked, "There's not a card like that for me?"

"Congratulations." Rose gave her a wobbly smile.

May whooped. "Wait until my mother hears! And Rose, you mustn't let this one refusal stop you. Begin another painting."

"It's not just this rejection that's discouraging. Monsieur Krug never once said that I had talent."

"He never praises anyone."

"He makes sure you get the first choice of where to set your easel. He pins your sketches on the wall." Rose tucked her *refusé* card beneath a pile of letters.

"I've been painting for most of my life! And it's no disgrace to be turned down, when thousands are refused."

"I'll go pick up the portrait. I'd like to give it to you for all your help, if you'll have it."

"Then the Salon's loss will be my mother's gain. She'll appreciate your portrait more than anyone else ever could." May looked back over the table. "You don't think my *refusé* card could have gone missing?"

"No. They send them out all at once. And of course they wanted your work."

The next day, May reveled in the embraces and congratulations of friends at the atelier. Then, except for the letters she sent to Mother, she tried to keep her joy quiet, until worry returned. What if the *refusé* card sent to her been lost? Could she have been wrong to assume her humble painting had been chosen?

On a warm April morning, she walked through Montmartre, crossed a curved bridge over the Seine, and heard washerwomen on the banks, scrubbing, slapping, and singing. Reaching the fashionable Grands Boulevards, she spotted the stems and leaves of tulips, hyacinths, and irises coming up, the closed buds of rhododendrons. She walked by the Louvre, then climbed the wide steps of the Palais de l'Industrie, listening to each of her footsteps. The big brick building looked golden in the sun. She walked through the doors, asked for directions, and made her way down a hall. She found a door with a sign that read *Administration de l'Exposition des Beaux-Arts* and knocked.

She was called in and asked what she wanted by a man sitting behind a desk. After she explained, he opened a ledger, flipped through its tall pages, drew his finger down a column, looked up at her, and said, "*Admise.*"

48

MUGUET DES BOÍS

*M*ay dressed in a bronze gown with a square neckline and tight sleeves. She pinned flowers on the bodice, slipped feathers in her hat, and fastened the six buttons on each of her long gloves. She and Rose walked past blooming chestnut trees along the Seine, then met Mr. Ramsey among the crowds around the Arc de Triomphe, where children sold bunches of bluebells, ground ivy, and lilies of the valley for those celebrating the first day of May. Mr. Ramsey filled May in on news of Jane and London while they joined a line that wound around the exhibition building. May had heard that more than ten thousand people were expected here today, and thousands more were apt to be turned away. Ladies in pink and yellow gowns with flounces held white parasols. Artists who hadn't shaved seemed to have at least combed their hair off their foreheads, paid attention to how they tied their cravats, pinned their shirt cuffs instead of just folding them back, and polished their boots.

After several hours in line, May and her friends climbed the wide stairway and entered halls adorned with portraits of queens and military men. Still lifes, *les natures mortes*, of Oriental drapery and Venetian glass were hung one above another, from waist height to the ceiling, in elaborately scrolled and gilded frames. Many mimicked the palettes of old Italian and Flemish masters, though they'd been painted that year by Messieurs Gérôme, Bouguereau, Carolus-Duran, and Meissonier. These paintings of Napoleon and his army, a serene Madonna, David fighting Goliath, and cavaliers in bright uniforms would fetch thousands of francs.

May's progress through the crowd was interrupted by friends who congratulated her on having her name in the *programme*. Fanny joined them, and she, Rose, and Mr. Ramsey shrieked, sounds barely audible over the surrounding exclamations and gossip, when they reached May's painting.

"You didn't tell us it was *en ligne!*" Mr. Ramsey touched her elbow, in recognition that it had been hung at the height of an average eye, rather than low, or worse, "skyed," hung so close to the ceiling that viewers had to crane their necks.

"I was lucky." May was satisfied that the bottle looked perfectly rounded. The apples glowed. She fanned her face to hide her pride that must have been apparent as she thought of how many artists had used costlier objects, and yet her little painting in its plain wooden frame had not only been chosen for the Salon, but had also been hung in such a coveted place.

She said, "Next year I expect we'll see your work here."

"And yours, too, again!"

May didn't want to think about this being her last chance. She felt slightly unsteady on her heels. The crowds made her dizzy, as if she'd been spinning too long at a ball, caught in a trap of frothy gowns. She looked around, trying to remember everything to tell Louisa about what might be the best day of her life. She hated to leave her painting, but since exhibitors were given a pass to return as often as they liked, she said, "Let's visit some other rooms."

Her friends protested that they couldn't see anything finer, but they moved toward pictures of a peasant girl in a golden field, hunters on horseback, and cows grazing in meadows. May pointed out a painting by Monsieur Gauguin. "He's a banker, who Miss Cassatt says sometimes buys Impressionist works."

"Have you seen her? It's a shame that her woman in yellow was turned down," Fanny said.

"I haven't visited her since the Salon choices were announced, I'm ashamed to say." It now struck May as selfish, but she hadn't wanted to chance having her own happiness dimmed by Mary's likely melancholy or jealousy.

"Didn't you tell me the last time one of her paintings was rejected, she stopped painting for months?" Fanny asked.

"She left Paris. But let's not talk of unpleasant things today." May asked, "What will you do when the ateliers close for the summer?"

"I'm going to the country outside the city. I heard some artists paint *en plein air* in Grez."

"Jane and I hoped you'd come back to London, May," Mr. Ramsey said. "They say that even bakers and blacksmiths buy art here in *La Ville-Lumière*, but it's hard to sell with so many artists competing."

"I've promised my family to go home," May said. "It's indelicate to say, but I'm running low on funds."

"Nothing is indelicate among friends. But you can copy Turner, as you did before. Didn't Mr. Ruskin say you were the best?" Mr. Ramsey said.

"London *is* almost on my way back to Massachusetts," May said. Then she turned as an old friend of Rose's, Miss Lombard, greeted them. Soon Rose and Miss Lombard headed into another *salle*, while May agreed to investigate some shouting that piqued Mr. Ramsey's curiosity. They entered a hall under a high glass dome where marble sculptures of nymphs, an Eve with her arms crossed over her breasts, and Lafayette arriving in America stood among pots of ferns, palms, and roses. Rows of busts set on pedestals included ones of Napoleon III and Balzac. The air smelled of cigars, lavender soap, hair lacquer, and roses.

The darkness of a tall bronze statue stood out among the white marble. Some spectators threw their hands over their faces or rushed away. May guessed this was not only because of the absence of a fig leaf on the nude man, but also because feeling seemed to rise from all the wrinkled, rippling surfaces, each jutting bone and muscle, which made a striking contrast to the polished pale busts with closed lips and unfurrowed brows.

"*The Age of Bronze* is the greatest art ever made," a man exclaimed.

"It's a travesty." Another man raised his fist. "Not really a sculpture. It looks cast from a human. And it doesn't even have a theme!"

May overheard that it had been sculpted by an *ornemaniste* who made a living by carving mantelpieces, lamp bases, and waterspouts, a Monsieur Rodin.

"It's superb. Though I wonder if such a work can stand the test of time, the way a peaceful statue does," Mr. Ramsey said.

"Its vitality reminds me of the work of a teacher I had back in Boston. I think Dr. Rimmer would have liked to see this." She wished he could see her work, too. Not that she expected he'd be impressed, but perhaps he'd see that she'd been serious. She fanned away cigar smoke as they headed back to the paintings. After passing portraits of John the Baptist, Jeanne d'Arc, and actresses from the *Comédie-Française*, Mr. Ramsey said, "I don't see any of the violet trees, green women, and butter skies I've heard some of the French are painting."

"So word of *les Indépendants* has reached England."

"I hear they admire Turner. It's sad that Frenchmen see more in him than our queen, who says his work should stay in drawers. There are enough pictures that look as if they'd been painted with prune juice."

"Don't talk so loudly. You may be challenged to a duel."

"Chiaroscuro was fine in the Renaissance, but since then, science has taught us about paint and light."

Soon they left through the wide doors and strode down the Champs-Élysées. Ladies in exquisite silk dresses headed for fashion shows, which were timed to take advantage of the crowds attending the Salon. May would like to wear a Worth gown with pearls beaded at the neckline, a Reboux hat with ostrich feathers, a diamond bracelet, but she'd rather be holding a program with her name in it. Though she hadn't stopped wishing for a beau who might congratulate her by kissing her neck and drawing her closer. *Stop*, she told herself. She was lucky.

Stalls stacked with books and prints stood by the bridge to Montmartre. Church bells tolled. Girls holding lilies of the valley called, "*Muguet! Muguet des bois!* For your lover on May Day."

It seemed strange that people paid for flowers that May had once picked freely from under the old elm tree. She looked down at the river crowded with dinghies, skiffs with square yellow sails, and barges piled with coal. On the banks, too, it seemed everyone was out on this fine spring day. Some men held fishing rods, while others stuffed straw into mattresses they put on frames, where women stitched them. May's heart thudded as she noticed a pair of shoes left by the brown water.

"Is something amiss?" Mr. Ramsey asked.

Water lapped the land. A young woman waded back, laughing, dropping the damp hem of her dress, bending to pick up her shoes.

"No." May looked back to a park, where the bushes and trees were clipped and the pebbled paths raked. She missed the sprawl and tangle of grasses, the tumble of stones along the Concord River. She paid for a bunch of flowers, tied with a bit of straw, from a girl's basket and held the ivory-colored blossoms to her nose.

❧

STRAWBERRIES HAD RIPENED BY THE TIME MAY knocked on the studio door. After hearing a dog yap, she wondered if Mary was pretending not to hear because she didn't want to see her. The dog barked again, then Mary opened the door.

"You're here!" May exclaimed.

"Where else would I be?" Mary crouched down to keep her small dog from jumping. Behind her back, a sulky girl in a lacy dress sprawled on a big blue chair. "I had to finish painting a sleeve before I could answer. You didn't think I'd fled to the mountains because the jury disapproves of my palette?"

"You said that when your work was rejected before, you left the city."

"When I was young and foolish. And last year, I darkened my canvas to impress them. I won't do that again." Speaking in perfect French, Mary told the girl she could play. As she slid off the chair, her mother put down her knitting and said they'd go to the park and be back soon.

"That's a lovely dress," May told the little girl.

She stared at her and said, "Your hair is pretty."

May nodded her thanks and touched her necklace. How long had it been since anyone said that? As the mother and child shut the door behind them, Mary said, "My model was starting to wiggle. And the light is changing. Anyway, I've been meaning to see you and congratulate you on your Salon acceptance. I admired the yellows in your apples and the greens in your bottles. If I'd known you were coming, I'd have put champagne on ice. Will you make do with tea?" Mary set a kettle over a spirit lamp, measured some cherry-bark tea, and arranged shell-shaped cookies and jam tarts on a plate.

"I'm glad the refusal didn't make you downcast." May looked at the pictures of women reading a newspaper, crocheting a scarf, or holding a baby, who looked soft as cake. Some brushstrokes remained rough, so that the signs of Mary's work, and how she loved it, showed. The colors reminded May of the froth of clouds or nougat, but the rigor of her lines balanced the delicate palette.

"I mourned for a day or two. Then Monsieur Degas asked me to show my work with *les Indépendants* next spring."

"That's wonderful! Won't you be the first woman to be included?"

"Berthe Morisot has exhibited with them. But I'll be the first American woman." Mary's smile was wide. She coaxed the dog onto her lap with a madeleine.

"So we both have cause to celebrate. It's just too bad that all the people who come to the Salon won't see your work, and buy it."

"That's why *le Société des Artistes Indépendants* holds a show the same time as the Salon, to take advantage of the crowds who come to the city. Monsieur Degas believes those who exhibit there should snub the Salon, but Messieurs Renoir and Monet have families and need to sell wherever they can. They fight about this, what they should call themselves, and what walls which paintings should go on."

"Now you will have a chance to argue."

"Yes. Some advocate painting *en plein air*, which enrages Monsieur Degas. He says all you need is a crumpled napkin to paint the sky. That there should be a special brigade of *gendarmes* to guard against artists who insist on painting from nature. Not to kill anyone. Just a bit of birdshot sent out as warning."

"You do admire him."

"Once I mentioned my loneliness. I didn't mean he should give me this dog." Mary scratched the griffon terrier's ears. "I was touched, as he doesn't even like dogs, or the country, or the seashore. All he cares about is his pictures. He sells some, then asks to have them back, with excuses that he needs to change the color of an elbow or add a layer of varnish. Then he keeps them. Monsieur Faure has taken to chaining his paintings to the walls, then tells him he lost the keys."

"You don't hole away your work."

"For all his gruff ways, he was the one who asked me to join the group. And it was he who invited Mademoiselle Morisot—now Madame Manet."

"She's married? Is she young?"

"Berthe is our age, with twenty years of painting behind her before she wed a year or two ago."

"What is her painting like?"

"She doesn't care for line as much as I do, but she paints women on balconies, or by windows, or the edges of gardens."

"Do you think she might have a baby?"

"I hope not. It's best to be thankful to miss the dangers of childbirth, then the diapers, the scuffles, and the noise."

"There are pleasures, too."

"Maybe I'd feel differently if there ever comes a day when little girls are given paintbrushes along with dolls. But for now, women must choose. We can be artists *or* mothers. It's not a sacrifice, really. Artists get at least two lives. The one we live, and the ones we bring into the world with paints and brushes."

May's heart beat with a sense of possibility she'd pushed down. So a woman could make art, find love, and, even at her age, have a child. She put down her china cup. "I'm afraid this call might be one to say good-bye. I'll be leaving Paris soon."

"What a shame!"

The genuine sorrow in her voice unsettled May, so that she revealed more than she'd intended. "I'm going to London for the summer, where I can put higher prices on my work now that I can say I've shown in the Salon. Then I'll go back to Massachusetts. Louisa has done more than her share. She writes about Mother's woes, but she suffers, too. Ever since John died after enduring pain like hers, she worries about how much time she has."

"None of us know that," Mary said. "But I understand. It is hard when a family member is ill." Her eyes strayed to the wall, where she'd tacked a drawing of her sister seated at a tapestry frame. "I'm grateful that Lydia still feels well enough to pose. Even if I could afford to pay a model, it would be scandalous for me to stop by the fountain at Place Pigalle as the men do."

"She doesn't mind sitting for portraits?" May asked.

"She doesn't complain of being bored or sore from holding a position."

May hadn't meant just the ability to keep from wiggling, holding an arm until it ached, but being the quiet sister, whose name would never be as well known. "Lydia never wanted to paint?"

"Oh, no. I don't think so. She always preferred anonymity to attention."

"A creative life has pleasures besides fame."

"She enjoys needlework and crochet, and listening to music."

Could that be enough? May wondered if she was the only person who'd competed with her sister for as long as she could remember. Was she greedy, or was it natural, having been making art so long, to want recognition? She asked, "Did you read my sister's book? It's wrong to complain, when Louisa is so generous. I didn't even pose. But it was difficult for me to see myself painted in words as I don't see myself."

"You didn't let that stop you from becoming who you wanted to be. Will you paint her?"

"I'd like to paint her in a crimson dress." May smiled as she stood, then took Mary's hand. "Your painting was turned down by the Salon for its power."

"This refusal gave me permission to use all the oranges, yellows, and reds I like most." Mary fixed her sharp dark eyes on her. "You should come to the Impressionist show. And see Berthe's work. I'll introduce you."

"I have so much to do to get ready to leave for England." May had already sent Rose's portrait of her with Miss Lombard, who was returning to Massachusetts, along with a program from the Salon and a note about how she wanted to take advantage of her chance to sell paintings before coming home. She picked up the dog, who wiggled in her arms.

"Will you come back here?"

"I want to." May knew that wasn't really an answer. She

wished she could say that she'd come next year, when Mary's paintings would be shown with the Impressionists. She looked at the half-finished painting of the little girl on a blue chair, then turned to pastels of a sister and mother, Mary's, though they might be anyone's. May felt warm and safe as if a blanket had been pulled up to her chin. All ambition, even jealousy, slid away. Could standing here among pictures of women tending babies, pouring tea, making tapestries, or reading newspapers be the best day of her life? How could she know? She rose on her toes as if for a closer look at a picture she hadn't yet seen but knew would be painted. A woman held a baby and a palette and paintbrush, too.

49

AN ARMFUL OF VIOLETS

he first morning that May returned to the room with wide drawers filled with Turner's pictures of storms, winters, and bogs, the other copyists stood and clapped softly, congratulating her on having a painting in the Salon. They welcomed her back, then sat back down at the long table. The caretaker's keys jangled as he filled cups with fresh water. Soon May set down translucent layers of ginger, vermilion, and cobalt blue to recreate storms and sunsets. She blurred outlines with a sponge, creating a sense of mist, or rubbed pigments into paper with a cloth instead of a brush, as Turner was said to have done.

On days when the National Gallery closed, she joined Jane in a studio where they split the rent. She painted panels of pale blooms that contrasted with black backgrounds, which remained popular, as were her still lifes. She also enjoyed evenings at the boarding house, joining mostly businessmen for dinners of joints of beef, legs of lamb, and Stilton cheese. Most of the men were ten or twenty years older than she was, and were glad for the company of a woman besides Jane or Mrs. Hammond, a young married woman who was usually busy with her little boy. May spoke brightly, with her eyes often shifting to a young man whose pale, slender face stood out among those that were rounder and ruddier. His loneliness hadn't hardened like that of the older men.

After dinner, some gathered in the common room to play dominoes, checkers, or whist. Sometimes May coaxed the men to put down their newspapers and play Hide the Thimble with four-year-old Harry Hammond. They also played Mother, May I?, they rushed about the room blowing to keep a feather in the air, and they tossed cards into a hat on the floor. Sometimes May told stories to Harry, who liked to sit on her lap and touch her hair. The young man, whom she'd learned came from Switzerland, seemed particularly enchanted when May abandoned fairy tales to tell about life growing up in New England with her sisters.

One evening, the young man brought down his violin and played a German folk tune. Firelight glowed on his soft mouth, chiseled nose, and pale throat, revealed by the top button of his linen shirt left open. His green eyes widened, then closed, as the poignant notes deepened. He coaxed his violin to hover on the edges of high notes it could never quite hold.

When he put down his bow, May asked, "Do you play in an orchestra, Mr. Nieriker?"

"Call me Ernst, please. My violin adds sweetness to my life, but I don't call myself a musician."

"Why not, when you play so well!"

"I love music, but few can make a living at it. I'll have a family to support one day."

"You're too young to think about such things."

"Not at all too young. I am twenty-two. Isn't that what everyone wants—to have a family?"

"My mother wanted her daughters to be able to earn a living." Her mouth felt dry as she did the calculations and realized there were sixteen years between them. How much she would have liked meeting a man like him, handsome, a bit shy, when she was younger, but she resolved not to waste moments by looking back or ahead.

"That's unusual, isn't it, for girls? Or maybe not so unusual in your country. My mother makes sure my sisters learn about art and music, but she would be surprised by someone like you, making a living with your hands. I think she would like it. She would like you."

"My mother would enjoy hearing such playing as yours." At least without any chance of a romance, she might confide in him as a friend. She said, "I worry about her. My sister's letters are about how her stomach ailments are worse, which could be a crisis, or just the expected troubles of age. I expect the latter. My mother writes that she doesn't need me."

"Your mother would not lie."

"I'm afraid she would, to make me feel better. I won't go back till spring, to care for her the way she once did everything for us. She made sure we had not only food and a roof, but costumes to dress up as pilgrims or princesses." May shook her head. "Most girls grow out of their dreams."

"Your mother must be proud to have daughters who wouldn't give up."

May thought she'd been wrong to choose such an intimate subject, and she changed it. "You haven't told me much about your work."

"Our company arranges to ship ore from South America. We supply metals to scientists who want to make a new sort of gas lamp. They seek materials that will glow but not burn out when a current passes through. This electricity is being studied by Thomas Edison, an American. Do you know him?"

"America is a big country."

"Yes. Someday I hope to visit."

"You must," May exclaimed, then she made her voice even. "Please explain. I don't understand how light can come from—nothing."

"The scientists have made clear glass bulbs, and they want to make filaments that will glow with heat, but won't burn out like wicks. Imagine, no more smoky lampshades to clean."

His English was good, but she kept her gaze on his lips in an effort to understand his German accent, sounds that seemed to rise from deep in his throat. She asked, "Then you like your work?"

"Only an American would ask that." He laughed. "My job has less science than I hoped. I oversee numbers and correspondence. But I look forward to the evenings."

She shook her head again, aware the firelight might catch in her hair. "Do you want to play a game of chess?"

He nodded, and they set a board on a hassock between their chairs.

As the evenings grew longer and chillier, more people stayed by the hearth, which they kept feeding with logs. May and Ernst often played chess, a game just for two. When he leaned forward, she could smell the starch of his linen shirt. Sometimes their hands almost touched. It seemed harmless enough, a pleasant way to end long days of work. She sketched London sights and could now fetch sixty or seventy dollars for some Turner copies. She recorded her sale figures and purchases in a small notebook—every bit of lace, each thumbnail-sized block of paint, every sold picture. For the first time, the row of money coming in was more than what she spent. She wrote to her family saying that since she was making enough money to support herself, and wasn't sure when that could happen again, at least not by selling art, she'd decided to stay through the fall and winter. She hoped they would understand.

❧

LATE ONE AFTERNOON, MAY RUSHED OUT OF A STORM into the boarding house anteroom, shaking cold rain from her skirt. Making her way around a jumble of drying umbrellas, she looked up to see Ernst, with his lovely mouth slightly open. Behind him, Harry Hammond sat on the stairs, bumping his way down.

"Hello, my little chipmunk." May crouched and opened her arms, but Harry didn't rush toward her. His round face was curiously solemn. "My mum wants you."

May looked up to see her coming down the stairs, holding an envelope edged in black. As May tore it, a small, coiled lock of gray hair fell. Tears filled her eyes even before she read the note in Louisa's hand: "Marmee is at rest."

May sank to the carpet, her skirts skimming around her. She threw her arms around Ernst's knees and kept holding on as if his body held her to the earth. His fingertips lightly touched her head. She tried to stand, and she stumbled. He helped her to a chair, where she bent under the force of her tears. Why hadn't Louisa or Father sent a telegram, or written more to her sooner? Why hadn't she paid attention to the warnings?

She excused herself and went upstairs to her room. She threw herself on her bed and sobbed. She'd never expected this; she should have expected this. Why did her mother have to die now, without May there to brush her hair from her brow? Had the portrait Rose painted reminded her mother of her or just her absence? Had she been glad about what May was doing or simply lonesome?

In a while, Jane brought up a plate of beef with a roll and a tumbler of sherry sent by another concerned boarder. "Everyone sends their sympathy."

"Please thank them, and tell them I'm all right, but don't want to be disturbed." May asked her to bring back the food she couldn't eat, then fell back on her bed. During lulls in her tears, she could hear soft footsteps that paused outside her door as if her sentinel were listening to be sure she breathed. She heard a whisper with a German accent, and the word *alone*.

Alone. Had she ever really chosen that? What she felt that night, and through the following days, was less a longing to be by herself than finding she didn't want to talk. She had no words for her exhaustion from all the things she hadn't done.

She couldn't complain that she'd been sent away, for she'd made that choice herself. She reread Louisa's letters and put the lock of hair on her mantelpiece, along with the note it had been folded between: "A talisman for you. All the silver Marmee left."

It took an effort to get out of bed in the morning and open her sketchbook. Even as she lifted her pencil, tears blurred her vision. She heard Harry race up and down the hall, then bounce a ball against her door, which she finally opened. He bolted in and announced that his mother didn't feel well and he had nobody to play with. She helped him name the colors in her paint box and wound the crank on her music box so he could dance.

That evening, she came down for supper. Afterward, she sat with Ernst in the common room. Her throat felt scraped as she said, "I was wrong. I don't want to be alone."

"Of course not. Will you tell me about your dear mother?"

"She was elderly, but she'd endured so much that I supposed she'd live at least ten more years. Still, I should have been there, making gingerbread. Such things gave her a little pleasure."

"She must have been glad her daughter saw lands she could not."

"I hope so. She was forgiving and strong. She loved music. I wish she could have heard you play the violin."

"She would have liked Mr. Edison's invention. You turn a crank, like on a music box, but the phonograph is bigger. You can hear many kinds of music, not just one tune."

"Yes, she might have enjoyed that. She should have gone to more concerts. There was always so much plain sewing to do that she never had time for fancy work. She tended to potatoes and carrots, but she never grew roses. Did she really prefer lilies of the valley, or did she think she had no choice? At least she knew I'd had a picture in the Salon. But now that I've finally done something she can be proud of, she's gone. Every painting I ever made, I wanted her to see."

"Miss Hughes told me you haven't yet been to your studio. It was your work that kept you here. It would be wrong to stop."

"I don't know what's right or wrong."

But as the December days grew long and dark, she supposed it was foolish to stay upstairs, adding sticks to the fire, when she could sit by a shared hearth. Ernst read to her or played his violin while she sewed. The slightest motion of his slim, pale hands brought out deep and wildly varied notes, vibrations that soothed an ache inside her. He sang German lullabies in a low voice that seemed to tremble through her body. She looked up from her mending to his chiseled chin, his nose with its little dent near the top.

Many people at the boarding house left for Christmas and New Year's, but May arranged pine boughs around the picture of Mother on her mantel and was pleased that Ernst stayed in London, too. They often sat in the common room, where he talked about his seven sisters and one brother, who he deeply missed. At this time of year, his mother made star-shaped cookies or rolled ones filled with chopped nuts. He told May that he was becoming more frustrated with his job and was looking for one that might make better use of his talents.

"My father runs a shop, where I used to help, and thinks I should be grateful for my good position. I could not be contented as he is selling cigars. The way of the future is with big stores, like Harrods, where busy modern women can buy clothing, medicine, perfume, fruits, and vegetables. Some ladies enjoy going from shop to shop, but working women like you want everything in one place."

"And don't forget your music."

"I won't. And you must promise me you'll paint."

The next day, May went to the studio, which seemed filled with so many memories and regrets that it was all she could do to stand still. She left after twenty minutes. But day by day, her breathing grew more even, and she stayed longer. Loneliness may have sharpened her vision, but her wrist and elbow didn't move with its former verve or conviction. Nothing felt worthwhile, though she worked on another painting of the stuffed owl she'd brought from Paris, brushing on layers of oil paint and shellac to make the canvas darker and shinier. She planned to submit it to the Ladies Exhibition and perhaps the Salon, which would be accepting entries again soon.

One evening, not for the first time, Ernst asked to see some of her work. She brought her old sketchbooks from France and Switzerland to the common room.

"I have never seen the mountains as you've drawn them. And what charming chalets. And the goats!" He turned the pages enthusiastically, then stopped and frowned at one. "Who is this young man?"

"He was the son of our landlady in Brittany."

"What odd clothing." He flipped to the next page in her sketchbook, his mouth relaxing as his gaze fell on poppies in a churchyard. "These are as fine as anything done by Rembrandt. By Raphael!"

"Such different artists." May spoke quickly, to hide her pleasure in the compliment, though she thought she'd labored too long over the flowers, rendered too much detail, when the blossoms might be more recognizable as dabs of red. "One man is Dutch and shows some flaws in his portraits. The other is Italian and paints everything rosier than it can be."

"I'm afraid I know little about art. I haven't been to Holland or Italy."

"There are paintings by Rembrandt and Raphael right here in the National Gallery."

"I've never been there either."

"When you've lived in London for months?"

"Perhaps I've been waiting for the right guide. Will you show me around?"

An outing seemed inappropriate while she was in mourning, but how could she refuse, when he'd been so kind? She put on a dress that was a brighter blue than those she'd recently worn, with a skirt gathered in puffs and rouches. She couldn't help enjoying walking beside a man who was almost as tall as she was, whose cravat was almost the same plum color as his mouth, and whose shirt was probably from Charvet. He took her arm and kept it within his as they maneuvered down a crowded sidewalk to Bedford Square, where an old woman sold hot potatoes from a barrow. A one-man band held pipes under his chin, while beating his elbow on a drum worn on his back, clanging cymbals by tugging a string tied to his foot, and ringing a triangle. Ernst listened to a musician with a torn, baggy coat. He nodded in appreciation and dropped a few shillings into his open fiddle case. May stopped to watch a little girl raise her arm to toss a stone onto a hopscotch square drawn in chalk on the sidewalk. Her petticoat peeked from under her coat as she lifted one leg and hopped on the other. Landing on the last square, she triumphantly lifted her sharp chin.

"See the sunlight caught in her hair?" May said.

Ernst gently pushed her forward, so she wouldn't block pedestrians. "Did your mother think twice before sending you on errands? You must have been gone for hours."

"I did get scolded for dawdling, but Louisa wasn't any better. She'd come home with stories. Father often forgot altogether why he'd been sent out, and Beth was too shy to go. My poor mother had to rely on Anna." She looked back at the girl who hopped over the chalked squares. She was about the age May had been when she'd handed out flyers for her father's talk. She couldn't explain how the sky had seemed to lift, but she told him about being mistaken for a beggar.

"I hate to think of you as being sad." His soft forehead wrinkled, and his hand moved toward hers, though they didn't touch.

At the National Gallery, she showed him paintings by Turner and Constable, artists who could say so much with clouds. Then, remembering why they'd come, she led him past blue-robed angels in a room of Italian paintings. She pointed to a Madonna with a round-headed baby sprawled across her lap. "That's by Raphael."

"What woman could look at that and not long to have a child?" His eyes returned to her hand, which she dropped.

"I believe we're supposed to think of the Nativity." She stepped over to Raphael's *Vision of a Knight* for a look at a man seeming to have just woken up on the ground. He'd raised himself on an elbow to peer at a fair-haired woman holding a lily. Beside her, a woman with brown hair raised a sword and a book. May said, "He's supposed to be choosing between Aphrodite and Athena, goddess of wisdom."

"Of course he will choose the goddess of love."

May smiled as if he'd meant this as a joke, then led him to a room of Dutch paintings. She pointed out Vermeer's honey-colored light and said, "It's better to look at Rembrandt in the morning, when this room gets more sun."

"Once incandescent lights are perfected, the museums should be the first places to get them."

"I wish I understood more about this electricity. I'm afraid science didn't have much place in my father's curriculum. Nor business practices, not once we'd learned our sums."

"Who would have expected the daughter of a philosopher and the son of a businessman to become friends?"

May blushed and turned to *A Woman Bathing in a Stream.* The woman who lifted her chemise above her thighs to wade in green, golden, and red water wasn't young or slender, but the light made her bare skin glow. "Rembrandt usually painted on commission, but they say he painted this one only for himself."

"The lady was his lover?"

"She might have been." May's face grew still warmer. "It's not as finished as his other work. See the left shoulder and the shadow under her chemise? Scraping away can have as much effect as a stroke of paint. But you look like you might have had enough art for one day."

They walked through a park, then warmed up in a tea shop

where footmen hovered behind ladies, watching their umbrellas and shopping baskets, and where silver sugar tongs, tiered trays, dishes of marmalade, and teapots glistened. They ate small sandwiches filled with watercress or cucumbers sliced as thin as leaves. May bit into a scone smeared with clotted cream that spread deliciously to every inner surface of her mouth. She said, "We don't have such cream in Massachusetts. I suppose our cows work too hard."

As winter passed, they began walking every weekend. On a Saturday in March, they strolled on a pathway near the Thames. Massive brownstone breweries, smokestacks, and turrets cast reflections on the water. They saw canal boats tugged by old horses and lumber boats with yellow sails, but it was still too chilly for pleasure barges to be out. May told Ernst about the Concord River. "It's narrower and slower, but I suppose that's why more can grow in it. Pickerelweed has pretty blue flowers. Once I rowed before dawn to see water lilies open."

"Rowing so early in the morning? By yourself?" His forehead wrinkled.

She didn't want to talk about Julian. She'd only remembered folding her hand around the slick stem, the closed petals that fit in her palm. She said, "I went with a friend."

"Did you have many friends?"

"Not so very many."

"Who could not adore you?"

Her chest grew warm, though she told herself he was being kind, not romantic.

"Darling," he said, and he entwined his fingers with hers.

She didn't pull away her hand. She longed to unbutton her

glove and feel his skin on hers, keep hearing the river lap and Ernst's breath not far from her neck. As he linked her arm through his, he tugged her close enough to feel the heat through their clothing. She said, "We'll go rowing one day."

"When the water gets warmer. But May, I won't be here long. I wrote to my father that I am not so happy in my work, as you've said I must be. He contacted a friend who helps manage one of the *grands magasins*, the big stores that sell most everything in Paris. There could be a job for me there."

"You're leaving?" She pushed her lips into a fragile smile, reminding herself that she had expected this, or she should have. Her throat felt cool again, her breath short as she understood his endearment had been casual. She'd been foolish to allow herself to think he could be expecting they might have more than this afternoon.

"May, I haven't spoken because I don't know what to do. My office also offered me a position in Russia."

"Choose Paris! If I knew what would happen to my mother, I never would have left."

"Then we would not have met! I'd like to see Paris through your eyes. But each asks that I work for at least a year. How could I leave you for that long?"

"Ernst, I mustn't keep you from your future."

"My future! May, it's nothing without you. Would you be sorry if I left?" The green flecks in his eyes darkened.

"Of course I would."

"But would it be dreadful? Would you wait for me? I must reply to these offers, but how can I leave when your heart hurts?"

"I'll go back to Massachusetts after the danger of spring

storms is past. And you must follow the work that brings you happiness."

"All my joy comes from you. Even in your time of grief, you bring me more than I thought possible. May . . ."

"You mustn't say such things." She pulled out her lace-edged handkerchief and shook her head. "I thought I was over my crying."

"You must not apologize for tears."

"Sometimes it seems as if my mother died just days ago. Sometimes it seems like years."

"You're mourning."

"And Louisa would be horrified if she knew I was out strolling."

"You haven't written to your family about me? Why, I've written pages about you to my mother and brother!"

"Of course I've written about you."

"And what did you say?"

"That I met a charming young Swiss gentleman." She felt something tremble in her throat, and she forced a prim tone. "Who comforts me in my sorrow. We should turn back. I'm poor company today."

"I like your shining eyes, but you are beautiful, too, when you're sad."

The sun was starting to set. Their elbows jostled as they headed to the boarding house, silently walking through Bedford Square. Near the statue of the duke stood a pale girl wearing a torn dress that fell in loose folds from her waist. Holding a basket of violets in one hand and a tin cup in the other, she cried, "A bunch for a ha'penny."

Ernst took a gold coin from his pocket. "We'll take them all."

He scooped the violets from her basket and filled May's arms. She buried her face among the loose leaves and purple blossoms. Tears blurred her vision, so the edges of the flowers blended.

"I wish it could be a whole garden." He opened his arms and pulled her to him. The violets crushed slightly, which brought out their fragrance.

Stepping back, she said, "I don't have enough vases. Where will I put them all?"

"Enjoy them just tonight," he said.

At the boarding house, she left him at the landing, which smelled of beef and cabbages cooking for supper. Alone in her room, she dropped the violets on her bed. Breathing hard, maybe from hurrying up the stairs, she unlatched her paint box, poured water from her pitcher into a cup, and mixed colors on her palette. Without stepping back to consider perspective, she swept her biggest paintbrush so the bristles splayed on the thick paper. Her hold was confident but loose as a stem in a breeze. She was lavish with water, so the colors blurred. No certain lines separated grief and love, life as it is and hope, all the reasons not to love and all the reasons why she should.

She tossed a few broken branches on the hearth, held a burning stick under the lamp's glass globe, then went back to painting the coverlet she changed from blue to lemon yellow on her paper, so the blooms would stand out. Her wrist remained loose, but she was choosing every stroke, catching colors that would never glow just as they did now. She made more bold strokes even as the growing darkness made it hard to see the differences between green and purple, the unfurling or withering of blooms, with an imperfect beauty all their own.

At last she put down her brush. How long had she been painting? She breathed deep and fast, as if she'd finished a long race, but her arms and legs ached with an urge to move. And she was hungry. She headed downstairs. Ernst was at the bottom landing, pacing the way he had when guarding her door after her mother died. He said, "May, I'm sorry. I should never have dared to speak, but . . ."

"There's nothing to be sorry for. Nothing was said." She held up her hand, then swallowed to soothe the sting at the back of her throat, a blistering as if she'd tried to reach impossibly high notes of a song. "I was painting."

"Good."

"It may be the best work I've ever done."

"Can I see?"

"Now?"

"Please."

She went upstairs and brought down the watercolor of a river of violets on a sun-colored spread. "It might not look finished, but I like the sense of possibility that's left."

"It's beautiful." His green eyes were wide open. She believed that he saw not only the red and purple violets, but also all her grief and hunger. He might even understand that she didn't paint only for sales or acclaim, but that she wanted people to see what she saw. This painting, more than any she'd done before, seemed full of revelation. Whatever happened now, she had this painting, with its shimmer like that of a river that never stopped moving.

"Do you know if anything's left from supper?" she asked.

"It's late. The cook went home hours ago. Maybe the woman who sells potatoes on the square is out. Can I get you one or two?"

"I'll go."

"Please, let me come with you."

She got a shawl, then they walked to the dark square. An old woman wrapped in a blanket perched on a stool, hunched over a barrow of glowing coals. She might have been sleeping. She didn't raise her head until May and Ernst stood close enough to feel the heat, then asked, "How many?"

"One for me."

"Two, please." Ernst told the woman, who uncurled her chapped hands to grasp a fork she used to poke and lift large potatoes from the glowing coals. "Should I break the skins?"

"Leave them, please, so they'll keep warm," Ernst said.

The woman scooped salt from a tin into brown paper. She sliced a bit of butter and a slab of Cheshire cheese off a block, handed everything to Ernst, then wrapped herself deeper in her blanket.

May and Ernst stopped in a shop for a bottle of wine, then brought their meal to the common room. It was late enough so that everyone had gone upstairs. May put a log on the fire. She unbuttoned her shoes, slipped them off, and sat on the rug while Ernst poured the wine. He handed her his pocketknife, but May broke the wedge of crumbly cheese in two. Food and wine warmed her mouth. She ate with appetite, then turned to Ernst and ran her fingertips, slightly slick from the butter, along the sides of his beautiful face. He kissed her softly, so she felt the curves of his lips and hers. She tasted the salty corner of his mouth, heard his heart pound, smelled the grassy scent of his linen shirt and burning firewood.

May leaned back. "We mustn't. We should go back to our rooms."

"How can we sleep?"

"Is it too late to walk to the river?"

"It's not too late." He stood, then reached for her hand, which pulsed as if with small fireworks. They headed through the gaslit streets to the Thames. Barges and boats tugged on lines that held them to wharves. London Bridge loomed, dark and Gothic, guarded by sentinels holding lanterns. People in tattered clothes huddled in its shadows, trying to keep out of the wind.

"I don't ever want to leave you." Ernst folded her hand in his and faced her. His eyelashes hid his eyes for a moment. Then they lifted, and his gaze fixed steadily on hers. "Will you marry me?"

May nodded, slightly, not because the answer *yes* didn't fill her body, but because it filled it so much she couldn't speak. Her breath caught in her throat, then rushed through her chest. Their embrace made it catch again, then move still faster. She stepped away.

"But you should know. I've never told you. I'm thirty . . ." She was about to add the "seven," but seeing his chin drop, she swerved from truth and said, ". . . or almost."

"Impossible! You look . . ." He nodded too many times, even as he said, "It doesn't matter."

"You can change your mind."

"No."

"We've only known each other for a few months."

"So it would be wrong to lose even one of the days ahead. We'll find a ring. If we wait, I could afford a diamond."

"I don't want a jewel. Paint could catch in the setting. And I can't stop painting now. I've worked hard to get this far."

"I would never want you to stop doing what you love."

"It's hard for a woman to paint if she's managing a household."

"We'll find a housekeeper, one who cooks. And one day, someone to mind our children."

"Children. I don't even know if that's possible for me."

"Anything is possible. Haven't you told me that? We must have at least four. At least two of them girls. As beautiful as you."

"You think everything should turn out perfectly. Just as easily as that?"

"Why not?"

She touched the soft skin below his eyes, the lovely dent near the top of his nose. Her mouth opened over his. His arms circled her trembling body. They kissed, then let go. He lifted her, leaning backward, then gently set her down and shouted, "We're getting married!"

"Shhh," she said, though neither the bridge guards nor vagrants turned to look. "When? Where?"

"Anywhere!"

"You spoke of taking a job in Russia."

"France is closer. We could cross the Channel to visit each other."

"To visit? We were talking about marriage."

"I could work for a year before our wedding, and save money."

"Let's marry first. Then I can come with you. And not lose a day."

"Darling, a year isn't so long."

"A year is forever." May looked out to the river, where the browns and green-golds were restoring themselves, as if by a painter who'd scraped everything off her canvas then began again with a certain hand.

"Do you forget I have sisters? I know how long it can take to plan for bouquets, a cake, and champagne. It may take a year to have a gown made fit for a princess. And I'll need to earn money for our home."

"I don't care about a fancy wedding. And I could live with you anywhere."

"Don't you want time to go see your sisters first? Or give them time to come be with you?"

May thought of how she'd crossed the sea safely a few times, but there was always a chance a ship might strike icebergs or sail into storms. She was only a little afraid of all the younger women Ernst might meet in a year. She was lucky, but she was old enough to know how swiftly luck could turn.

"My sisters would understand I had my great chance and took it."

"Then I suppose my family might come to England, or would you rather see my home in Switzerland? We could marry in our church."

"I've waited long enough." May wondered what his mother

would think of a woman who might not be much younger than she was. And how would she tell Louisa that she wasn't coming back? If they married in a few weeks, there would hardly be time for her letter and a reply to cross the Atlantic. She wouldn't have to hear what Louisa thought about a wedding so soon after Mother's death, or know if she could forgive her. She said, "Let's get married right away. Then we could travel together to your new job. If we go soon, the chestnut trees will be in bloom."

They ducked under the bridge's long shadows.

"The business owner hoped I would not delay. Do you really think you could be ready to go by April?"

She ran two fingertips down his neck and said, "Even sooner."

20

THE GOLD RİNG

May propped up her looking glass, pinned back the front of her hair, then curled the back locks. She put on the silk gown she'd worn to opening day at the Salon, after stitching topaz bands of piping above the hem and around the cuffs she'd shortened to show her wrists. She went downstairs to say goodbye to some gathered friends. Then she and Jane climbed into a carriage that took them to the Registry. Ernst was waiting with Mr. Ramsey in a ledger-lined office. An official asked a few questions and seemed satisfied with short answers. There were no lacy veils, admiring crowds, fiddles, dancing, or sisters by her side, but what mattered were the plain gold band Ernst slipped on her finger and his simple words: "I do. I will."

They took a train to the harbor, where May mailed a brief letter home about the wedding, promising to send her sisters her new address the minute she was settled in France. She expected they'd be surprised, maybe even shocked, though wasn't a kind and handsome young man what she'd always wanted? May and Ernst boarded a ferry with yellow rails and a green roof. Seagulls opened their wings as if they carried the sky above the English Channel. Ernst wrapped his hand around her wrist as they stood on the deck, their sides rocking together. He whispered, "May," over and over, which seemed what she'd wanted for so long. For someone to say her name with all his breath. Then he said, "A gift from the blue sea you love." He handed her a box with pearl earrings that were rounded, smooth, and caught light, like the buds of water lilies.

"I wish it could be more, and it will. A necklace one day," he said.

"Darling, I have everything."

In Le Havre, they left their trunks and portmanteaus in the customs house, took one valise, and wandered past piers, fishing cottages, taverns, and casinos, looking for signs that said: *Chambre à louer.* When they found a promising suite, May introduced herself to the innkeeper as Madame Nieriker, feeling giddy as a girl playing house. Her heart pounded even more once she and Ernst were alone in a room. She looked at the view of the water, then shut the curtains. He gently unwound the band on her hat, ducked under the brim, and kissed her softly. Her head felt light as he took off her hat and set it on a bureau. Their lips pressed open each other's mouths, urgently but without haste. Her knees gave. She placed his hands on her hips.

He bent to kiss each of her hands. "Let's put away our things and make everything nice."

She smiled. She hadn't expected him to be shy. "Aren't we staying just for the night?"

"I like it here, don't you? Let's stay a few days before going on to Paris." He put his starched and ironed shirts in the oak wardrobe. As he lit candles, he sang a Bellini aria so softly that his voice was more vibration than sound.

May pulled down the crimson coverlet on the canopied bed. "I've always loved red."

"And blue. And yellow and brown and green."

He slid his lips over the back of her neck and unfastened the long row of buttons. Her dress rustled as it fell to the floor. She slipped her fingers through his thick, wavy hair. "I want to take off your clothes."

He blushed as she unhooked his cuff links and kissed the downy tops of his wrists. She pushed the buttons through the slits in his shirt, then pulled it off. She wanted to kiss his long neck and collarbones, but she made herself stand back and look as carefully as if she were going to draw him. The hair on his chest was lighter than his hard, chestnut-colored nipples. Ernst pulled down his trousers and drawers. He touched himself with a look of both pride and embarrassment. He was so young, his skin smooth over the firm muscles in his chest and thighs. She moved close enough for him to reach under her petticoats and slide his hand upward. She pulled him onto the bed, where he lifted her chemise, unhooked her corset, and peeled down her silk stockings.

"May I touch you?" he asked.

"Yes."

"Here?"

She nodded.

"Here?"

"Yes." She loved his manners, his skin warming hers. Candlelight cast shadows on the ceiling. Her breath plunged deeper than she'd known it could go. Something inside her throbbed. She cried, then laughed. Who would have thought that pain, when touched, could pass into pleasure?

The next morning, the innkeeper smiled when they came down late for breakfast, and again when, leaving their milky coffee in glass bowls, they returned to their room. They spent most of the next few days on or under the crimson bedspread, sleeping curled around each other, waking to find their hands on each other's bodies. One afternoon, after much unlinking, unbuttoning, and uncovering, May dipped her fingers in rose-scented oil and drew a map over her body, marking places where she wanted to be touched. The warmth of his hands lifted the fragrance from her neck, wrists, the sides of her torso, and between her thighs.

Neither wanted to leave the room, but they needed to look for a home before Ernst's work began. They took a train to Paris and found a room in Montmartre to let. In the morning, they began looking for an apartment in the neighborhood where cats slept on cracked stone steps, horses pulled yellow wagons loaded with cartons of eggs and baskets of cheese, and boys milked goats before customers' doors. In a park, men played dominoes under plane trees. All the apartments they considered seemed not quite right, but this didn't touch their happiness that evening, as they ate dinner at the Moulin de la Galette, then danced under the globed lamps strung between acacia trees.

The next morning, they viewed a few more apartments, which were discouraging enough for May to suggest reviving their eyes with some art. They headed down the hills and walked by the Seine, where boats with four-sided sails cast shadows shaped like fins. They crossed a bridge and entered the Jardin de Tuileries. Tulips, hyacinths, and irises grew in crescent, circular, and fleur-de-lis patterns. *Bonnes* pushed prams or watched over children who crouched by the edge of a circular pool, prodding toy sailboats with sticks.

In the Louvre, May headed straight to the *Venus de Milo*, which made Ernst gasp. As they made their way past other art, she noticed he looked more at people than at statues and paintings, the way Louisa had at museums. She heard someone call her name and turned to see two women whom she'd met in Monsieur Krug's studio. After excited greetings, she introduced Ernst to Fanny and Caroline. Their words were gracious, but she could see the surprise on their faces. May's friends in London were used to Ernst, and the French weren't quick to raise eyebrows, but these Americans reminded May of how much younger he was than she was.

Caroline, who wore a gown embroidered with peacock feathers, asked May if she had a painting in the Salon.

"It will open soon, won't it? I didn't submit anything this spring." May thought of the past months in which her mother had died, she'd fallen in love, and she learned to paint with a looser hand and brighter colors. She'd had every reason not to send something to the jury; still, she was sorry that she'd missed a chance. "And what about you?"

"No luck yet."

"I'll leave you to get reacquainted," Ernst excused himself and sat on a bench, watching a little girl who kept trying to break away from her mother's hand to dance.

May asked her old classmates if they'd seen Miss Cassatt.

"I heard she didn't submit work to the Salon this year," Caroline replied. "The Impressionists demand that no one may show with them and at the Salon as well. She agreed, only to have this year's Impressionist show canceled. No galleries were willing to rent them space, not when they can make more money from all the tourists coming to the World's Fair. People who might want a real painting as a souvenir, not scratches and scrawls that are insults to the old masters."

"Have you been to the exposition, May? You can walk through the head of the Statue of the Liberty, which will be sent to New York soon," Fanny said.

"We hope to go. There's so much to do. First, my husband and I must find a place to live. Now I'd better go find him."

"He's handsome," Caroline said, but after May said goodbye and began searching for Ernst, she heard her say to the other, "I suppose he knows she has a rich sister."

May's face burned as she greeted Ernst. They walked through a few more galleries before heading down the grand stairs for another look at the *Venus de Milo*. On their way out, they stopped at the shop, where he bought a plaster copy of the statue with a forthright gaze, broken arms, and perfect breasts and torso. He whispered, "She reminds me of you."

She wanted to throw her arms around him right in the museum and kiss him deeply, coming up only for air. But even in Paris, all she could do was smile and ache and wonder if they were right to look for a home in the city. Maybe there were too many rooms in the Louvre, too many cabarets in Montmartre, too many soirees where she might want to show off her ring, and too much gossip. All could become distractions from what was important.

That night, she suggested they look for homes outside the city.

"But you love Paris," he said.

"We wouldn't move far, but find a town on the rail line so you could get to work without much trouble."

"Won't you miss your friends and the museums?"

"Now that I have you, I don't care so much about company."

"You were so eager to show Miss Cassatt your violets."

"I'll show her later. Right now, we need to make a home."

"If it's what you want, then we will look for a little house in the country."

The next day, they heard about a cottage in Meudon, which was about seven miles south of Paris. They took the train there and toured the kitchen, parlor, and two bedrooms.

"It's charming," May said. "Though isn't the rent more than we should spend? And what a view!" Beyond rose and currant bushes was a hill where lime trees grew around an abandoned château with partially burned towers.

They went into the other bedroom, where Ernst opened the tall window. "We can see the river!"

As she stood by his side, he grabbed her by the waist and lifted her. "We'll get a rowboat. You can find your water lilies. I'll gather them all for you." As he put her down, he lifted her hair off her shoulders. She felt a breeze on the back of her neck.

❧

THE COTTAGE CAME FURNISHED, BUT BEFORE ERNST began work helping manage a *grand magasin*, they unpacked and fixed up the rooms. They bought pots of pink geraniums for the windowsills. May rubbed the bedposts with beeswax and piled satin pillows under the blue canopy. She hung some of her landscapes in the *salon* and gave the portrait she called *La Négresse* the place of honor on an easel. She set her stuffed owl on a table in the second bedroom, by the French windows that opened like a door. "This will be a fine room for a studio."

"Yes. I'm sorry you'll be taken from it when we have guests."

"I love being just with you. Let's wait a little longer to have company." She expected that he might have written to his mother that she was a "few" years older, which was what she'd written to her family. Now that they had an address, she must write to her sisters. She didn't expect Anna to leave her boys, but Louisa might come to visit.

"It will also be a good room for a baby," he said.

"Hush." It seemed bad luck to want too much. "We have everything now."

"Of course. But children would bring even more joy."

"Do you still think you can have everything you want?"

"I never expected so much. Then you told me, *yes*. I have more than I ever dreamed was possible."

Soon they hired a *femme de ménage*, though after kissing Ernst good-bye each morning, May busied herself with housework, too, for Adrienne didn't always do things just the way she liked. May swept the floor and set a bowl of cream on a windowsill for the neighbor's cat. She exchanged a few words with the girl who stopped with her wheelbarrow of carrots and turnips. Meudon didn't seem much bigger than Concord, but May's French wasn't good enough for her to become familiar with most neighbors. But having grown used to starting work after a hike from her rooms to a studio, she walked in the morning, passing a man leading a donkey pulling a milk wagon, women carrying straw baskets, and clerics in long black robes headed to church. She sometimes climbed the hill to the château for a view of red-roofed villas, windmills, woods, and the river winding through the valley.

She returned home, then brought her watercolors to the garden, which smelled of clover, meadow saffron, mallow, and mint. She filled her palette with blues, reds, and yellows, then, rather than trying to sketch the details of every stem and blossom, worked as lightly and quickly as the leaves blown in the wind. Before the paints had a chance to dry, she swiftly chose whether to tip her paper to let the colors run or follow a mistake to somewhere new. She let her brush flutter as often as it landed, creating a gray-blue sky that blurred the lines between the distant hill and flowers near her feet, the way memory shaded the present.

Late in the afternoon, she tacked her watercolors on the wall to dry. The housekeeper fixed dinner, then tactfully disappeared just before Ernst came home.

"My darling," he shouted one evening, as if they'd been apart for weeks instead of the day. He handed May a long loaf of bread and a Delft vase.

"It's beautiful." She held up the vase to the light, standing by their mirror with a black-and-gilt frame, which he'd already brought home and which was tall enough to reflect the whole *salon*, with its deep scarlet rug and drapes they'd bought at the *Bon Marché*. "But no more presents. We promised to watch our money."

"We must celebrate our first month of marriage."

She kissed him, and said, "More mail came."

They unwrapped a package from his parents, a handsome box with May's new initials, "M. A. N.," embossed in gold. Inside were rows of silver forks, spoons, and knives padded in velvet. Ernst began translating the letter his mother had written in German, then hurried through it and summed up. "My mother is surprised, of course. Her first child to marry and she wasn't there, but she understands we didn't want to wait. She's anxious to meet you."

May opened the letter from Louisa, who wished them luck and enclosed a check. May was grateful, but she couldn't help feeling the money was not only a gift but also a message that Louisa didn't believe the two of them could make their own way.

A few weeks later, May polished the candelabra, cut back the geraniums, and arranged to rent a piano. She left up her watercolors of the garden but took down the nude drawings of Ernst she'd tacked on the bedroom walls. Adrienne's cooking was good, but May gave her some days off and experimented with several fancy dishes. At the last minute, she decided against them all and asked Ernst to bring salmon salad, Gervais cheese, and a pâté back from Paris. She arranged fruit in their grape-leaf bowl and rolled pale yellow napkins to set beside the shining silver. She picked up the cat, who smelled of lavender after napping in the garden.

The next afternoon, she and Ernst walked to the train station. Smoke spewed from the locomotive as it slowed to a stop. Ernst ran toward his mother, sister, and brother, who took turns lifting each other and pounding each other's arms. A slim woman wearing a nicely tailored traveling dress looked from her sons to May. Beside her, a young woman wore a pink dress with a black band around her waist. Both were quite tall and had blond-brown hair. Ernst's mother's hair was a little darker and his sister's a little lighter than May's.

"May, is it all right if I call you that?" Madame Nieriker walked forward. After hesitating a moment, she put her hands on May's arms. She twisted around and said, "Ernst, you never told me how beautiful your wife is!"

"*Maman,* I told you in every one of my letters!" Ernst introduced Sophie, then pulled off his brother's hat. "Max, race you to the house!"

Their feet stirred dust as they ran. When Ernst sprinted ahead, Max threw out an arm. They scuffled, laughed, yelled, and ran again. As the women climbed the hill, May pointed out her favorite chestnut trees. Madame Nieriker exclaimed over the cottage. "*C'est adorable!*" She proclaimed the *salon* charming and headed straight toward the painting May called *La Négresse.* "That's such an attractive easel. I'd like to set up one like it. It makes the room look so artistic."

"And a good painting," Sophie added.

"Yes. Ernst, you didn't tell me how talented your wife is!"

"Of course I did, *Maman*!"

After supper, May, Madame Nieriker, and Sophie, who was about fifteen, played cards. Ernst and his brother lounged on the sofa with their arms around each other, laughing and talking in German, English, and French. Ernst spoke of his work in the department store, and Max described what he did as an architect in Baden. Ernst pored over the plans he spread on the table, then said, "I only wish the buildings might be lighted incandescently. Scientists know how to do it, but they aren't certain how to divide electricity so it can be measured as easily as gas is rationed."

The brothers argued about whether the British Mr. Swan or the American Mr. Edison had the better ideas. Ernst mentioned that some men traveled to Brazil to get platinum to test as filaments in light bulbs.

"We should go!" Max cried.

"Your brother has a wife and responsibilities." Mrs. Nieriker looked up from the cards in her hand.

"They say there are dazzling flowers high in the treetops. May could paint them," Ernst said. "And she says I must follow my heart. I love the violin, but my dream isn't music. I want to help create a clear light."

Madame Nieriker shook her head. May, too, felt uneasy hearing about traveling to another continent. Soon she helped her mother-in-law and Sophie get settled in the blue room.

During the next few days, Max accompanied Ernst to work or stayed curled up with *The Origin of Species*. Madame Nieriker played the piano or knitted. May gave Sophie painting lessons.

"You know so much about art," she said.

"I used to hold classes back in Concord. I think of teaching again, but of course American girls cross the sea for lessons with French painters, not from me. Rosa Bonheur started a free art school for young ladies under twenty. I don't expect I'll ever be as successful as she is, with her grand paintings of horses, but I'd like to start a school like that someday."

"I'd enroll," Sophie said.

"If you're serious about art, you must live in Paris," May said.

"I wouldn't know who to take classes from, or where to live, or buy clothes, or anything," Sophie replied.

"That's a problem for many. There should be a guidebook," May said.

"Ernst says you have a writer in the family. Perhaps such talent runs in your blood. Why don't you write such a book?"

"I have learned a lot during my travels." May had recently looked through a slim book called *How to Take Care of Your Eyes* that Louisa had sent, noting that it was part of a series with practical advice overseen by Mr. Niles. "I have a friend who might consider publishing such a guidebook, but I'm so busy now."

"You'll be even busier after your babies come. Take my advice, please." Madame Nieriker put down her knitting needles. "Don't give up your art. I had help with my children, but there were always quarrels to settle, cups of milk to pour, lost toys to be found, or small heartbreaks to help mend. But I made sure to spend twenty minutes a day at the piano. It made a difference to shut the door."

Tears brimmed in May's eyes; she was touched both by the

kind words and the thought of children, which she rarely let herself consider. She, who'd always hoped, didn't dare to hope that much.

❧

ON SATURDAY MORNING, EVERYONE WALKED TO THE river, where water splashed the sides of rowboats that curved up in front, like tipped crescent moons. May could hear women talk as they scrubbed clothes and linens in a washhouse boat. While waiting for the ferry, May watched children chase butterflies with green nets.

They rode the boat to the Pont de l'Alma, where Ernst dropped a franc into the cup of a blind woman who sang "Sweet Marie." He hailed a carriage to bring them to the World's Fair Exhibition Palace, a huge building with long corridors filled with shops and displays of china dolls, antique pistols, and a pyramid of watch cases. They looked at paintings of military victories and surrenders, medieval tapestries, a lighthouse lamp, a model of a deep-sea diver, and stacks of mattresses arranged like a castle. Ernst and his brother liked the huge looms from Birmingham, a demonstration of a Swiss embroidery machine with three hundred needles, and other machines. One turned out folded newspapers. Another cut, weighed, and wrapped soap. Their favorite exhibit was the gold-prize-winning display on the new kind of gas.

After a long wait in line, they climbed up inside of Frédéric Auguste Bartholdi's large copper head of Liberty. May squeezed into a place to look out a window in the crown, over the treetops and crowds. It was hard to breathe with people crammed so close, or maybe she'd drawn her corset strings too tight. She was glad to walk back to the boat, and when everyone talked about going back tomorrow, she offered to stay behind to get dinner ready and tend to the garden. It had been good to be in Paris, but it was coming time to plant peas, cantaloupes, and herbs.

※

THAT SUMMER, MAY OFTEN PAINTED IN THE GARDEN, concentrating on passing light more than solid shapes, letting poppies spill off the page rather than stand in the center. She used the wrong end of a brush to scratch or scrape away paint to expose the white paper and suggest texture. The spaces made what she left more vivid. She stopped painting outside only after blossoms fell and leaves turned to shades of russet and gold. On the first anniversary of Mother's death, she arranged a garland of dried leaves around her picture and spent most of the day crying.

Winter came without the drama of New England blizzards. Cold rains fell, as well as snow that quickly melted on the grass or streets. Still, May couldn't ever get quite warm even sitting right next to the fire. Her chilly hands were too tight on a brush, so instead of painting, she began writing the book she hoped would be of use to artists trying to make their way in Europe. She offered advice on travel arrangements and safe, economical places to stay in Paris, London, and Rome. She named reputable teachers, studios, and shops, and she even gave tips on how to roll, pin, and pack clothing and the usefulness of a bit of dried ginger aboard ship.

❧

SOMETIMES SHE JOINED ERNST ON THE TRAIN TO HIS work, getting off at the Montparnasse station to visit her old friends at Monsieur Krug's atelier. They asked questions about Ernst and her painting, but May missed what could be said only when hour after hour, day after day, were spent together. When they showed her work they might send to the Salon, May promised that this year she'd send a painting, too.

After she and Ernst spent New Year's day quietly at home, she painted several still lifes, then she chose to submit her portrait of the woman from northern Africa, for she still liked the interplay of warm and cool tones, a suggestion of something both direct and shy in the gaze. And since she'd painted it in the class with Monseiur Krug, she could put his name by hers.

After Jury Day, she told Ernst, "I'll spend the next six weeks painting and waiting to collect another *refusé* card."

"That's not possible!"

She squeezed his hand, moved by his belief in her, but also feeling a need for company who understood the odds. She sat at her little desk by the window and wrote to Louisa:

Our life here is simple. Truly, you would hardly know me in this village with no theater or galleries. All I need now is Ernst and my paints. The French way of life would suit you, too.

Houses are small, so there's less to clean. We hired a femme de ménage, but even without Adrienne I could manage, as the French have all the baking, washing, and ironing done outside the home.

We have a second bedroom that I've readied for you with a blue china bowl and pitcher I set on the washstand and sewed blue cretonne curtains I hung around it. You'd have the best view in the house. The hills of Fleury and a castle. Lu, if you could see what I have, you would understand why I stay here.

May thought of writing about the river, where they might row and forgive each other for everything. But she signed her name, sealed the letter with honey-colored wax, and left it by the kitchen door for the postman.

24

İN THE GARDEN

*M*ay gripped Ernst's hand as they made their way through crowds exclaiming over paintings of Napoleon, a maiden holding a jug of milk, foundlings reading prayer books, and Renoir's mother with two children. A portrait by John Singer Sargent, an American whom May had met last year at the Cassatt's soirees, attracted an admiring circle of ladies wearing spangled gowns and men holding gold-tipped canes. Ernst whooped when they reached May's painting. He said, "*La Négresse* is almost as beautiful as the woman who painted her!"

"Hush, people are looking." Her face turned warm.

"Naturally they are looking at this masterpiece. Let me see in my *programme* who painted it. Why, it says M. Nieriker. What a talented lady she must be. And how much does it cost? Ah, it's not for sale." He snapped the program shut. "A pity for so many, but who could put a price on such a work?"

"I'm happy that my first Salon acceptance wasn't just luck. Two paintings make a career seem likely. Come, there's much more to look at."

"We've seen the best. And I wanted to surprise you with a dinner reservation, but I had to make it early in order for us to get back to Meudon before the trains stop." He ran his hand down the back of her silk dress. She felt the fabric tug slightly between the buttons and reminded herself to be more cautious around the croissants and cheese that Ernst brought home from the city. Though on recent mornings, perhaps anxious about the reception of her Salon painting, she could only sip weak tea at breakfast.

They went to a restaurant where the candlelit room with varnished black walls held just half a dozen tables covered with crisp white linen. Waiters took silent steps toward and away from them, filling their glasses when the water was still near the rim. In movements that seemed choreographed, one man whisked away a plate, while another put down a fresh one holding beautifully arranged meat, vegetables, or cheese. A waiter poured champagne, which didn't taste quite right to May. Another man brought a bouquet of yellow roses, saying, "These came for Madame Nieriker."

He set the jar of flowers between May and Ernst, who, delighted with his surprise, grinned like a boy. She squeezed his hand under the tablecloth, then leaned past the fragrant buds, just opening but big enough so no one might see their kiss behind the drape of petals, as if they were in their own yellow room.

THE NEXT WEEK, MAY JOINED ERNST ON THE MORNING train to Paris. After he headed to work, she toured the Salon with friends. On another morning, she met Mary Cassatt at a café. Mary's dark hair was swept under her Reboux hat, with an extravagant burst of ostrich feathers. Her gray dress with jet buttons down the front, an edge of lace showing at the cuffs, was the height of fashion, though below the accordion pleats, May spotted her flat-heeled British shoes. Mary's dark eyes were steady, and her lips pressed together, an expression that reminded May of Louisa. Was that why she'd put off seeing her, afraid she'd criticize her choices as her sister might? Instead, their conversation flowed as if little time had passed. Mary congratulated her on her painting in the Salon. Her eyes brimmed with tears as she said, "There's little worse than a mother dying." As they walked to the Impressionist show, they talked about their work and May's marriage.

No lines wound around the building to get into the show with pictures of people in gaudy clothing and chairs the color of egg yolks. These were viewed from the side or below instead of straight in front. Some portraits were sliced at the edges of canvasses. Instead of everything being shaded as if it were at the back of a pantry, light seemed cast by the noon sun, with shadows as brilliant as whatever cast them. Paintings by Claude Monet, Camille Pissarro, Edgar Degas, and Paul Gauguin showed streaks and scratches left by brushes and palette knives. May felt caught between shock and longing for this bright, lush world that reminded her of a dark river turning petal-pale, a room full of people pushing up their sleeves, whispers turning to shouts. She overheard people demanding back their *entrée* fee, complaining, "Five slashes as fingers! My children could do that!'"

"Sky isn't the color of butter."

"Those women look like they have cholera or jaundice. Or are dead."

May thought that all the paintings she'd seen, and which she'd loved, had been like looking to the past. Within these plain white frames she saw the gleam of the present and the future. She asked her friend, "Where are yours?"

Mary led her to a gallery with eleven of her paintings and pastels, including *Little Girl in a Blue Armchair*, one of Mary's sister in the loge of a grand theater, and another of her holding the reins of a carriage with determined hands and an intent expression. The portraits of strong and sensual women had the softness and colors of babies and cakes, not the ones May used to make, which were dense with molasses, but the light ones with spun frosting that gleamed from cases in pâtisseries.

"These are bound to win the medals," she said.

"There are no prizes. There were so many fights putting up this show. Where to hang what, and Monsieur Degas went into a rage when someone suggested bringing in a couch. He doesn't want an audience unwilling to stand. But one thing we agree on: The Impressionist credo is no jury, no medals, and no awards. Why should we compete with each other, when we're all different?"

"I like that. Though I do think yours are the best."

"So have you become an Impressionist?"

"No, but I understand more. I've worked on the rules for so long, I can't throw them all out."

"What you need remains in your hand. None of it is wasted. One makes the new ways her own. Père Tanguay, who takes Monsieur Cézanne's paintings in trade for brushes and canvas, won't sell black paint in his shop. But I don't reject lines or contour. I want to show form as well as light."

May understood that beauty changed. Artists had to keep up. She followed Mary into a room filled with pictures of washerwomen, ballerinas, acrobats, and seamstresses with wrinkled skin. A woman bending over a tin tub looked rather too pink, but her loneliness and beauty shined through. May asked, "And how is Monsieur Degas?"

"He works as much as I do. He infuriates me, then shows me something I hadn't seen. We went to the Louvre, where he pointed out how Botticelli's Madonna had her fingernails worn down by fieldwork. Some of the toes curved in as they do from wearing shoes, not bare feet or sandals, as Virgin Mary would have worn. The painting is exquisite, but why not show women as we are?"

"Then you don't miss showing in the Salon?"

"No. The crowds here are bigger than they were two years ago, and a few works have already sold. I'm the only woman with paintings here this year, since Berthe had a baby in November—did you hear? A little girl named Julie. She promises she'll have work next year. I'm certain she will."

"They are both well?"

"My mother worried that a first baby from a mother who's thirty-seven would mean difficulties, but everything was fine."

"You said a woman must choose between art and motherhood."

"Everything changes, and why shouldn't Madame Manet lead the way? Berthe has already painted some since the birth. She has a strong will and a *bonne* to help with the child." Mary set her black eyes on May's. "You must have that, too. Might I have a baby to paint, with her dear mother soon?"

May glanced down. It had been a while since she'd bled, but that had happened before. She hardly dared to hope and wished she could consult with her mother or Anna, who might tell her about signs. "I haven't said anything to Ernst yet."

"One child, Berthe agrees, maybe two. Beyond that, a woman's chances to keep painting are slight."

"Ernst comes from a big family and misses the bustle. But we'll have to see. One little girl or boy sounds nice."

⊂⊃

LATE ONE AFTERNOON, MAY FILLED THE DELFT VASE with mint and roses, though their scents seemed a bit too sweet. After Adrienne took a chicken from the oven, May told her to go home early. She went to the bedroom and brushed her hair until it crackled, plumped the pillows, opened the windows to let in the smells of spring, and took away the dish she'd set out for the neighbor's cat, now licked free of cream.

When Ernst came home, she threw her arms around him. He laughed, then pushed up her sleeves to kiss her wrists, then elbows, then the skin behind her ears. He pressed his lips against her neck as they moved into the bedroom, where the tall windows let in the croaks of frogs and hum of bees. He gently pulled clasps from her hair. She bent to take off his shoes and socks, curved her hands around his long, elegant feet, then stepped back. "I haven't drawn enough today."

"May! Now?"

She grabbed her sketchbook and ordered, "Take off your clothes."

He unbuttoned his shirt, shrugged out of the sleeves, and sat on the edge of the bed. She rapidly sketched his head, chest, and arms, then tugged down his trousers. She said, "The folds of the cloth aren't as interesting as what's beneath."

After a few minutes, she set aside her charcoal stick and put her palms on his hips. He pulled off her gown, petticoats, and stockings. As they settled on the bed, she tasted the salty skin around his ear, then the soft creases of his throat. He swung his legs over her hips. She wrapped her arms around him. Their eyes never left each other's as they rocked together.

Afterward, she watched the room turn darker while Ernst played Haydn on his violin. She put on her *robe d'intérieur* and went to the kitchen. She wrinkled her nose at the chicken Adrienne had roasted with onions and bay leaves, and she brought a bottle of *Clos de Lampes*, the local wine, fresh bread, a wedge of cheese, and a bowl of plums back to the bedroom. She spread the feast on the coverlet and tore apart the crusty loaf, handing him a piece. "I could live in France just for the bread."

He set down his violin and bow and spread the Brie, which was warm, a bit melted. "And why would anyone live in a country where there were only one or two types of cheese? Not when we can live where there are dozens."

"I love to hear you play. You should devote yourself to music."

He swept his arm over the food and wine. "Where would all this come from if I left my job?"

May ripped apart the bread, then fed him a plum. "Then you've given up thoughts of traveling to South America, helping to make that clear light?"

"I won't go now, but I don't know that I'll want to keep my job for more than a year. I'm young. I want . . ."

"Do you regret marrying me?"

"Never! It's just, I have dreams. I've always . . ."

"Please don't talk of traveling!" She took a deep breath, then heard a thud in the second bedroom. "What was that?"

They ran to the next room. The neighbor's cat had pounced onto the sill of the open window and snatched the stuffed owl. The cat bounded back outside with its prey.

"Not my owl!" May cried.

Ernst leapt onto the windowsill. She tossed him her robe, which he threw over his bare shoulders. He crouched, dropped to the ground, and chased the cat up a tree. The cat stopped on a high branch and dropped the speckled owl.

May pulled on her nightgown and ran out to pick it up. She looked up at Ernst among the green leaves, with her blue robe falling open. What a devoted father he would be.

After he scrambled down, she hugged him and said, "I want you to have your dreams. I just don't want our children to grow up poor as we did. And I don't want to paint flowers in Brazil! A jungle is no place for a baby."

"Our children?" He stepped back, grabbed her bare arm,

and studied her face. "Darling." He lifted her in the air, while she waved the owl.

When he put her down, their kiss was warm and moist. She said, "I'm not sure. It doesn't seem possible."

"Just think, there will be three of us. A family." He stroked her belly.

"You can't feel anything yet!"

"Of course I can. A little girl as beautiful as her *maman*."

"You're terribly silly. And I love you."

He kissed her eyelids, the bridge of her nose, and the sides of her mouth. He sank to his knees and lifted her nightgown. "Let's have a big family."

"You don't want to go to South America?"

"I don't need anything but you." He stood again and caressed her neck. "Wait until my mother hears. Shall I write to her, or do you want to? Should we wait? We have so much to do. What should we name her?"

"We have time. Besides, the baby might be a boy."

"Girls run in your family as well as in mine. We could name her after your mother."

"That would be nice. Though I never cared for the name *Abigail*."

"We could call her *May*. How we'll spoil her."

She pulled Ernst to the ground, kissing him until her breath filled her hips and she could hardly tell it from his body inside her. Around them, she heard boughs rustle, rise, and fall.

◦⟨∞⟩◦

THAT SUMMER, MAY PAINTED POPPIES, LAVENDER, irises, and biscuit-colored foxgloves. Working amidst buds that swelled before spilling open, changing butter-and-cream colored blossoms to blue on her paper, turning leaves larger than they were, sweeping paint to every edge and corner, her hand seemed to pull the world closer. Sometimes she touched her curving belly and thought of how she'd never be lonely again. Now that she felt quite certain that she was with child, she sent a letter to her family with her news and begged Louisa to visit. Louisa sent back congratulations but wrote that Anna had broken her leg and needed her. She didn't feel well enough for a sea voyage now and was busy reading Mother's old letters and diaries to write a memoir, which Mr. Niles had promised to publish.

As the months passed, May's fatigue deepened. Ernst insisted that she see a doctor, who said that he could do nothing for the backaches that began to plague her and warned that, especially at her age, she should expect discomforts. She didn't suppose he meant the way her throat burned when Ernst left for his job in Paris. Sometimes now silence felt like a threat, instead of a kind of company. Her paintbrush trembled or slashed in one wrong direction. May made herself keep working, unscrewing the top of a tube containing a blue so vibrant that it was almost purple or opening a tube of sunny yellow paint. Gradually, her vision and hand felt all of a piece, though the muscles in her throat tightened the way they did when she listened to Ernst's violin strain for high notes. She left a short unfinished stroke, a scrubbed-away patch on her paper, to acknowledge what was crucial, what escaped, how her paintings might never match her vision. Would her sense of imperfection ever leave her? Was that what made her an artist?

At noon, she stopped for rice with marmalade and a tumbler of milk, and she looked through mail. Louisa sent old issues of *Scribner's* and *The Atlantic Monthly*, a pattern waist that May could wear instead of a corset. Each time she unpacked a baby frock, booties, a little knitted cap, or a thick biography of Turner, she saved the note Louisa had enclosed to look at last. Surely Anna's broken leg had healed by now and Louisa could leave that memoir? No, not yet.

May was grateful for the gifts, though she slit open the boxes feeling that each measured the distance between herself and her sisters. Louisa sent a check, which May folded without yet looking at the numbers. She was afraid that a grand sum would mean that Louisa didn't plan to come. May knew she'd be fine, but she wanted a sister's advice, as well as that of Adrienne, who'd given her the name of a trusted midwife. May tried to remember what her cousin Lucy had said was necessary. She'd made it sound simple. Clean, strong hands and kind eyes, she believed. Louisa would know. May hadn't yet accepted the offer from Ernst's mother and sister to be there for the birth, since that might mean there wouldn't be a room for Louisa.

⁂

AS THE DAYS GREW DARKER EARLIER IN THE EVENING, time itself seemed to narrow and press in on her. The sun fell at a sharper slant. Drumming crickets, the slightly burnt scent of drying grasses, gave the air an edge. Fallen leaves left bare branches, which brought the tolling of church bells closer. The bees had flown away. Birdsong grew fainter. May touched her big belly, willing away loneliness, but something clutched in her chest. The coming anniversary of Mother's death felt harder this year than last, perhaps because she carried a child that her mother would never hold. May addressed another envelope to Louisa. *I need you to help*, she wrote. *Help* was a word her sister understood.

In October, a large package arrived, holding a quilt stitched by Anna and Louisa. May pressed her face in the soft fabric, the splendid array of blues. She waited until Ernst got home to open the letter tucked underneath.

Dear May,

We are all well enough here, with Anna's leg recovering nicely. She was shocked when you wrote that you have plenty of clothes for the baby, that a few little gowns and a blanket would be sufficient. She said, "Oh, that poor girl, all alone and ignorant." She says those frocks will be soaked in minutes and you must have fresh, dry ones, so we are sending more.

I have given up the idea of writing a book about Marmee, though there could be no worthier subject, one bound to cheer and instruct readers. Perhaps she poses too great a theme for my pen, and Father stays with philosophy, so we are burning her diaries and letters. This is the best way to ensure that someone who didn't know her as we did does not attempt to write her life.

Father continues with his lectures but as ever has no sense of business. I must manage for both him and Anna, so I cannot be spared for a visit now. Perhaps I can come next spring, when your baby is here. I have some pains, as you know, and am afraid of being a burden to you when I mean to help.

Love, Louisa

May threw down the letter.

"Darling, what's wrong? Is it your father? Is he ill?" Ernst asked.

"How dare she!" May's hands trembled. "Louisa's worst fear was having her stories burned, but she destroyed our mother's diaries! She had no right. She was my mother, too."

"May, sit down. Your face is turning red."

"Louisa could never stand the truth. I suppose Mother complained in her diaries, and Louisa won't let anyone think that our family wasn't as idyllic as she described."

"You must calm down. You're delicate."

She shook her head. She'd never felt stronger, but the world seemed more fragile. Bare branches scratched the window. She heard dry leaves rip in the wind. "Louisa was there for Beth and our mother, and she'll never let me forget it. Why should she? She's good, and everyone knows it. I hate her!" May rubbed her aching hands, understanding that she missed her sister as much as their mother. She sobbed. "I love her so much."

"Of course you do."

"She must hate me for not being there with our mother at the end."

"No one could dislike you. You say that because of the

baby you carry. My mother told me it can make some women say strange things."

She supposed that could be so. Bouts of unease were followed by periods of calm. She thought that Louisa's presence might calm her. Had it ever? "She sent money. She thinks we can't survive without her help. I wish we could send it back."

"She is kind. But we can manage without help, if you'd rather."

May wiped her tears with the back of her hand, thinking they couldn't turn down a gift when there were doctor bills and expenses like cradles and perhaps a nursemaid to think about. "She's not coming."

"We thought she wouldn't, didn't we?"

"The last time I was in Concord, I promised to give her something wonderful. I couldn't even imagine what it might be. But now I see that I want her to hold our baby. And when she's a little older, to take her hand while she learns to walk."

"She will visit us."

"You don't understand. She would only come if she thought she could be of help, such as with a newborn. She won't come now. Not ever."

"Then we will go there. Someday, when our little girl is old enough to travel and remember what she sees."

"Could you leave work that long? It would be expensive."

"We'll find a way. Then she can see Anna, too, and her cousins. They'll adore her!"

"We'll have a boy. I know it."

"Then can we name him after my brother, Max? But we won't have a boy."

"I'll be happy as long as he or she has your nose." She tried to steady her voice. "Ernst, perhaps I am too much alone here."

"You must meet more of our neighbors."

"When we first moved here, I only wanted to be with you or to paint. Now I suppose they think I'm a snobbish American."

"How can they not love you?"

She felt tears well again as her eyes ranged over the crimson drapes, the mirror with its lavish frame, the reproduction of the *Venus de Milo*. She wanted to hear milkmen's clattering tins, boys shouting news as they sold papers in the mornings, and, at twilight, watch lamplighters lift sticks to light gas jets. May missed the atelier, painting while surrounded by other women's determined, shifting elbows, and the way Mary Cassatt tried to lure her with pastels. Even if she didn't go to the café concerts with yellow chairs and blue benches, she'd like knowing they were close.

"Let's look for a place to live in Paris," she said.

"You love it here!"

"I know you must work, but the train takes about thirty minutes each way to Paris and back. That's an extra hour when I might be with you."

"You won't be alone for long. My mother and Sophie are coming soon."

"They'll be happier in Paris, too. Sophie shows a talent for painting, and I might be able to arrange lessons for her with Monsieur Krug. Your mother would enjoy the concerts and ballet." May thought how they'd have places to go to, leaving time when she could be alone with Ernst and their baby. "We won't need much, but just enough room so we can rent a piano for your mother."

"You seem to have it all worked out." He smoothed her hair, twining his fingers in her curls. "Won't you miss the garden?"

"I'll have everything I ever wanted."

22

EVERGREEN

*M*ay heard church bells ring as she set pots of geraniums by the tall windows. They'd sold the red carpet and drapes and the gold-framed mirror. Now that she was with child, she wondered why she'd ever cared about such things. They bought a secondhand rug and cotton curtains, so except for the broken-armed Venus, which they couldn't give up, the parlor reminded her of the one in Concord. May tacked her garden pictures to the bedroom walls, satisfied with the way she'd shown that lines shifted, like the edges of rivers or clouds. She set Mother's picture next to the old music box on the mantel, glad that she'd kept it all these years, for it would be lovely to wind the crank to play tunes for a newborn.

Early in November, Ernst's mother and sister moved into this apartment on the Left Bank to help prepare for the baby's arrival. Having them around reminded May of how everyone in her own family had stayed home. Still, she smiled when Madame Nieriker took the quilt, rag, or broom from May, called Sophie, and amiably chided, "We came to be of use!"

May gave painting lessons to Sophie, who did the shopping and brought up any mail that had been left at the table where the elderly landlady sat with her little dog. Fewer packages arrived since they'd moved, but one day, she brought up a package May tore open to find a copy of *Studying Art Abroad, and How to do it Cheaply.* She ruffled through the pages looking for a check, snatched it out, and waved the book through the air. She looked through it, satisfied that all her words seemed clearly printed and grateful that Mr. Niles hadn't asked for a preface from her sister.

Madame Nieriker cooked a celebratory dinner. Afterward, they sat in the *salon* for champagne, followed by pistachio *macarons* that Sophie brought back from the neighborhood pâtisserie. Ernst dramatically read aloud a few pages, then said, "This is the best book ever written. Soon you will be as famous as your sister!" he declared.

"Who is her sister?" Madame Nieriker looked up from the hat not much bigger than her fist that she was knitting.

"*Maman*, we told you," Sophie said. "Some of my friends are devoted to those four sisters. They told me there's a beautiful girl in the book. I'm not much of a reader, especially in English. But they ask if she's like you, May."

"I'm luckier. I found your brother." May stiffened as a pain shot through her lower back.

Ernst picked up his violin and bow, but he stopped playing

when she winced. "Is it time to call for the midwife?"

"No, no." May shook her head.

"I know you're happy with the one our landlady recommended, but I've talked to some fellows at work. They say you'll be safer in the hands of a doctor. That's how it's done here these days."

"Midwives did fine by me," Madame Nieriker said. "I don't claim to understand modern ways, but I wouldn't have wanted a gentleman present."

"Your mother knows what she's talking about. She had nine." May glanced at Sophie, who kept her face close to the forget-me-nots she was embroidering around the neckline of a small gown. May put her hand back on her round belly, thinking how she might have once felt embarrassed by a strange man in her bedroom. Now that she was getting close to her time, all her old worries had been replaced by a conviction that all would be well. "If a doctor would ease Ernst's mind, I don't object. We should find someone soon."

MAY WAS SLEEPING WHEN HER WATER BROKE, SOAKING her thighs. She pushed Ernst out of their bed, asking him to get his mother. Madame Nieriker tore off the damp sheets and put on fresh ones, while May wiped her sticky skin. Then she lay back down with Ernst, waiting for pain that ebbed and returned, waiting for her baby.

After the sun rose, Madame Nieriker told Ernst to fetch the doctor, then moved books and bracelets from the table, opened and shut the windows, rearranged the blankets, and murmured about this or that little thing. This first irritated, then calmed May. Hearing horses *clip-clop* on cobblestones, she stood at the window and looked down at a woman selling bundles of grape leaves and bay branches. She screamed as pains shot up toward her chest.

"Lie down," Madame Nieriker said.

"Will it ever stop hurting?" May asked.

"My poor dear. Let me brush your hair." Madame Nieriker settled May in the bed, then left the room when she heard footsteps. A minute later, May greeted the doctor with smiles and grimaces. He assured her that everything was going as it should and promised to come back soon.

Madame Nieriker banished Ernst to the parlor.

"Don't go!" May cried.

Madame Nieriker took her hand. "I'm here."

May squeezed her hand, then yanked back her arm. Heat flared through her body and behind her eyes. She clenched her mouth. Why hadn't anyone told her how torn she could feel inside, what heaving through her hips? How much could she endure? She longed for her mother and called, "Ernst!"

He cracked open the door but left after his mother sharply spoke a few German words.

"He's pale. Is he all right?" May asked.

"Yes. He's getting the doctor."

The doctor returned as the pains grew more intense and frequent. Was his jacket stained with blood? Was it hers? May screamed as everything around her funneled into her belly, which felt torn in two. "Am I going to die?"

"Darling, one thinks that, but we don't." Madame Nieriker wiped her forehead. "It will be over soon."

When it seemed that she could not bear another pang, May lifted herself on her elbows, cried out, fell back on the bed, and raised her knees. At last, with shrieks, gasps, shaking, and wonder, she felt a baby slip into the doctor's open hands. He patted May's legs with cloths. After he cut the cord, she struggled to sit up, crying, "Where's my baby? Is she all right?"

"The baby is fine." Madame Nieriker cradled her in her arms and shouted, "Sophie, bring warm water! Ernst, come see!"

Ernst kissed May's neck, shoulders, and hands. He dabbed tears and sweat from her face before looking at the crying baby. He whispered, "She's a girl."

May reached for her child, her exhaustion lifting. "I never thought I'd have a daughter, not really. How I wanted one!"

Madame Nieriker finished wiping blood from the baby before handing her to May, who asked, "Shouldn't she stop crying?"

"She will," Madame Nieriker said.

May pressed her to her chest, then touched each tiny, curled finger. Her fingernails were translucent pink and white, like seashells. Her feet were as crinkled as tubes of well-used paints. Her eyes were *bleu ciel*. Her nose looked rather flat and long, like her mother's, but that was perfect, too. She wrapped her hands around the tiny feet and gently pressed her nose against her belly. "She isn't too thin, is she?"

"She'll be plump soon enough. Now let's wrap her up so she doesn't get chilled," Madame Nieriker said. "You haven't told us her name."

"Louisa?" May looked at Ernst. "That's a good name, isn't it?"

"Louisa May Nieriker," he said. "I like that."

"We must send her proud aunt the news at once." May touched the skin by Ernst's green eyes. The pain was ebbing now, the way everyone had said it would.

❧

DURING THE NEXT FEW LONG DAYS, MAY SLEPT IN short blocks of time, waking when the baby cried and putting her to her breast. Each small sound posed a challenge to figure out what the baby wanted. Each leg unfolding, each hand curling, was part of a conversation May must respond to, and she did, even when dazed or dizzy from sleeplessness. When she managed to soothe wails or wiggling, she felt the perfect understanding she'd longed for.

May padded about in her nightgown and robe, never entirely dressed or sure of the time or day. Her belly hurt, so she only nibbled the edges of crêpes or ate a few Muscat grapes. Sometimes Madame Nieriker brought little puddings, but it grew hard to lift a spoon or swallow. She and Ernst arranged pink roses and ferns sent by friends they turned away, asking them to come back later. May wasn't sure she'd ever need to see another person, but she said, "Soon we must show our darling to everyone."

"You won't always be so tired. You need to get back your appetite," Madame Nieriker said.

Sometimes pains shot through May's belly and back. Her

head throbbed. She couldn't keep up with the conversations about doctors. All she longed for now was to hold the baby and sleep. One afternoon, she woke to the sounds of voices, then confident, heavy footsteps the length of Louisa's stride. With a racing heart, May threw aside blankets, letting a bootie, which were always falling off the baby's feet, skim to the floor. She knew her sister couldn't stay away! She called, "Come in," amused that she would knock.

But it was Mary Cassatt. Her dark eyes were wide and her mouth slightly open as she faced May, who wondered if she looked so alarming. She wished she'd at least put on a clean robe and brushed her hair.

Mary set down a hatbox. "What a beautiful baby! Your mother-in-law let me admire her, then told me no one was to be let in to congratulate the mother. I assured her I wouldn't stay long."

"Yes, isn't Louisa darling? I'm glad you came. I'm so happy, so lucky. Just a bit tired today."

"I brought you something." Mary lifted a plumed hat from the box, then dropped a fistful of paint tubes onto the bed. "I expected you'd get enough booties and blankets. A new mother needs fresh paints and a Reboux hat."

May scooped up the bouquet of tubes of carmine, yellow as brilliant as daffodils, and another the hue of butter in winter. She read the labels on several shades of blue: *L'azur, l'indigo, bleu de prusse.* "These are lovely. I'm sorry I haven't seen you since the Impressionist show. Was it successful?"

"Yes. For the first time, there was a profit."

"Congratulations! I hope I can get to your studio soon.

Who would have thought a baby would leave me in bed so long?"

Mary turned and, for the first time, looked at the garden paintings tacked to the wall. "These are new. And magnificent. Here is the world as *you* see it, and no one else."

"It's not what people want."

"Not yet, perhaps. Sometimes people buy art because they don't understand or even admire a piece. They like to pretend that they do." Mary propped up the pillows behind May.

May leaned back and closed her eyes for a moment. "Do you remember the morning we watched paintings arrive at the Palais?"

"Of course, on Jury Day."

"You said that one day you hoped to have paintings worthy of being shown among the old masters. Mary, you already do. Your work will be remembered."

"Your *life* will be remembered. Your happiness is an achievement." Mary kissed her cheek.

EVERY MORNING, MAY EXPECTED HER FATIGUE TO LIFT, but as the days passed, her arms and legs often felt so heavy that she could barely manage to shuffle from one room to another. After another few days, she could hardly hold the baby. Chills wracked through her feverish body, then her skin felt as if it were on fire. As she slept, minutes blurred into hours. Pain slashed through her back and belly. Her eyes stung so that she could barely keep them open. When Ernst returned from work, he held cloths on her hot forehead and handed her a teacup. He said, "You need to keep up your strength."

The broth smelled foul to her. She put down the cup with shaking hands. "I'm trying."

"Of course you are."

Madame Nieriker hired a wet nurse and asked the doctor to return. May couldn't lift her head to make out much of the murmurs and raised voices beyond her shut door, words about medicine, time, and unclean hands. Fever pulsed through days that had no shape. Sophie set advent candles in the windows and green boughs across the mantel. May craved the scent of pine, the garlands like those she and Louisa had arranged at Anna's wedding. Where were her sisters, her mother? *Where are the lilies of the valley?* May couldn't tell dreams and nightmares from waking, minutes from hours. Who were all these people crowding around her? She waved everyone, or their shadows, away. A baby cried and cried. Church bells clanged. She heard someone say, *It's the sickness. It's the medicine.* They knew nothing. They were so kind.

Then at last, the mist lifted, and her room was filled with a clear light. May's lips were cracked, her dry skin was flaking, but her tongue felt soft instead of swollen. She pushed off the covers. Who had put all these quilts on her? She wiped sweat from her forehead and neck and cried, "Ernst!"

He rushed to her side. His worried face became radiant as he turned to call, "Her fever broke!"

May stared at her husband, who looked as if he hadn't shaved for days. Where had be been? Why did he look so scared?

Madame Nieriker appeared in the doorway. She threw out an arm to hold back Sophie and said, "We must check the baby."

May kissed the corners of Ernst's mouth, the side of his neck, the skin under his ears. When they drew apart, she saw that her watercolors of violets, poppies, and roses looked too bright on the walls. Nothing was as she meant it to be. She swung her legs over the side of the bed. They buckled as she tried to stand.

"What are you doing? May, you're better now, but you must rest," Ernst said.

She put an arm around him and hobbled to her wardrobe. She began pulling out dresses, dropping them to the floor. "I'll send these to my sisters."

"May, you'll wear them again. The doctor says women often get such fevers after childbirth. My mother says it happened to her."

"I need to put everything in order!" Her voice was sharp, surprising even her.

They folded her gowns, the blue for everyday, the golden silk that she'd worn to the Salon and to her wedding. Ernst helped her take the watercolors off the walls and stack them. She touched the painting of the violets he'd given her in London, the day she'd understood that even as petals unfurled, then darkened, something new would bloom. "Darling, you won't let anyone forget my paintings? I worked so hard." She touched his face, which was pink with held-back tears. She rested her finger in the dent on his nose. "I'm sorry I can't give you more."

"You gave me everything."

"Will you help me back to bed? Where is Louisa? When is my sister coming?"

"Soon, dearest."

"I promised to show her the water lilies. She'll never find them herself. They're so close, but she won't look."

"It doesn't matter."

Nothing mattered. Everything mattered. She was dying, she knew it, and she'd never truly thanked Louisa for all that she'd given her. May was so proud of her; had she ever told her that? How many sisters pay to send another across the ocean? Louisa was the best of sisters and daughters and aunts. She'd known everything about love.

"You're right. I need to rest," May said.

After Ernst shut the door, she cried not from the pain, which the medicine eased, but as she'd cried after Beth died, after her mother died. But she didn't have much time for grief. She felt life closing around her, and her hope channeled into a single desire. Exhausted, but also restless, she managed to slide from her bed, dragging a blanket. Her pulse ran fast. With an effort, she opened her trunk, remembering another one that had been filled with a tattered tablecloth, scuffed boots, and crushed hats, worn by girls who pretended to be pilgrims, princesses, or pirates. Why hadn't they known they were perfect just the way they were?

She knelt and filled the trunk with her small notebooks with accounts of silk stockings, yellow gloves, lace, watercolor paper, and sales from her paintings. She tied a thin blue ribbon around her old diaries and letters, tucking in her green *refusé* card and a pine twig that would turn brittle but that might leave a scent. She packed her antique dagger, her jewelry box, and the locket with Mother's picture. Before including her work basket, she took out her scissors and snipped off a lock of her hair. She sealed it in an envelope, which she labeled: *May, December 1879.*

She pushed herself off the floor to gather her stack of watercolors. She crouched before the hearth like the girl in Louisa's book, but it was her own masterpiece, not her sister's, that she moved toward flames that rose yellow, orange, blue, and silver-gray. Embers glowed and swelled. These paintings of violets, roses, and geraniums were the best work she'd ever done, but Louisa hadn't asked to see them. Her sister already knew May had won places in the Salon and had a husband and baby she adored. Enough jealousy had come between them. Why shouldn't May spare her from seeing paintings in which she'd shown joy and grief in the same space?

She pushed them toward the fire. As edges blackened from the heat, hissed, and curled, she snatched them out. A scream caught in her throat as she scorched her fingertips. She yanked back her hand, dropping a painting in the coals. It was caught by a larger flame, swallowed, puffed, then crumbled into ash.

She blew on her fingers to soothe them. She remembered standing by the old bridge, promising to give Louisa something that mattered and to be with her when she was dying. Wasn't Louisa's worst fear to be alone? May picked up a fallen bootie, curled her hand around it, and dug her fingernails into her palm. She called, "Ernst! Please! Bring the baby."

He dashed into the room and crouched beside her. "What are you doing on the floor?"

"I was cold."

"Yes, your hands are freezing."

"Please. Bring Louisa."

He helped her back to bed, then brought in their child.

With hands that smelled slightly smoky, May stroked her sweet-smelling head. She looked up at Ernst. "Our baby's healthy, isn't she? That's all that matters. "

"No! That isn't enough." Ernst looked as horrified as May had felt when Anna had said almost the same words, years and years ago. May loved him for this innocence. He was young and beautiful and had eyes that always seemed to be on her and not the baby, who'd grown so much during the past weeks. May touched her lips to the top of her downy head. Her whole face puckered in delight.

"Promise me something," she said.

"Anything, dearest," Ernst said.

"If I don't live, I want Louisa to raise her." Her voice scraped up, deep and urgent.

"May, the baby is fine. And so are you."

"Promise." She didn't know how many words were left to her, and she couldn't waste one. In his grief, Ernst might neglect this precious girl. She knew that his mother and Sophie would mind her for a while, but they had other cares, too. Madame Nieriker already had children. Sophie was likely to marry before long and have babies of her own.

"I don't know what to say when you're this way."

"Just say yes. Oh, Ernst, if only Louisa could know a little of the love we've had. I want to make things right for her."

"May, I need you."

"And I want you to be free." She looked him in the eye. "You'll go to Brazil or look for Mr. Edison. Someday you'll find another wife."

"There never could be anyone else."

"I had everything I wanted. You and our baby and painting. Now you and our beautiful girl must be free. She's small, but born in France, raised in America, she'll know that two continents can be hers."

"May, you must get better!"

"This is Louisa's only chance for a child."

"She's not young. You've told me she's not well."

"A baby will make her feel young again."

"Perhaps your sister Anna would care for a baby, if you insist on such things."

"She has her boys. It's Lu who needs someone to care for. Ernst, she would teach her right from wrong. She wouldn't let her waste her time on foolish things." Maybe Louisa would brush her hair and tell her stories about her *maman,* a pretty woman who was sometimes selfish, sometimes vain, but who had followed her great dream. And for as long as she could, for as well as she could, Louisa would assure their girl that she wasn't alone.

"If it will give you peace, I'll promise. But I won't let anything happen to you."

Her heart ached for him, but she felt strangely calm, too, as she kissed the baby's eyelids. She had loved France, but she wanted her daughter to know the hills she'd known as a girl. She wanted her to draw on the walls of her old home, to tug her grandfather's white hair, and, when she grew older, to try to scramble up his bookshelves. May's child should meet her cousins, boys who'd teach her to skate around the river bend, and, in summer, to swim and row a boat.

She handed Ernst the baby, letting her palm slip from the round, precious head. "Will you write a letter to Louisa for me? Tell her I was happy." May closed her eyes. She was lucky. That hadn't changed. She'd married a man she loved with her whole heart and gave birth to a daughter. Friends and strangers in Boston, London, and Paris had chosen her flower panels for their walls. She had climbed a mountain in the Alps. She'd published a book of her landscapes and written a guidebook she hoped would coax other women to travel and paint in England, Italy, and France.

Ernst twined his fingers through hers.

May wanted to stay with him and see their baby grow, but the room was turning dark. The cradle creaked too loudly. Had she fallen asleep? Was her fever worsening? Her breath became ragged. Did the church bells clang thirty-nine times, one for every year of her life? Were those the songs of robins, wood thrushes, and phoebes? She clutched as if reaching for a long stem beneath bobbing blossoms. She must hold on. She must let go. Why was everything so dark? Why was she shivering? The flames in the hearth burned brighter. The room was getting smaller, or was it the world, or the hours?

As her breaths shortened, pictures from her past expanded. Lilies opened all at once, turning the river white and gold. Standing by the bridge, Louisa urged her to go to Paris. Striding down the Champs-Élysées, May held a *programme* with her name in it. Ernst's hand stroked her hair. The baby scrunched her perfect mouth. A girl waved her father's handbills in the park, a coin folded in her hand under the sky that had always touched her and the earth.

23

TWENTY-EİGHT DRESSES

Louisa pinched the edges of her shawl together, trying to keep out the cold New England wind. Around her on the wharf, people waved to passengers waiting to leave the ship. Louisa quietly gazed at the ocean, blue in the afternoon sunlight, but saw nothing beautiful in its waves or wideness. She slipped a hand into the pocket that held May's last letter, sent by Ernst a year ago. She'd memorized some words: "Whatever happens, I want you to know that these past two years of happiness made it all worthwhile. Everything is perfect."

But it wasn't, Louisa thought. She'd grieved ever since she'd found Mr. Emerson in their parlor, standing before the portrait of May in her blue hat. His eyes looked almost unbearably sad as he said, "May's husband wrote to me so that you might hear the news from an old friend. If only I could prepare you."

"I am prepared. I expected this," Louisa said. Those were the only words she could find that kept her from falling into his arms and embarrassing them both. After Mr. Emerson shut the door, she tipped her head, the way May used to do before an unfinished painting, picked up her bolster pillow, threw it against the wall, and screamed.

In spring, a ship had brought trunks from Paris. Louisa had kneeled before one to take out a sewing basket, notebooks, and a tin of watercolors with tubes labeled *bleu de ciel*, *géranium*, and *terre d'ombre*. She shook out dried pine needles as she unfolded gowns that May had worn to all her fancy dinners and her blue smock. What had May thought she could do with clothes she wouldn't wear, paints she couldn't use, and diaries written in handwriting she'd never see fresh again? Why had she sent paintings she couldn't bear to hang?

But the baby! Sending her was the worst idea of all. The infant had been too young to risk the crossing in spring, then that summer, Louisa was plagued by a fever that flared off and on for months. It hadn't been until six weeks ago that she'd sent a nurse overseas to fetch the baby. Now she wondered if she should have waited even longer. Maybe May had had everything she'd ever wanted, but why did she think everyone wanted the same things she did? Whatever had made her think that at forty-eight, Louisa was fit and willing to start raising a child? She already had Father, Anna, and her boys to worry about.

The harbor grew noisier as passengers hurried down the gangplank, shouting greetings. Louisa spotted the short, plump nurse, but Mrs. Giles's arms were empty. Where was May's child? The ship's captain walked beside her, and so did a tall young woman whose loose hair blew in the sea breeze. She held a baby on her hip.

For a moment, Louisa felt as if she might be waking from a nightmare and that May was coming home. Then she realized that the woman must be Ernst's sister, who'd insisted on coming to see May's daughter safely to Massachusetts. It had seemed a waste of time and money to Louisa. She'd offered capable Mrs. Giles a handsome salary for her help. But there was nothing Louisa could say, since the Nieriker family was paying Sophie's way. Louisa just hoped that Ernst's sister didn't expect to be entertained. She'd made a list of good, clean inns where a young woman might safely stay and meant to encourage her to spend most of her time in Boston.

Louisa greeted Mrs. Giles, introduced herself to Sophie, and shook hands with the captain. Then her eyes fell on the baby. Her round face looked rosy. Her eyes were the same blue as the forget-me-nots stitched along the neckline of her frock.

"I'll see that our luggage gets where it should," Mrs. Giles said.

Louisa nodded as she briskly set off.

"Thank you for everything you did for us." Sophie gave her hand to the captain, who held it a bit too long, then bowed as he excused himself.

"He was so sweet to our little traveler." Sophie tightened her grip on the little girl, who clutched Sophie's bonnet and tried to yank if off. Failing that, the child tugged at the ribbons of her own little hat.

Sophie laughed, then gently pushed away her soft small

hand. "She hates hats. We put them on. She takes them off. I'm afraid she got a bit brown, but you know how small those cabins are. We could hardly keep her inside all the time."

"I expect the sea air was good for her."

"Yes. May was always opening windows. And she so loved the ocean!" Sophie's eyes brimmed with tears. "How you must miss her. Through those terrible weeks, she kept asking for you."

Louisa nodded curtly. She thought how it wasn't only that Sophie Nieriker wore her hair the way May did, but she was selfish like her, too, thinking that everyone must want to hear whatever she felt like saying.

"We dressed May in white and covered the casket with flowers," Sophie said.

Louisa looked away. Wouldn't she ever stop talking?

"Did my *maman* write you that Ernst left for Brazil? He needs to forget. I mean, of course he'll remember. He has work there, and . . ."

"Work is the best medicine."

The little girl tugged her hat again, this time managing to pull it off. She threw it down to the wharf, revealing puffs of reddish-gold hair.

"Lulu, no!" Sophie sighed, smiled, and bent to pick up the hat. "She's determined. And clever, too."

"You call her 'Lulu'?"

"'Louisa' seemed like such a long name for a baby, so we started to call her 'Lu.' May told us she used to call you that. She babbles all the time, but she's said some words, including 'Lu.' Her own name! The little darling was so proud. She'd say it over and over, so we began calling her 'Lulu.'" Sophie hoisted up the small girl. "I'm sorry. You must think me selfish, keeping her to myself. Lulu, you must meet your dear aunt."

Before Louisa could speak, the child was in her arms. Lulu twisted her head to see who was holding her, then squirmed out of Louisa's arms to the wharf. She dropped to her knees, sped off on hands and knees, pushed herself up, and started to walk, wobbly and quick on her short, chubby legs.

"Stop!" Louisa's heart pounded as the little girl toddled toward the edge of the wharf.

Sophie lunged forward and caught her.

Lulu laughed, shrieked, and threw out her arms as Sophie picked her up.

"You must listen to your aunt." Sophie firmly handed her back to Louisa, who squeezed her to her chest. Her heart raced. Why hadn't she held her harder, run faster? She could have fallen into the sea! Why hadn't May asked Anna, who would know what she was doing, to raise her daughter?

Louisa pressed her face in the small girl's yellow-red hair. Why hadn't she gone to see May? Why hadn't she told her about all the hours Mother had gazed at her portrait during her last illness, how she read her letters over and over and said her name moments before she died? Why had she assumed they had as much time as they could need? She should have told May that even when she and Mother had missed her, it had brought them pleasure to know that somewhere in the world, a woman was doing exactly what she wanted.

"Isn't she young to walk?" Louisa asked.

"She started just before we left France," Sophie said. "My

mother says that's not terribly unusual at her age, but she is advanced, don't you think?"

"She doesn't like me." Louisa tightened her arms as Lulu wiggled.

"It's not that. She's curious about everything."

"I don't know anything about raising a girl."

"That's what I thought at first, too, but she lets you know what she needs."

"Lu, lu, lu, lu, lu," the little girl babbled.

"She already knows a few words in French, German, and English," Sophie said. "She's quite a genius. Maybe she'll be a writer, like her famous aunt."

"I hope not." Louisa saw Mrs. Giles raise her arm as she stood by a carriage. She looked assured, directing the driver, but Louisa wondered what she could know about her niece.

"You'll have a lot to teach me." Louisa linked her free arm through Sophie's. "Will you come stay with us for a while?"

"Thank you. Oh, you're as good and generous as May said you were." Sophie's eyes welled with tears again. "I'm going to miss her."

Of course she would. No one who'd known May could forget her. Louisa squinted in the sunlight, thinking of her third book about the March sisters, in which she'd made Amy be a contented artist, wife, and mother to one darling girl. She'd begun writing it when May was expecting her baby, then put it away when May became ill. But she hadn't destroyed it. She was done filling up a room with smoke. Recently, she'd taken out the manuscript again, needing not only to make money for Anna's boys, but now May's daughter, too. It was painful to write about a woman who was teaching her daughter how to paint, something that should have happened in life. But Louisa owed this portrait to May, who'd yearned for stories of good wives and mothers who wouldn't squander the gifts of their hearts and hands.

"Come on." Louisa carried the small girl toward the waiting carriage. She looked into Lulu's eyes, hoping she wouldn't forget to one day tell her that blue was her mother's favorite color, and how she would have adored, even envied her eyes. "May. Can you say that? Your mother's name was May."

"Lulu lulu lu," the little girl chanted.

There were so many things to tell her about her mother. Louisa hoped she had time, while spoiling her with silver mugs, gorgeous dolls, picture books, boxes of colored chalk, and twenty-eight dresses at a time. For now, she'd take her home, with one backward glance at the sea and the wide, unpredictable sky.

My fascination with May Alcott Nierker (July 26, 1840–December 29, 1879) began when I was a girl playing *Little Women* and my older sister claimed the role of Jo. Even then, I thought there was more to the youngest sister than mangling words, obsessing about fads like pickled limes, and worrying about her nose. As I studied art history as an adult, May's name, along with those of other nineteenth-century women artists, reappeared. I remained somewhat haunted by the way Amy stops making art in *Little Women*, saying that it's only worth doing if you're a genius. I wondered both why Louisa May Alcott never entirely acknowledged her own genius and how her real sister had reacted to seeing her fictional counterpart give up a quest for beauty that defined much of her life.

Questions like that led me to old diaries, letters, memoirs, fiction, and biographies by or about the Alcotts, as well as those focused on Concord neighbors such as the Hawthorne and Emerson families, Henry David Thoreau, and Daniel Chester French. I read books about women artists of the period, particularly Mary Cassatt, and other expatriate artists working in France at a time when academic art was being challenged by Impressionism. May was mentioned in some of these books, and a 1927 memoir by Caroline Ticknor put her at the center. But because much was missing, as I researched in libraries, historic houses, museums, and at riverbanks, I drew upon my imagination to develop my sense of May. Much as a portrait painter begins with a particular face that changes as she chooses colors and brushstrokes, I began with descriptions of real people, places, and events to form impressions. Dependent on both facts and mysteries, I elaborated upon summaries to create scenes that comprise a work of fiction.

Biographers believe that May's death was likely from the effects of puerperal fever, which she contracted during childbirth, probably from an infection that rose from unsanitary conditions common at the time. May was buried in the Montrouge cemetery in Paris, though Louisa arranged for a marker in the Concord cemetery, which simply bears her initials. The year of her death, Louisa began writing *Jo's Boys*, her third and final book about the family at the center of *Little Women*, in which we find Amy has grown up to become an artist, "one of those who prove that women can be faithful wives and mothers without sacrificing . . . [their] special gift."

Louisa raised May's daughter, who the family called Lulu, until Louisa died in 1888. At the request of the Nieriker family, Anna Alcott Pratt then brought ten-year-old Lulu to Zurich to live with them. Lulu spent most of the rest of her life in Switzerland, where she married, raised one daughter, and died in 1975.

Some of May's paintings remain in Europe with the Nieriker family. Others are displayed in historic houses in Concord, most importantly in Orchard House, where the gods and goddesses May drew on her bedroom walls and the flowers and owl in Louisa's bedroom have been preserved. Some art works have likely been destroyed, lost, relegated to attics, or hung on walls where they're seldom looked at. But there will always be people who pause to consider paintings May left behind and wonder about the woman who held the brush.

ACKNOWLEDGMENTS

So many librarians deserve parades every day, but here I'll just thank those at the Houghton Library at Harvard College, the Special Collections at the Concord Free Public Library, and the good people at Jones Library in Amherst, Massachusetts and Forbes Library in Northampton, Massachusetts: You have helped make research a delight. I'm grateful to everyone who works to make history accessible, particularly those at Louisa May Alcott's Orchard House, overseen with such skill and devotion by Jan Turnquist.

My writing group makes my work possible. For twenty-five years, Bruce Carson, Dina Friedman, and Lisa Kleinholz have raised bars, asked the right questions, and cheered at all the right times. I've also been lucky to have wonderful writing teachers and students. There are too many to name, like my good friends, though I'll single out Karen Lederer, who's kept a folder of stories with my name on it since we were students at UMass-Amherst, and Amy Greenfield, for a conversation by the Concord River that led me to take out the manuscript that had long gripped me one more time. Always, I thank my husband Peter Laird, and our daughter, Emily, who make life so very sweet.

ABOUT THE AUTHOR

photo credit: Peter Laird

JEANNINE ATKINS is the author of books for young readers featuring women in history, including Borrowed Names: Poems about Laura Ingalls Wilder, Madam C. J. Walker, Marie Curie and their Daughters. She is an adjunct professor at Simmons College and the University of Massachusetts-Amherst. She welcomes readers to visit her online at:

www.jeannineatkins.com.

SELECTED TITLES FROM SHE WRITES PRESS

She Writes Press is an independent publishing company founded to serve women writers everywhere.
Visit us at www.shewritespress.com.

Hysterical: Anna Freud's Story by Rebecca Coffey. $18.95, 978-1-938314-42-1. An irreverent, fictionalized exploration of the seemingly contradictory life of Anna Freud—told from her point of view.

The Rooms Are Filled by Jessica Null Vealitzek. $16.95, 978-1-938314-58-2. The coming-of-age story of two outcasts—a nine-year-old boy who just lost his father, and a closeted young woman—brought together by circumstance.

Bittersweet Manor by Tory McCagg. $16.95, 978-1-938314-56-8. A chronicle of three generations of love, manipulation, entitlement, and disappointed expectations in an upper-middle class New England family.

A Cup of Redemption by Carole Bumpus. $16.95, 978-1-938314-90-2. Three women, each with their own secrets and shames, seek to make peace with their pasts and carve out new identities for themselves.

The Sweetness by Sande Boritz Berger. $16.95, 978-1-63152-907-8. A compelling and powerful story of two girls—cousins living on separate continents—whose strikingly different lives are forever changed when the Nazis invade Vilna, Lithuania.

What is Found, What is Lost by Anne Leigh Parrish. $16.95, 978-1-938314-95-7. After her husband passes away, a series of family crises forces Freddie, a woman raised on religion, to confront long-held questions about her faith.